a.k.a.

"Trouble"

Martin J. Roddini

Dedication

This work is dedicated to the memory of Robert (Bob) Glidden and William (Bill) Stillman – good husbands, good fathers, great men.

This is a work of fiction. Unless otherwise indicated, all the names, characters, businesses, places, events and incidents in this book are either the product of the author's imagination or used in a fictitious manner. Any resemblance to actual persons, living or dead, or actual events is purely coincidental.

Also by Martin J. Roddini:

Saving Kings

They Can Hear

The Apparition

Jack

a.k.a.________________________________

“Trouble”

Chapter One

A Calculated Risk

It was a Saturday afternoon in the fall, and, as usual, Rocco was in the neighborhood park with a few of the many friends that he had. They were all at an age where the topic of "what do you want to be when you grow up" was one of the main points of discussion. The usual vocations that the guys spoke about were police officer, fireman, and astronaut among others. The girls focused on such positions as nurse, teacher and model. It was a time when imaginations soared and dreams melded into possible realities.

When Rocco Deloberti closed his eyes, he could see himself snugly engulfed in a NASA spacesuit sitting in the cockpit of a space capsule that was mounted on top of a Saturn rocket. He was ready to blast off to some foreign celestial body.

However, upon opening his eyes, he was well grounded onto the cement foundation of the park that he frequented with his friends. This imaginary escape was so real that Rocco could almost feel the gravitational pull as the rocket blasted through the earth's atmosphere. As soon as Rocco closed his eyes, his friends knew that he was once again envisioning that ride through space because they had witnessed this same scene many times before. They didn't interrupt the imagined space ride, but as Rocco opened his eyes and came back down to earth, his closest friend, Dennis, was the first to ask how it was. Rocco was always embarrassed after being so involved in his dream, but everyone knew that with a little luck, Rocco Deloberti would one day actually blast into space. So, they all just laughed together as everyone let their imaginations run amuck.

As the friends grew up, some of them also grew apart. However, there was a small cadre of friends that remained close and still "hung out" together. This close group remained friends throughout high school and even as some registered for different colleges. Whenever there were breaks in the college schedule, the group looked forward to getting together and rehashing "old times" or revealing the latest adventures that they had experienced. The big difference, however, was that they had to start thinking seriously about what the future would hold. They could no longer depend on the positive effects of an imaginary journey, but had to realistically direct their focus on the rest of their lives.

Rocco and his best friend, Dennis, had registered to attend the same college. Although their majors were different, they were able to take many of the same classes together. However, there came a point when Rocco decided that college, at least at this time, was not the best choice for him. He had taken the New York City Police examination and was waiting to be called for an academy class. Although he just tolerated college, his grades were better than average. Timing was everything though, and as the semester was ending, Rocco got called by the New York City Police Department. Dennis thought that the decision was the wrong one, but he could not persuade Rocco to stay in college.

Following an in-depth background investigation and numerous health checks, Rocco followed his heart and reported to the New York City Police Academy. Of course, he kept in touch with his friend, Dennis, and learned that many of the male college students were in fear of the fact that they might be called into military service by way of the draft. The Vietnam War was going on and military service was not viewed by anyone as the ideal place for a progressive future. In fact, many thought that service in the military could easily result in possible injury or even death. So, college males were employing different methods to avoid being taken into the military. Fear was so high that some guys punctured their ear drums to fail the army physical. Others resorted to such things as paraphernalia that would increase the possibility of having flat feet which also excluded one from serving.

Rocco felt that if he were called, he would enter the military with the same approach that he had faced other events in his life, with enthusiasm, commitment and a desire to do the best that he could. However, Rocco Deloberti was presently a brand-new recruit in the academy class of the New York City Police Department. He didn't dwell on the "what ifs" in life but focused on doing his best as each day progressed.

He had been in the academy for only about two weeks when Rocco received his draft notice to appear for military service. He was disappointed because he was on his way to joining the ranks of the New York City Police Department, and this notification would delay his entry into this coveted group. He was going to wear another uniform, however, one which would surely take him into harm's way. He accepted that, but was troubled that he had to put his police ambitions on hold.

The day following the receipt of his draft notice, Rocco went to the academy to present his military papers to the desk sergeant. The sergeant was a by-the-book officer who had more than the required years to be able to retire. To say that he was not a person one could get close to would be an understatement. There were a number of recruits waiting to see the sergeant, so Rocco waited his turn which only took a few minutes. When Rocco appeared before the sergeant, he was greeted with: "And what do you want?" The greeting, if you could call it that, was toned in more of an order than a question.

Rocco was more or less taken aback by the gruff and almost intimidating salutation by the sergeant, but he took a deep breath and spoke: "Good afternoon, Sarge." Rocco was interrupted with another comment in the form of a rhetorical question from the sergeant: "What's so good about it?" Rocco said nothing but just smiled and continued: "I received my draft notice from the army, so I will not be able to continue in the academy." As he was about to present the papers to the sergeant, the sergeant reached over and grabbed the papers right out of Rocco's hands. In a demanding and almost disconcerting manner, the sergeant barked: "Give me those papers and get back to class."

Police Recruit Rocco Deloberti was surprised with the sergeant's response and following the sergeant's direct order, he went back to class. Rocco never heard another word from either the police department or the military about his draft notice. Unbeknownst to him, a police officer position was considered an essential occupation and was, therefore, exempt from the draft. To say the least, Rocco was shocked and surprised to hear that he was exempt, but he was more gratified that he was going to be able to finish his training and be sworn-in as a New York City Police Officer.

Although, at times, the training in the academy was trying to say the least, Rocco was happy to be there. When he used to get together with his friends in the park, being a police officer was discussed but really didn't rank as being on top of the list. But here he was, he was training to become a police officer. It all happened so quickly and without much thought. He had separated himself, at least temporarily, from the designs of college life and while he was deciding on his future, he was called by the police department. Things just fit into place, and with a little luck, he would graduate the academy and join the rank-and-file members of the New York City Police Department.

Although Rocco still kept in touch with Dennis, his contacts were now few and far between. Dennis was one of those individuals who was drafted and was serving in Vietnam. Many times, Rocco thought how life dictates its course. Here he was ready to accept a tour of duty in the military, while others were looking for any way to avoid the draft. He becomes a police officer and is deferred from the draft. What a twist of fate!

The academy training was intense and rigid, but because of the fact that "teamwork" is a necessary element in the training, new friendships are easily forged. For six months of constant training, you are exposed every day to the same people in your particular class. One cannot avoid the close camaraderie that builds as the class continues as a unit through the training. Competition builds as the classes face each other in exercises that are geared to what a police officer might encounter in the street. Unfortunately, as all police officers ultimately discover, the academy training is, by no means, a reflection of the street experience.

Rocco's academy training turned out to be far different than what an ordinarily scheduled academy class would encounter. While Rocco was training in the academy, riots broke out in the streets of New York. In an effort to demonstrate an overwhelming show of force, police academy recruits were assigned to the street wearing the regular blue uniform of a seasoned officer. Unbeknownst to all, the recruits would never be wearing the gray recruit uniform again. Yes, this academy class was far different than those that came before or those yet to come.

Rocco and his academy cohorts were in the street knowing very little about what to do and never again going back to the academy to finish their formal training. For them, it was a baptism by fire. There were no more curfews, and the recruits were introduced to real police work. The police department had been in a real crunch, and in a desperation move, utilized police recruits. They took a calculated risk with a liability factor that was off the charts, and it had worked without incident. However, some recruits never recovered from the unanticipated and unprecedented premature entry into the real world of law enforcement.

Chapter Two

The Letter

The final stage of the academy journey is the field training assignments. Although this academy class had already been out in the street for the riots, they were now going to work with individual units for a taste of teamwork and guidance from experienced police officers. Rocco and a number of other recruits were assigned to different teams in the Rapid Response Task Force. Although the name indicated that these officers were available to respond quickly in emergency situations, they were also available to complement the officers in any precinct. The task force officers could blanket an area that was having problems and through targeted pressure eliminate the incidence of crime. These units had a reputation. The community knew that when the task force arrived on the scene, whatever was causing specific problems in the neighborhood, would soon be eliminated.

Academy Police Officer Rocco Deloberti was assigned to a task force unit that was working the East New York area of Brooklyn. He was on foot patrol with two other police officers who were assigned to the unit. As they approached the El (the elevated track structure of the subway system) on Myrtle Avenue, their attention was drawn to a huge crashing sound from under the El. The officers ran to a location where they could see what caused the loud noise. They were shocked to see a vehicle wrapped around one of the steel support columns of the El. The senior task force officer started running toward the crash with his partner alongside. Rocco trailed behind and was waiting for directions to act. Those directions came quickly as the officer told his partner to direct traffic away from the crash and ordered Rocco to follow him to the passenger side of the vehicle.

Apparently, the vehicle, which was occupied by two young men, had been going at such an advanced rate of speed that the steel column was now located in the front seat of the Ford Mustang. The car had been traveling on the narrow street underneath the El. The street was divided into two opposite lanes and is also a designated bus route. It became obvious that the driver of the Mustang decided to pass a vehicle which was moving too slowly in front of him. As the Mustang driver pulled around the slowly moving vehicle, he apparently misjudged the distance of the oncoming bus in the opposite lane. In a desperate move to avoid the bus, the driver floored the accelerator pedal and lost control of the vehicle as it careened into the steel support column.

The car was steaming, and the senior officer was afraid that the vehicle could burst into flames. The task force officer told Rocco to grab onto the door handle and help him open the passenger side door. They both pulled as hard as they could, and finally the door gave way. The officer looked at the passenger and then directed Rocco to hold the head of the unconscious individual in such a way as to reduce the stress on the neck area. There was blood all over, and Rocco was having a hard time holding down the contents of his stomach.

After placing Rocco in the proper position, the officer ran to the driver's side of the car and forced the door open. He tugged at the driver, who was pinned in his seat by the steering wheel. Ultimately, the officer was able to extract the driver from the car. As the officer laid the driver on the sidewalk a distance from the car, he realized that the young man had expired. Sirens could be heard as the ambulance, which had been called by the traffic control officer, arrived on the scene. The first EMT ran to the passenger side of the car and ushered Rocco away from the apparently seriously injured individual. As Rocco released his grip on the head of the passenger, it fell to the side where it became obvious to Rocco that he had been holding a head which had been partially severed from the body. In shock, Rocco moved away from the car and almost backed into oncoming traffic. Following their examination, the EMTs declared both victims to be D.O.A. (dead on arrival).

After the officers collected the necessary information, and the ambulance and tow truck were leaving, the two task force officers looked questioningly at one another and realized that their recruit Police Officer Rocco Deloberti was nowhere in sight. As they started to look around, a passerby notified them that he had seen an officer bent over in a nearby alley, and it seemed that he needed help. The officers walked to the alley where they found Police Officer Rocco Deloberti dry heaving after having vomited all the contents of his stomach. The officers remarked that they had never seen that particular shade of green which was masking Rocco's entire face. Although they made light of Rocco's condition, they were also affected by what they had seen. The difference was that they had been present at similar scenes and had built up a defense mechanism to ward off the attack of the green monster.

After helping their charge to breathe more deeply and escorting him back to the station house, the officers went back out on patrol. Recruit Police Officer Deloberti, however, stayed behind in the station house where he spent the remainder of his tour beating a path to and from the bathroom. Rocco was not sure that he had chosen the right vocation in life, but he was reassured by other officers that, out of necessity, one builds up a tolerance level. This tolerance allows an officer to deal with experiences that are gut-wrenching and which the average individual never comes upon. These seasoned officers also mentioned that Rocco was not alone, and that they also had a similar first-time green experience. They assured him that although there will still be sights that are shocking and upsetting, experience helps build that immunity barrier that allows officers to continue on. Rocco had, apparently, planted the first building block which cemented the foundation for the barrier construction to begin.

Rocco completed his six weeks of field training and was anxious to come back to the academy from which he would finally graduate. To say the least, his fellow recruits exchanged many unique experiences that just added to the overall adventure of which they were to be a permanent part. With graduation day just around the corner, much of the academy time was focused on rehearsals. The Police Academy graduation is always a big event, and it is always televised on the local T.V. stations. The Police Department naturally wanted to put its best foot forward, so the recruits were forced to rehearse endlessly to make sure that the event went on without a hitch. The graduation was also always well attended by city and political figures filling their reserved seats on the stage.

The graduation lasted for about ninety minutes after which the newly graduated officers said goodbye to their academy mates. Although some might be going to the same precinct, the majority of officers would be spread out throughout the city adding to the rosters of the individual commands. The graduates had already received their assignments, and many were going to enhance the patrols in high crime areas. Police Officer Deloberti was one of those officers who was assigned to the Crown Heights/East New York area of Brooklyn. This is a high crime area, and seasoned officers always remarked that it is in these areas where "you learn the job." These active precincts demanded response to many and varied calls for service, so the potential for learning the job was greater in an active command than in a slow command.

After all the good wishes and goodbyes were completed, the graduates, now full-fledged police officers, met with their families and friends. Rocco's parents couldn't be prouder, and his father was far beyond that. Rocco was the first police officer in the family, and he landed a job that was both honorable and well-respected. His father shook Rocco's hand and hugged him so tightly that Rocco almost lost his breath. His girlfriend, Janet, was also there with her parents and although there was pride on her face, she also worried about the everyday dangers that her boyfriend was about to face.

When all of the congratulations and best wishes were over, the family and friends left the academy auditorium and went on their way to a local restaurant to continue celebrating. For Rocco, only one thing was missing. His best friend, Dennis, wasn't able to be there. He was in the jungles of Vietnam for reasons not clearly annunciated by the government. The war had been going on for a long time, and it was the consensus of opinion, that one: we shouldn't have been there in the first place, and two: if we had to be there, we should be fighting to win. Although these thoughts were floating around in his head, Rocco was not going to dampen the celebration with the talk of war. That discussion always resulted in differences of opinions and hard feelings that usually evolved into accusations and political rhetoric.

Rocco's mother had been in such a rush to get to the graduation ceremony that when she picked up the mail on the way out, she unthinkingly kept it in her hands. On the way to the academy, she browsed over the mail and saw that there was a letter from Dennis Salerno, her son's best friend. She knew that Rocco would be happy that Dennis wrote, and most appropriately, it arrived on the day of Rocco's graduation.

When they arrived at the restaurant and after everyone ordered their meals, Rocco's mom remembered that she had Dennis' letter in her bag. She told Rocco that she had gotten the letter and gave it to him. Rocco couldn't be happier, and one could see it on his face. It would have been rude for him to open the letter at the restaurant, so he waited until the congratulations and the day came to an end. He thanked everyone for their best wishes, and the group went their separate ways. Janet, however, went with Rocco and his parents to continue a private celebration back in their house.

When they arrived home, Rocco excused himself for a few minutes so that he could open Dennis' letter. Janet was excited for him and went with him to his room. He excitedly tore open the letter and began to read it. The happy and excited expression on Rocco's face slowly changed into a serious and concerned look. Janet saw the change and asked: "Rocco, what's the matter?" He hesitated and looked at Janet with a worried concern: "Dennis got shot, and he is in an army hospital. He most likely will be leaving the military with a medical discharge."

"Does he say what the extent of the injuries is?"

"No, but he mentions that he will probably suffer the resulting effects for a very long time."

The excitement and celebratory mood that minutes ago had filled Rocco's day was now replaced with the worry and concern. Rocco was concerned about how badly Dennis would suffer with the ramifications of a battle wound that would stay with him more-than-likely for a lifetime.

Chapter Three

A Missed Meeting

Dennis Salerno was medically discharged from the army and back in the states. He had contacted his good friend, Rocco, and made arrangements to meet with him in a local bar. While he was waiting for Rocco to complete his tour and come to the bar, Dennis was having drinks with some other friends. The wound that he sustained in Vietnam damaged the dexterity level that he once had in his right hand. Although the bullet smashed into his right shoulder, the damage filtered down to include his right hand, and his ability to hold items tightly in that hand was greatly reduced. This was an unfortunate occurrence since he was a right-handed individual. At times, he would forget about his reduced capability and utilize his right hand with faltering results. However, Dennis had seen far worse injuries that impacted many of his comrades-in-arms. He considered himself lucky and fought every day not to dwell upon his disability but rather celebrate the fact that he had been in combat and survived.

Dennis and his friends had been in the bar for quite a while, and at this point, no one was feeling any pain. One of the participants decided to make a toast to the long-lasting friendship that had endured amongst the group. Everyone picked up their glasses and raised them to cheer. However, when Dennis, who was closing in on inebriation, attempted to raise his glass from the bar countertop, his right hand gave way, and his grip on the fully refilled drink did not hold. The glass and its contents landed squarely on the lap of the woman who was sitting directly next to him. Following a blood-curdling scream, the woman's boyfriend, who was sitting on the opposite side of the woman, rose from his chair and approached Dennis in a less than friendly manner. In fact, he approached with a half of a beer bottle that he had smashed against the bar.

The boyfriend caught Dennis by surprise, and before he knew it, a jagged edge of a beer bottle was being pressed against his throat. Although it was definitely an accident, the aggressor, who was also alcohol-influenced, saw it as an intentionally disrespectful act against his girlfriend. As Dennis raised his hands in defense, the irrational, bottle-holding boyfriend pressed harder against Dennis' neck and penetrated the skin with the sharp edge of the broken beer bottle. By the time that Dennis' friends were able to intercede and stop the attack, the increased and continued pressure on Dennis' neck had caused a constant stream of blood to escape from the wound. Dennis started losing a lot of blood and that caused him to feel dizzy. He collapsed to the floor.

As all this was going on, the bartender had called the police who were now arriving on the scene. They took the crazed aggressor into custody and proceeded to wait for an ambulance. Dennis lay unresponsive, spilling an increased flow of blood onto the floor. A police officer applied direct pressure with a towel that the bartender had given him. If the blood flow didn't stop, Dennis could surely bleed out.

As Rocco approached the bar to meet with his friend, he saw a cascade of flashing emergency lights. Both police vehicles and an ambulance had responded to the bar so there were flashing lights as far as the eye could see. At first, Rocco wasn't sure that the emergency vehicles had responded to the bar or maybe to some other location, but as he got closer, he saw that the bar was the location to which the first responders were directing their efforts.

Rocco quickly parked his car and ran to the bar. He had his police I.D. in hand and was able to maneuver his way past the blue barrier and into the bar. It was a chaotic scene with police officers and EMTs working together to save a life and de-escalate a situation that could easily have evolved into an uncontrollable display of misplaced rage. As he got closer to the action, his friends recognized the fact that Rocco had arrived, and they all started to speak at the same time. Rocco identified himself to the investigating officer and inquired as to what had occurred.

As he was listening to the officer, he realized that Dennis was not among the friends who were still in the bar. Rocco interrupted the police officer and asked about Dennis. He was told that his friend suffered a deep laceration to the neck and was already in the ambulance. As Rocco turned and ran to see his friend inside the ambulance, it pulled away and began its emergency ride to the county hospital.

Although the rest of his friends were still in the bar, Rocco was more concerned about Dennis. So, he headed to his car to drive to the hospital. As he ran past one of the police vehicles, he noticed an individual, who he believed to be the perpetrator, seated in the rear of the cruiser. Seeing the attacker brought Rocco's building anger and frustration to the forefront. He opened the rear door and confronted the hand-cuffed man. The man's disconcerted attitude pushed Rocco to the point of no return, and he began administering street justice. Rocco landed a number of well targeted punches before other officers and a sergeant were able to pull Rocco away from the individual. Police Officer Rocco Deloberti was now in a world of trouble.

The sergeant on the scene called for the duty captain to respond since the situation now also included potentially criminal actions by a police officer. Rocco was escorted to one of the other police vehicles and was ushered into the back seat. He knew that he had violated a strict tenet of police work. He had let his emotions overrule his professional conduct, and he had inflicted punishment upon a defenseless prisoner.

It seemed as though the duty captain was taking forever to respond to the scene, and Rocco patiently waited for a determination which he knew would not fare well for him. He dwelled on the fact that this one foolishly impulsive action could easily end his law enforcement career as well as deem him a criminal for assaulting another individual. Oh, how he wished he could have that moment back. Although he had been incensed about what the individual had done, it was not up to him, a police officer, to become judge, jury and executioner. However, that was exactly what he had become.

Although he focused on what might ultimately happen to him, he wondered about how his friend, Dennis, was doing. Because of his uncontrollable actions, Rocco was not able to get to the hospital to find out specifics and to support his friend. He was worried because, in the brief time that he was at the bar, he saw an awful lot of blood on the floor. Rocco also knew that a wound to the neck area usually produces a lot of blood. He also knew that a cut to a certain area of the neck, the jugular vein, could easily spell the end of life for an individual. But again, because he let his emotions run away with him, Rocco was not able to know how serious a condition his friend might be in.

Finally, the duty captain arrived on the scene and was getting an earful from the sergeant who had originally responded to the bar. They were in conversation for a long time when the duty captain turned and walked to the police vehicle that was holding Police Officer Deloberti. The sergeant accompanied the duty captain and was ordered to take Rocco's gun and shield. The duty captain suspended Police Officer Deloberti and discharged him from any police work while the department awaited a decision from the district attorney on the possibility of criminal charges. Rocco had imagined what the worst scenario could possibly be, and his imagination had been right on the money. Rocco was told to leave but to remain local until the department notified him of further developments.

Dennis Salerno was in critical condition and unconscious as the doctors tried to save his life. He had lost an enormous amount of blood and was barely holding on to life. They were working on him for over an hour when their efforts no longer saw a successful conclusion. Despite employing every treatment that they had at their disposal, the attending doctor declared Dennis "dead" as of 6:15pm.

At approximately the same time, Rocco was on his way with his girlfriend, Janet, to the county hospital. Rocco was anxious to see Dennis and to make sure that everything that could be done for him was being done. When Rocco and Janet entered the waiting area of the emergency room, they were surprised to see that Dennis' parents were not there. For sure, Rocco thought that they would be there and probably pacing as they waited to hear something from the doctor.

Just as Rocco was about to approach the receiving nurse to inquire about his friend, he heard a commotion at the door that led to a room adjacent to the emergency room. He and Janet both looked intently at what was happening. Apparently, a woman had passed out and was being triaged by one of the nurses.

As Rocco and Janet looked more closely, they recognized the woman. Dennis' mother had just fainted, and his father was on his knees trying to help his wife. As soon as Rocco realized who the man and woman were, he ran over to them. Dennis' mother was coming around, and as soon as she recognized Rocco, she hugged him and kept repeating: "Oh, Rocco. Oh, Rocco." Dennis' father was alongside of Rocco, and he was visibly sobbing. Things were not looking good, and Rocco only imagined the worst. He turned to the nurse who was administering aid to Dennis' mother and father and asked: "What's happened? How is Dennis Salerno doing?" The nurse looked at Rocco and incorrectly had assumed that Rocco knew what had occurred. When she saw his bewildered expression, she whispered: "Dennis expired just a few moments ago."

Rocco looked at the nurse in disbelief. He wasn't sure that he had heard her correctly, so he repeated: "Dennis is dead?" The nurse just nodded briefly and then, once again, turned her attention to Dennis' mother.

Rocco released the hold that Dennis' mother had on him, and he was quickly replaced by Dennis' sobbing father who tightly held his wife. Rocco stood up and faced his girlfriend, who also had tears in her eyes. The remorse he had just felt a short time ago for acting aggressively and unprofessionally now dissipated and was replaced by seething rage. Rocco looked at Janet and said: "I should have killed him! In fact, I am going to kill him!" Rocco marched out of the hospital.

Chapter Four

You Can't Save Everyone

Janet ran after her boyfriend to try and calm him down. After a continuous diatribe of begging and pleading, Rocco finally agreed that he would not do anything more to jeopardize his future. He realized that the bottle-wielding, short-fused moron who attacked his friend would now be charged, at the very least, with manslaughter as a result of Dennis' death. The level of his revenge having been reduced, Rocco realized that the sentence that the court would levy on his friend's aggressor would be punishment enough. The individual would spend a number of years behind bars. Rocco felt that this would be enough because whatever he would have done would not have brought his friend back. Also, Rocco was not really a proponent of an eye-for-an-eye philosophy.

Rocco's wait for the determinations of the police department and the district attorney seemed like an eternity. However, the wait was well worth it. Although Rocco was suspended for fifteen days without pay, the charge of assault was dropped to a harassment violation and a fine. To say that politics does not play a huge role in city government would be a naive statement of an uninformed individual. The final determinations by both the department and the district attorney's office did not come about without the influence of political persuasion. Rocco's father had been a long-time member of the political party which was now in power in the city. In fact, he had formerly held a minor office in the party. With a few phone calls and a large donation to the party by his father, Police Officer Deloberti did not forfeit his law enforcement career.

Rocco was assigned back to his original precinct, and was given a hero's welcome by the other police officers. There were many times that these other officers would have liked to do the same thing that Rocco had done. They would have liked to administer street justice. Rocco did it, and with a little more than a slap on the wrist, he was able to escape real punishment for his actions.

Police Officer Deloberti was, of course, still a rookie cop, and rookie cops usually got the bottom of the barrel when it came to assignments. On his second day back in the precinct, he was assigned to secure an area in a private home where an individual had apparently hanged himself. This area, the basement of the house, had to be secured until the incident was formerly deemed a suicide. The body of the individual had to be protected until the technicians from the Medical Examiner's Office released it.

Rocco was working a day tour and upon his arrival at the home, he relieved the officer who had been assigned on the previous tour. The officer explained to Rocco that the family periodically insisted on wanting to go into the basement to be close to their relative who apparently took his own life. The officer also explained that emotions were running high, and that many times they included yelling and crying and attempts at pushing by the officer. Rocco knew that this was a crime scene until a preliminary investigation proved it not to be, so the immediate area had to be secured.

Police Officer Deloberti positioned himself at the bottom of the stairs that led to the basement. His first look at the hanging victim was one which he would never forget. Apparently, the individual, a federal law enforcement agent, had been hanging for quite a while before he was discovered. As a result of gravity exerting its pressure on the extremities, the arms and legs were distorted replicas of the shape they once had. Liquids in the body all filtered down into these locations and the body took on monster-like proportions. It was difficult for Rocco to cope with this, and the family would be even more devastated upon seeing the distorted misshapen body of their relative. So, securing the area actually served two purposes: it preserved the crime scene area for further investigation, and it protected the family from a shocking sight that would remain with them forever.

Rocco was a little nervous being alone in the basement with the hanging body. He was going to experience a lot of firsts, and this was surely one of them. To say the least, the whole idea of protecting a dead person was in itself kind of eerie, but this body was misshapen and scary to look at. As much as he could, he looked at everything other than the body. And although it was trying when the family wanted to come into the basement, for Rocco it was a distraction from the silence and eeriness of the situation. Unfortunately, there were some moments when Rocco had to use a certain amount of force to prevent the scene from being contaminated by relatives; however, cooler heads in the family realized that the officer was only doing his job.

Rocco had been there for over two hours before the techs from the medical examiner's office arrived on the scene. There was a male and female, and they were dressed in hospital-like white gowns. When they entered the side door which led to the basement, they were greeted by Officer Deloberti who was quite relieved and more than happy to see them. All he got was a nod from them as they proceeded down into the basement. One carried a metal pale while the other had what looked like a doctor's instrument bag. Of course, with the arrival of the techs, the family became more interested in what was going on, so they attempted a few more times to enter the basement. However, Rocco was there to make certain that no one but authorized personnel entered into the secured area. It was a more difficult task at this time because even the calmer, cooler heads wanted to know what was taking place.

The technicians were very direct and to the point. There was no conversation as each tech knew what the other had to do. Rocco had his back to the techs when he heard what he thought was a gurgling sound. It, in fact, was a gurgling sound. It was one of the techs slitting open an extremity to allow the built-up liquids to drain from the body into the pail. This procedure was repeated on all of the extremities until the body was drained of all the pooling liquids. Only then, after the body was free of these liquids, did the technicians cut the body down from the rope that was tightly wound around the victim's neck and attached to a basement beam.

If it wasn't for the distraction of the family attempting to enter the basement, Police Officer Rocco Deloberti would, once again, have emptied his stomach all over the floor. Luckily, he had to pay attention to the efforts of the family and not to those of the technicians who went about their business as if they were just planting flowers in the front yard. They had, apparently, built up that very strong wall of immunity that the other officers in the precinct had been speaking about. Rocco thought about it and knew that he would never be able to erect such a barrier. The natural emotions and reactions that human beings experience as part of life are sometimes just too much. He might be able to handle them a little better than the average person, but he would never be immune to them.

The local funeral home was notified and the body was turned over to the director. Rocco was finally free from the disturbing assignment that, according to the other police officers, would make him a stronger cop. The entire morning had been filled with guarding a crime scene, deterring a grieving family and listening to the efforts of a robotic medical team. Before he knew it, his assigned meal time had arrived. For some "strange" reason and for one of the very few times that he could remember, Police Officer Rocco Deloberti had no appetite and was going to skip a meal.

Rocco was back in the station house sitting at a table where other officers were eating their lunch. The smells, aromas and sounds all combined to turn Rocco's stomach into a potential volcano about to erupt. He had to leave the lunch room and get some fresh air. The green mask that he had once worn was slowly beginning to cover his face again.

As Rocco stood on the steps of the precinct station house and awaited his next assignment, he noticed a car approaching the intersection at an excessive and dangerously high rate of speed. Crossing at that same intersection was a young boy who was apparently released early from school. As is usual for young kids, he wasn't paying attention as he should have been. The light was just changing red against the driver, and he decided to beat the light. The driver of the car only saw the boy at the last minute and didn't even have time to apply the brakes. Rocco saw the young boy fly into the air and land about twenty feet away from where he had been standing in the crosswalk. The vehicle never stopped.

Rocco ran down the station house stairs and knelt down next to the child who was unconscious and not breathing. His training immediately coming to mind, Police Officer Deloberti started CPR on the boy. An off-duty Emergency Medical Technician who had just finished his shift happened to be passing by. He saw Police Officer Deloberti administering CPR on the child and immediately left his car and ran to help. Rocco was heavily into the CPR repetitions and was unaware that help had arrived. Applying CPR repetitions is tiresome work, so the EMT relieved Rocco and continued with the repetitions. The young boy was not coming around. Rocco took over again and vigorously continued with the CPR measures. By this time, other police officers were out of the station house, and an ambulance had been called to the scene. Rocco continued with the repetitions, and when the EMT wanted to relieve him again, Rocco refused to stop.

An ambulance arrived in a very short time and the responding EMTs tried to take over, but Rocco did not move and just continued with the CPR repetitions. It became obviously apparent to the EMT's that the boy had expired at the scene. However, Rocco, who had been administering CPR with the help of the off-duty EMT for well over 15 minutes, would not stop applying the measures. The EMT's nodded to the other officers who were at the scene, and the officers had to forcibly remove a reluctant Rocco away from the boy's body. Rocco pleaded with them to let him continue so he could save the little boy, but the responders all knew that nothing was going to bring the boy back.

Police Officer Rocco Deloberti went limp in the arms of his fellow officers and sobbed at his failure to save the child. On this day, Rocco Deloberti was definitely the poster-boy for the mantra that states "You can't save everyone."

It had been one hell of a day for Rocco, and he wondered if there were any positives to the job for which he had contracted. As he sat in his room at home, his cell phone rang and Janet's name appeared on the screen. He said "hello", and waited for Janet to respond. She said: "Hi Rocco, how was your day?" All she heard were sobs at the other end.

Chapter Five

Square One

Police Officer Rocco Deloberti had a rough introduction into law enforcement, but things seemed to have calmed down just a bit. Sure, as a rookie cop, he continued to get the least desirable assignments and posts, but he realized that everyone had to pay their dues, and he was in the process of doing just that.

It would have been easier to spot a white buffalo prancing down Main Street than to see a rookie cop assigned to a sector car with another police officer. However, through a number of unanticipated circumstances and the scarcity of additional police officers, Rocco Deloberti found himself sitting in the front seat of a radio car and assigned with another police officer to a specific sector in the precinct.

Rocco's partner for the day was a police officer who had about five years on the job, and who had oddly worked in a number of different precincts for four of those years. He was only in Rocco's precinct for a very short time. He was not the most experienced officer, but he had answered many calls for service. To Rocco's relief, his partner seemed like an easy guy to get along with. He had not yet been tainted by the attitude of some of the older officers who had been working in the precinct for many years. Having said that, however, he was the senior officer in the car, and he let Rocco know it.

The day started out with just a few calls that amounted to the completion of very little paper-work. For the first four hours of the tour, Rocco was the "recorder," which meant that he was responsible for all of the reports and paper-work. For the last four hours, Rocco would become the "operator," which meant that he was responsible for all of the driving.

A sector car had to show activity, so Rocco's partner, Police Officer Jamie Weston, drove to an area in their sector where he knew cars would be parked illegally. In addition to showing activity and clearing up a precinct problem, writing summonses in this neighborhood would give Rocco more experience in this area of police work. Rocco was more than happy to cooperate and learn from his partner. Jamie was correct. The parking situation in this particular location was atrocious with cars double parked, blocking fire hydrants and parked in safety zones. It was the commercial part of the precinct, but that didn't mean that parking and traffic regulations were going to be ignored.

Police Officer Weston did the right thing and slowly drove through the area letting everyone know that the police had arrived, and that the possibility existed that summonses were going to be issued. After his second drive through, Jamie stopped his vehicle, and both he and Rocco exited the car with summons books in hand. Even though it became obvious that the officers were going to issue summonses, there wasn't an onslaught of people rushing to their vehicles to avoid being ticketed. To some of these people, the convenience of being parked close to a particular location was well worth the amount of the summons. Between the two officers, fifteen summonses were issued with no complaints or incidents. Rocco was amazed with the lack of concern that these people had regarding the issuance of a summons. This commercial location was not new to the issuance of summonses; it had been classified as a "post condition" which meant that it was a problem area. Jamie and Rocco had addressed the post condition.

They left the commercial strip and were on their way to answer a complaint about harassment. Jamie pulled alongside a vehicle that was waiting for a red light to change. Rocco looked over at the vehicle, and the driver noticed Rocco. The driver turned away and then gunned his car right through the red light narrowly missing another vehicle which was going through the intersection. Police Officer Weston and Deloberti engaged the siren and emergency lights and were now in pursuit of a vehicle that had run a red light. However, the car looked vaguely familiar to Rocco. It closely matched the description of the hit-and-run vehicle that was involved in the recent killing of the young boy in front of the station house. The officers might be in pursuit of the hit-and-run assailant who was now wanted for vehicular homicide.

As procedures mandated, Police Officer Deloberti put the pursuit over the radio. The vehicle being pursued was reaching speeds of over seventy miles an hour on side streets. Rocco kept relaying the direction and speed as the pursuit continued. Both vehicles were traveling at breakneck speeds and other police officers, with their guns drawn, were now lining the projected streets as they awaited the fleeing vehicle. To both Jamie and Rocco, the situation was becoming increasingly dangerous. They feared that if the police officers began firing, there was a good possibility that rounds might enter their own vehicle and both of them could become possible victims of friendly fire. Jamie told Rocco to advise the central dispatcher to order that all police officers holster their weapons. The dispatcher did as Rocco requested, and, at least, the possibility of being shot by another police officer was removed.

In Police Officer Weston's opinion, the pursuit was continuing for much too long a period of time. Sooner or later some innocent people were going to get hurt. Weston turned to Rocco and told him to take out his weapon and fire at the suspect vehicle. Rocco couldn't believe what he was hearing, and he just looked at Jamie with a "Did I hear you right?" expression. Jamie emphasized his order with: "Do it!" Rocco drew his weapon, and extended his head outside of the car window. He took aim and fired several times, hitting the rear end of the suspect vehicle. The surprise and impact of the rounds caused the driver to lose control of the car, and he crashed into a parked vehicle. However, he was not injured and fled the vehicle with Police Officer Deloberti in pursuit. Rocco was able to cut off his path of escape and tackle the fleeing man. The suspect resisted, and Rocco used the necessary force to maintain control of the individual until his partner arrived.

The driver was placed under arrest and turned over to the precinct detectives for further investigation. Through excellent police work and detailed investigative accuracy, the detectives were able to connect the driver of the redlight violation to the hit-and-run killing of the young boy. Both Police Officer Weston and Police Officer Deloberti were awarded "Excellent Police Duty" medals. It was the third medal for Jamie and the first for Rocco. However, in years to come, firing a weapon at a fleeing vehicle would be prohibited, and the actual pursuit would have been called off by the patrol sergeant. But this day, none of those regulations were in effect, and the officers were rewarded for their actions.

Rocco was feeling good about the fact that the individual who had ruthlessly slaughtered a young boy would now be punished for what he did. Of course, nothing would bring the young boy back, but his death would not remain an unsolved case where justice was not exacted. For a young rookie cop, Rocco Deloberti was getting a full dose of police work. Unfortunately, he was still a rookie cop and that meant that he was still getting the assignments that the other more experienced cops didn't want. He was still paying his dues.

Unfortunately, the majority of the assignments that Rocco was still being assigned had to do with "fixed" posts. This meant that he had to stand in front of a specific location, many times a house of worship, and remain there for the duration of his tour. He was responsible for the safety and security of that location. Understand that it is demoralizing for someone who becomes a police officer to remain as a security guard in front of a specific location. In Rocco's case, it was even more demoralizing since he had a brief taste of real police work. The days became very long and the nights even longer. Unfortunately, the command that Rocco was assigned to had a large number of "fixed" posts, so escaping them was not going to be an easy task. For sure, most of these posts were assigned to the rookie cops, and there were more fixed posts than rookie cops. This ratio most assuredly dictated that rookie cops were going to become those stationary security guards assigned to posts that were created by the combination of political payback and religious influences.

For six months, Rocco and the other new cops were assigned to these stationary posts. At roll call, it was never a question of whether or not a rookie cop was going to be assigned to a "fixed" post, but rather which one of the stationary posts the officer would get. It became so demoralizing for Rocco and the others that going to work became a distasteful effort. It was so frustrating for Police Officer Deloberti that he had reached the end of his rope and was about to leave the police department. However, just before he formally handed in his separation papers, an order came down through the department asking for volunteers for assignment to scooter patrol. Although he knew nothing about this new patrol, anything was better than what he had been doing. Without hesitation, Police Officer Rocco Deloberti volunteered to become a scooter officer.

Shortly after he submitted his application for scooter patrol, Rocco was called for an interview. Since most of the older seasoned officers had their niche in the precinct and were not interested in scooters, there remained a number of openings for the new cops. Rocco aced the interview and was temporarily assigned to report for training at the Highway Patrol Unit. Since the Highway Unit utilized motorcycles in addition to vehicles, it was natural for this unit to be responsible for training all of the officers who were going to be assigned to the new patrol.

For approximately two months, Rocco along with the other volunteers were trained in the use of police scooters. They were taught how to ride, how to respond to certain calls, and how to use the scooter as a defensive weapon. Before long, the officers were becoming experts in the use of scooters for patrol. Upon their certification as motorcycle operators (a scooter license is viewed the same as a motorcycle license), the officers were assigned to the commands that were deemed pilot precincts for the project. This was great for Rocco because he was glad to get out of his former precinct that had more fixed posts than patrol posts.

When Rocco's name came up for precinct scooter patrol assignment, the training sergeant read out the precinct from which he had just left. Apparently, his former command was one of the pilot precincts. Rocco was going back to the only place where he didn't want to go. However, things had to be better because now he was a scooter operator.

Rocco's first post as a new scooter operator in his old command was in front of a house of worship where he utilized his scooter only for transportation to and from the fixed post. Police Officer Rocco Deloberti was back to square one!

Chapter Six

Youth Gangs

As with all new programs, the police department wanted statistics to see if the pilot project was succeeding. Fortunately for Rocco Deloberti, that meant that scooter officers had to actually go out on patrol. One cannot build up stats when he or she is assigned to a fixed post. Included in the statistical analysis was the number of hours the officer was actually patrolling on the scooter, so it was quite difficult for a commanding officer to fudge the numbers.

The commanding officer in the precinct to which Rocco was assigned had to develop a new scooter patrol chart. Accordingly, the hours for scooter patrol officers were limited to just two tours – 8:00am x 4:00pm and 4:00pm x midnight. This, of course, meant that Rocco and the other scooter officers would not have to work the dreaded midnight tour, the graveyard shift. So, becoming a scooter cop, now, not only eliminated the officers from being assigned to a fixed post, it also meant that the officers were excluded from assignment to the midnight tour. Finally, things were looking up for Rocco.

In addition to responding to minor calls for service, the scooter officers concentrated on the issuance of summonses. This showed patrol activity and added to the overall revenue that the city realized. With the statistics proving that scooter patrol was an asset to the operation of a precinct, scooter officers were sure to become a permanent fixture on the precinct roster sheets. In fact, scooter officers were being given specific assignments and locations where regular police vehicles could not easily navigate.

The youth gangs in the local parks were a major problem for the people living in the community. The gangs were taking over the parks and preventing families from utilizing these community assets for their children. The parks were riddled with drug paraphernalia and discarded sex items. They were also being frequented by the youth gangs in the late evenings with loud music blasting from the audio equipment that the gangs brought into the park. The precinct had received numerous complaints about the noise and the drug use in the parks.

===

The sergeant to whom the scooter officers reported decided that through the use of this relatively new asset, scooter patrol, the precinct was going to address the park problem and take back the parks for the community. The sergeant worked out a strategic plan for the most ravaged park. The scooter officers were going to enter through three separate entrances and push the youth gang members to the center of the park. With the help of back-up officers who waited just outside the park in their vehicles, the gang members would be summonsed and/or arrested and ushered out of the park. The officers would continue this strategy until the youth gang members no longer controlled the park.

Unbeknownst to the sergeant and the scooter officers, the youth gang had gotten word that the police were going to raid the park. The gang members had planned a surprise of their own. At ten o'clock in the evening, when the park had been officially closed for over two hours, all three scooter officers convened at the park entrances. They were waiting for the "go" signal from the sergeant to commence their raid on the park and the gang members. The sergeant made certain that the back-up units were in place, and that the scooter officers were ready to start their scooters and enter the park.

After carefully checking that all was ready, the sergeant gave the signal and the scooter officers started their scooters and began speeding into the park. The head lights on the scooters went on and the officers proceeded with the plan. However, shortly after the officers entered the park, Rocco noticed that the headlights from the other two scooters had disappeared. He thought it strange but proceeded with his part of the operation. When he arrived at the center of the park,

Rocco realized that he was alone with approximately thirty gang members. The other two scooter officers were nowhere in sight. The gang knocked Rocco off of the scooter and pushed him to the ground where they proceeded to punch and kick him. Rocco was helpless because of the number of assailants. Through the mayhem, Rocco heard the sirens of approaching radio cars and the gang quickly dispersed. However, the damage had been done, and Rocco was hurting as he lay on the ground waiting to be helped by his fellow officers.

The youth gang seemed to have been better prepared than the officers as they made off to different areas of the park where the police cars could not follow. Police Officer Deloberti was transported to the local hospital and treated for numerous cuts and bruises. It was there in the hospital that Rocco learned why the other scooter officers failed to follow the sergeant's strategic plan.

Apparently, the gang members were even more prepared than the officers originally thought. Across all three entrances to the park, members of the gang had strung piano wire at the approximate height of a cop sitting on a scooter. So, as the officers proceeded through the entrances, they were met with piano wire that hit the scooter wind screen and bounced off the helmets that the officers were wearing. The natural instinct for the police officers upon hearing and feeling the impact was to rear their heads back to avoid contact. This move, however, only added to the success of the trap as the officers were forcibly thrown backwards off the scooters. The other two scooter officers had sustained serious injuries and were in the same hospital as Rocco.

As Rocco waited for additional treatment, he mentally reviewed the entire evening focusing on what had gone wrong. A follow-up investigation had shown that there was piano wire mounted across all three entrances, but Rocco had escaped the potential for injury from the trap. He tried to recall how the wire had not forced him off of his scooter. He recalled that as he started to proceed through the entrance, he saw a red light appear on the scooter dashboard. As he looked down at the dashboard, he remembered hearing a sound bouncing off the wind shield and then an impact on the top of his helmet. At the time, he didn't pay too much attention to it. However, it was the fact that he had been bending and looking down at the dashboard that allowed the piano wire to hit off his helmet and glance over its smooth surface. Because of the downward angle of his helmet, the wire scooted off the back, and the piano wire trap failed. Rocco learned the hard way, however, that unfortunately, the trap was a success at the other two entrances.

The youth gang had won the battle, but in no way, were they going to win the war. Through street intelligence and intensified pressure, the precinct officers learned the location of an enclosure that was believed to be the meeting place for the youth gang. Having performed numerous off-duty clandestine surveillances of the location, the officers determined that their assumption regarding the enclosure was correct. It was, in fact, the headquarters of the gang.

===

Two weeks or so after the surveillance operation ceased, a call came over the radio on the 4 x 12 tour that there was an alarm of fire at a particularly familiar location to most of the officers. The uniformed officers responded, as always, to assist the firemen. However, they "carelessly" parked their vehicles in such a manner as to inadvertently block fire apparatus from immediate access to the fire location which was on an isolated one-way street. Finally, having cleared up the mishap, the fire officers reached the location. Unfortunately, it was too late for them to save the enclosure which had burned to the ground.

Not too far away from the burning structure was a vacant lot that was in line of sight to the flaming rubble. In the center of the lot, out of sight and on top of a small hill, stood three individuals who stared at the engulfing flames. They were friends, colleagues, and public servants who really had no interest in fires, but were totally curious as to the final destruction of this non-descript shelter. The fire having done the most damage possible, the three friends nodded to each other and proceeded to their vehicles. They coincidentally all had motorcycle licenses and drove off on their newly purchased scooters.

The precinct officers continued their raids on the community parks and were successful in giving back to the community this asset that was so sorely missed. The youth gangs in the area suffered losses as each of their headquarters locations suffered from the damage inflicted by the ravages of fire. The gangs were not totally dissolved, but they had to move on to other areas and find other meeting places where they could recruit more people and begin again. With criminal youth gangs, police officers never really eliminate the problem, but they force these advocates of disturbance and potential criminal behavior to ply their trade elsewhere.

To the people of the community, the problem of occupied parks had been solved, and families were able to enjoy what the parks had to offer. To the police, they had answered the complaints of the community and serviced its residents the best way they knew how, even if it was a bit unorthodox.

The youth gangs had won a battle, but they definitely lost the war!

Chapter Seven

The Pursuit

Things were going relatively well for Police Officer Deloberti, and he enjoyed the scooter assignment as well as the comradery of the other officers in the scooter patrol program. They patrolled together and socialized together. Rocco got particularly close to one officer, Joey (Red) Lelan. One could not miss Joey in a crowd. His red hair was a dead giveaway, hence the nickname, Red.

Included in the initial scooter training and the yearly retraining is the warning that scooters are not to be used to initiate a vehicle chase. That meant that if a car took off, the officer should just notify central dispatch and not start to pursue the vehicle. All of the officers knew the restriction, but sometimes when one is at the scene and the car takes off, the officer takes it personally. At that time, the "no pursuit" restriction goes by the wayside in favor of satisfying one's ego.

There were times when Rocco and Red had adjoining scooter patrol posts, and when that occurred, they got together and patrolled both posts as a team. It was safer and more enjoyable to have a partner on patrol. During one of these partner patrols, Red observed a vehicle go right through a stop sign and almost hit a pedestrian. Red signaled to Rocco, and they both followed the vehicle to the next stop sign where Red pulled alongside the car and ordered the driver to pull to the curb. The driver acknowledged the command and turned his head as if he was going to comply; however, he turned back to Red and yelled "fuck you," and sped off. Joey Lelan took the comment personally, and his ego dictated that he pursue the driver who insulted him. This was just what the training told the officers not to do. However, it's easier said than done when an officer is at the scene.

Pushing all his training and caution aside, Red began the pursuit. The police scooters were no match for a speeding vehicle, so Red had to hope that the driver would be caught in traffic and not be able to proceed. The offending operator would then be at the mercy of a very pissed-off police officer.

Rocco, who had been to the rear of the vehicle when it was originally stopped, saw that his partner was initiating a pursuit. In an attempt to curtail any further action and get to his partner as quickly as possible, Rocco inadvertently flooded too much gas into the engine. Rocco's scooter stalled. From experience, the scooter cops knew that once the scooter stalled, it took forever to restart. Rocco could only watch as his partner, at full throttle, was pursuing the vehicle. Even though the patrol supervisor would now know that Red initiated an unauthorized pursuit, Rocco put the pursuit out over the air. Red's safety was more important than his receiving a possible reprimand for violating procedures.

As Rocco radioed central dispatch, he kept his eye on his partner as he sped down the block after the vehicle. Rocco unsuccessfully tried to start his scooter a number of times and pounded on the gas tank in frustration. He only took his eyes off of his partner and the pursuit for a few brief seconds, but as he looked up again, he saw the illuminated red brake lights of the vehicle. The driver had jammed on his brakes so that the pursuing scooter cop would not be able to react in time and crash into the car. The vindictive driver's plan was successful. Rocco saw Joey Lelan crash into the rear of the vehicle and fly off the scooter over the car that he had been pursuing. Red landed in the roadway right in front of the vehicle. Apparently, and with no regard for human life, the driver proceeded to drive over the obstacle in his path, Red, and escape into traffic.

As Rocco ran down the street toward his partner, he called for an ambulance to be dispatched. Fortunately, there had been an unassigned ambulance in the area, and it responded shortly after Rocco got to his partner. Police Officer Joey Lelan was laying in the street and was unresponsive. Upon closer inspection, the responding Emergency Medical Technicians realized that the officer wasn't breathing, and they initiated the CPR protocols. Their efforts were nothing short of tireless, but Red was not responding. Additional police officers responded, and they all helped getting Red onto a gurney and into the ambulance. The EMT continued with the chest thrusts. With oxygen flowing through the face mask and CPR continuously being administered, the officers at the scene hoped that Red would pull through.

A small contingent of officers responded to the hospital and were available, as was the usual routine, to give blood, if needed. In the interim, a city-wide alert was dispatched with the description of the vehicle that was responsible for Red's injuries. With emotions running exceptionally high, there was a strong possibility that, if caught, the driver might experience some street justice. All precincts were on the lookout for the described vehicle. As it is with many incidents of this kind, sooner or later the vehicle will be spotted. The officers now knew, however, that the driver was capable of injuring and possibly killing a cop, so their approach would be a very calculated one. When the suspect vehicle was stopped, if there was any sudden movement from the operator of the vehicle, he would have put his life in jeopardy.

===

Shortly after the incident with Police Officer Lelan, a report of an accident came over the radio. The description of one of the vehicles involved in the accident matched the general description of the car that had hit Red. It was also reported that the operator of the suspect vehicle had originally stopped, but then floored his car and left the scene of the accident. A description of the individual and the vehicle was put out over the air, and it was accompanied with the warning that this individual could be the person wanted in connection with the incident involving Police Officer Lelan.

It was unfortunate that the suspect driver was able to flee from the scene into the neighborhood. If he was a local guy, and most likely he was, he would be able to find shelter with a number of people living in the area. There was no love lost among many of the local residents and the police officers in this high-crime area.

Through license plate information that was supplied by the driver of the other vehicle, it was determined that the individual went by the name of Austin Jones. Again, a city-wide alert was put out for Austin Jones who was wanted in connection with an assault on a police officer, and leaving-the-scene of an accident. Although the immediate responsibility for capture and arrest presently laid with the uniformed police officers, if capture was not imminent, detectives would soon get the case. Rocco knew that the longer the individual remained on the lamb, the harder it would be to capture him. However, Rocco's present concern was the condition of his partner and friend. He and the other officers waited patiently for news from the hospital and the attending doctor, but it was taking much longer than anyone anticipated. It was the consensus that the longer it took, the better the chance that the doctors were still treating a surviving Joey Lelan.

===

Joey's parents had arrived at the hospital, and they went right over to Rocco to find out about their son since no doctors or nurses were available. Rocco knew Red's parents very well and told them all he knew: "We are waiting for the doctors to give us some news. I am sure we'll find out shortly. We are all hopeful that Joey will be okay."

Joey's mother, through streaming tears, spoke first: "Rocco, how did Joey look? What happened? How did he get hurt?" Before Rocco could answer any of the questions, Joey's father spoke: "Someone said that a guy ran him over. Is that true?"

Rocco responded: "Mr. and Mrs. Lelan, we will have plenty of time to go over what happened, but right now we should focus on getting the information on Joey's condition from the doctors."

Joey's father spoke up again: "Rocco, if it did happen the way I heard, did we catch the son-of-a-bitch?"

"Mr. Lelan, we are still looking for the individual, and we have put out a city-wide alert for his capture. Sooner or later, we will get him."

"So, he is still out there, while my son is laying in the emergency room possibly fighting for his life?"

Rocco knew that Mr. Lelan was not expecting an answer to his rhetorical question. Joey's father was speaking out of pure worry, frustration and anger. Rocco just looked at Joey's dad, and the expression that Rocco had on his face confirmed the obvious situation to which Mr. Lelan was referring.

At that point, a doctor came out of the emergency treatment room, and as is procedure, he looked for the highest-ranking officer present. He spotted a lieutenant who had responded to the hospital. As the doctor got the lieutenant's attention and proceeded toward him, the doctor was intercepted by Mrs. Lelan who grabbed onto the doctor and pleaded with him regarding her son's condition. Not knowing who this woman was, the doctor looked at the lieutenant for clarification and support.

The lieutenant spoke: "Hey Doc, this is Mrs. Lelan, Joey's mother." Joey's father was standing right behind his wife, so the lieutenant also introduced Mr. Lelan to the doctor. The doctor asked Mrs. Lelan to sit on the chair that was next to her. She and the doctor sat down together: "Mrs. Lelan, we tried everything we could to save your son, but his injuries were just too severe. I am so sorry."

Mrs. Lelan just stared in shock at the doctor with disbelief at the news that she had just lost her son. This blank stare was followed by shrieking exclamations: "No! No! No! He can't be gone! He's my son! He can't be gone! Where's my Joey? Joey!"

Joey's mother collapsed in the chair, and the doctor called a nurse over to assist the grieving woman. Mr. Lelan also grabbed his wife and helped with supporting her.

Mr. Lelan looked at the doctor and asked: "Doc, was my son in pain?"

"Mr. Lelan, Joey never regained consciousness, and I'm sure he never experienced any pain. I am so sorry." The doctor left the group, and the nurse continued to assist Mrs. Lelan. Mr. Lelan, who could no longer hold back his tears, temporarily left his wife in the arms of the nurse, and went directly over to a tear-filled Rocco. Joey's father spoke in a whispered grieving tone: "Rocco, you have to find this bastard and make sure he doesn't live another day. Do you understand? For Joey, my only son and your friend, you have to find this son-of-a-bitch and avenge my son's death. Tell me you will! Tell me!"

In between sobs, Police Officer Rocco Deloberti confirmed to Joey's father that his son's perpetrator would not live for any length of time, and Rocco meant it. Joey's father, having received the answer that he was looking for, went back to his wife and consoled her as much as he could. Police Officer Rocco Deloberti went outside and yelled at the top of his lungs: "You can't hide! I'll get you, and you'll die just like my friend did. But you will suffer!"

The other officers gathered around Rocco and consoled him as best they could. The supervisor was there and was able to stop him from shouting. The ranking officer advised Rocco to take sick leave. Rocco agreed because sick leave would give him more time to find Joey's killer and administer his own form of justice. So, Rocco just answered the supervisor with a satisfying: "Yes, sir."

Chapter Eight

Vying for Plainclothes

Every day during his suggested sick leave, Rocco searched the neighborhood for the car that struck his partner. He looked carefully at every late model, silver/gray, 2 door coupe with dual exhaust pipes. Unfortunately, his search bore no fruit, and his sick leave was coming to an end. During his time off, he also contemplated his position in the department, and whether or not he should stay in the scooter patrol program. It was not going to be the same without Joey, and he had been in the program for quite a while. He had made a number of quality arrests and had issued far more summonses than the unofficial requirement.

Rocco had heard that one of the officers assigned to the precinct plainclothes unit was leaving to join the ranks of the city fire department. This meant that the plainclothes supervisor, in conjunction with the precinct commander, would be accepting applications for the vacant position. Rocco felt that he had just as good a chance as anyone else in the precinct, so he applied. It would be a welcomed change, and it would help Rocco put the devastations of the recent past behind him. He would never forget what happened, but the memories would fade a little as he addressed new challenges, worked with different officers, and explored new locations. As he thought about it, he not only wanted the plainclothes position, he needed it.

Rocco's interview lasted about thirty minutes, and he seemed to feel that it went relatively well. There were approximately ten applications for the position, but Rocco knew that just about four of those applications would be a "no-go" just because of the inactivity of the officers who applied. Rocco also had a negative stain that he had to deal with. He had that harassment complaint a few years back that stayed on his record; however, for the past few years, he had no complaints and had an active and clean record. He was hoping that the sergeant would take that into consideration.

Two weeks after the initial interviews, the sergeant called Rocco and another officer who applied for the position into his office. The supervisor conducted another separate interview with each officer. This time, however, the supervisor wanted to know why the particular officer felt that he should be picked, and why he would be a better choice than the other applicant waiting to be interviewed. The sergeant pitted both applicants against one another.

Rocco knew the other police officer but not as well as he knew others. He worked opposite tours than the other officer and, therefore, only knew about him. What Rocco had heard about his competition was that he was a good officer who was an active cop. He had a little more time on the job than Rocco but favored working day tours. Apparently, he had a growing family and preferred to be home at night with his wife and children. But didn't most cops want that?

During Rocco's interview with the sergeant, the supervisor referred to the recent tragic incident of which Rocco had been a part: "Officer Deloberti, how are you doing after what happened to your partner?" Rocco thought that the question would come up, so he was somewhat prepared for it: "Sarge, it is something that I will never forget, but instead of weakening or hampering my resolve, I believe that it has made me a stronger and even more cautious police officer. However, to say that my partner's death didn't devastate me at the time, would be a lie."

The sergeant continued: "Do you think that because of what happened that you would tend to be overly cautious when it came to certain operations? Being too careful could also become a hindrance not only for you but for your other team members."

"No Sarge, the incident with Joey has shown me that I should never take things for granted. It has shown me that just acting on assumptions alone could, sometimes, have negative and dangerous results."

"What's your opinion about your competition, Officer Prathers?"

"Sarge, I don't think that I am in a position to offer an opinion about Jake Prathers, but from what I hear from other officers, he is highly regarded and easy to get along with. I also believe that if he is successful, the unit would benefit by his acceptance."

"Thank you, Rocco. As you leave, please ask Officer Prathers to come in."

"Sure thing, Sarge, and thank you for the opportunity."

When Rocco Deloberti left the sergeant's office, he nodded to Jake who had been patiently waiting, and wished him luck. Jake Prathers thanked Rocco and entered the sergeant's office.

Police Officer Rocco Deloberti resumed his scooter patrol responsibilities while he waited for the results of the interviews. Even if he passed the supervisor's interview, he knew that the commanding officer would have the final say on any transfer. Two more weeks passed, and still there had been no determination on who would fill the vacant plainclothes position. Rocco didn't want to wait any longer, so he headed for the plainclothes sergeant's office. Just before he was about to knock on the door, the door opened and the sergeant was standing before him: "Police Officer Deloberti. Just the person I was coming to see. Please come with me to the commanding officer's office. He wants to speak with you."

"Sure Sarge, I'm right behind you."

The Commanding Officer, Captain Richard Geskasco, was a strict but fair individual. He was liked by most of the rank and file, and encouraged everyone to do more than expected of them. He was ranked very high among commanding officers and was expected to be promoted on the next go around.

The commanding officer greeted Rocco: "Have a seat Officer Deloberti. Do you have any idea why I asked to see you?"

"Yes sir. I was hoping that a final decision had been made regarding the precinct plainclothes position."

"Well, Rocco, a final decision hasn't just yet been made. It will be, however, when we finish talking. The sergeant here has recommended that you be transferred to the plainclothes unit. I have reviewed your record, and I see that you have been an active cop. We do not want any slouchers in plainclothes. I also see that you have a good attendance record and have not had any problems with supervisors. All that is good, but tell me why do you want to go into plainclothes?"

"Captain, I have been in uniform for almost five years and have been in the scooter patrol program for over two years. I believe that I can apply the experience that I have accrued to assist in the plainclothes operation. I also see the unit as one that will offer new challenges for me to explore, and I am more than happy to confront those challenges and possibly learn from them. Whenever I have garnered information that I thought the unit could use, I didn't hesitate to give it to them. And because of this interaction, I have come to know most of the plainclothes officers. I believe that I would fit in well with the personalities and expectations of the officers in the unit. I see plainclothes as a unit in which I could excel and work with other officers who have also proven themselves."

"Well, Rocco, that was a mouthful. I expected an answer, but I wasn't prepared for a campaign speech." Rocco was taken aback, but when the captain smiled, Rocco was relieved.

"Rocco, I consider myself as a fair but disciplined leader. I know what I am doing, and I do not need help from any outside source." Rocco did not know where the captain was going with his statement, but he continued to listen. The commanding officer continued with his remarks: "I did not get any phone calls from a priest, a political leader, the principal of a school, or the mayor's office trying to convince me that you were the right person for the plainclothes unit. Why didn't I?"

"Captain Geskasco, I didn't know that a phone call was one of the requirements that would lead to success. However, I am not that familiar with any one of the people you mentioned, and I felt that I should be able to get the position based on my own merits. Apparently, I should have worked harder to get some kind of endorsement, but that goes against my way of thinking. If I can't get the position on my own, then I don't deserve it, but thank you anyway, Captain."

Rocco rose to leave the captain's office, but he was asked to remain seated.

"Officer Deloberti, I have received no less than three phone calls regarding the possible transfer for Jake Prathers." Rocco understood, and he felt that there was no need for the commanding officer to continue to rub it in. However, the captain continued: "You have no idea how I hate those type of calls. This is my command, and I know the people, the officers, and what is best for the community. I do not need anyone else telling me what I should do. Upon the sergeant's recommendation and the results of this interview, you will be assigned to the precinct plainclothes unit as soon as possible."

The commanding officer rose from his chair, and walked to Rocco who was shocked that he had been chosen. He had incorrectly read the captain's original statement and was elated that he had. The captain shook Rocco's hand and congratulated him on his success.

The captain ended the meeting as any disciplinarian would: "Just remember Officer Deloberti that as quickly as I can assign you to the plainclothes unit is as quickly as I can transfer you out of it."

"Yes sir, I understand." Rocco expected nothing less from the commanding officer.

Chapter Nine

A Tough Decision

In the blink of an eye, Police Officer Rocco Deloberti was assigned to the precinct plainclothes unit. Since he was the newest officer in the unit, the sergeant partnered Rocco with Police Officer John Hallerin. Officer Hallerin had previously been assigned to the city-wide plainclothes unit, but because of a personality clash with the newly assigned supervisor of that unit, Hallerin was transferred to precinct duty. However, the commanding officer of the precinct, knowing the value of an experienced plainclothes officer, recognized Hallerin's expertise and assigned him to the precinct plainclothes unit.

Rocco was in awe of John Hallerin's experience and could not wait to learn from him. Hallerin, however, was not exactly thrilled with having an inexperienced partner. Hallerin made his feelings known to the sergeant, but ultimately accepted the sergeant's decision. He didn't need another problem with a different supervisor. Rocco knew that he had a lot to learn, and who better to learn from than someone who had been in plainclothes on a city-wide assignment. Rocco was sure that John had seen it all, and now Rocco was going to benefit from his partner's experience.

There was quite an age difference between Rocco and his partner, but that did not seem to bother either one of them. In fact, after a while, Rocco started referring to his partner as "Pop." Apparently, Hallerin didn't outwardly object to the nickname, and it stuck with the rest of the officers in the unit. Thanks to Rocco Deloberti, Police Officer John Hallerin was now known as "Pop."

Until he started riding with his partner, Rocco didn't realize how much he didn't know about the street. Pop pointed out things to his partner that Rocco would have never associated with criminal behavior. Pop called his partner's attention to such things as runners who transported bets and monies, lookouts who notified the participants of a big-time illegal card game that the cops were near, women who were plying their trade as prostitutes, young kids who delivered drugs, and gang members who were looking for the opportunity to enhance their position in their gang. There were so many things that Pop pointed out that the ordinary cop would never assume to be connected to any type of criminal behavior. Pop's knowledge of the street was amazing, and Rocco was overwhelmed with the wealth of knowledge that he was trying to digest. Rocco knew that he had made the right decision to apply for the plainclothes unit, and he was gratified that the sergeant had him working with someone who could show him the ropes of a plainclothes operation. Rocco was excited.

In a short time, Pop and Rocco became the most active plainclothes team in the unit. In fact, their activity challenged the numbers of the plainclothes units in adjoining precincts. They were getting a reputation, and it was a good one. Their work was recognized by the sergeant and the commanding officer. Pop and Rocco became the "go-to" team in the unit. They were given the better assignments and were involved in the investigations that were earmarked for a certain amount of notoriety. The boss had total confidence in the "go-to" team, and they didn't disappoint.

Although it was a far cry from the reality of the situation, at times the activity of a plainclothes officer resulted in the possibility of an interview for the detective squad. This thought existed in the far reaches of both their minds, but Pop and Rocco knew that there was a lot more involved than just activity. So, they concentrated on their present responsibilities and their ability to be that reliable team that the bosses counted on.

On one particular day, Pop drove to a local park where a number of older men sat at cement tables and played cards. For some reason, this was one of the regular stops for Pop. He always parked the car out of sight and told Rocco to wait for him while he did some surveilling of the area. This day, however, there were no advantageous spots, so Pop parked in a spot where his partner had a partial view of the "surveillance" that was taking place. Rocco eyeballed his partner, as best as he could, and he saw Pop going from table to table, conversing with one person at each table and accepting an envelope from that person. Pop then placed each envelope in his pocket and disappeared into the center of the card playing area.

The whole ordeal struck Rocco as being odd, and he decided that he was going to ask his partner what was going on. Rocco's original thought was that the men were giving Pop intelligence information, but Pop never shared that information with Rocco. Rocco's curiosity was aroused, and when Pop returned to the car, Rocco posed the question to him: "Hey, Pop. What's with the visits to the tables and the envelopes that the men give you. If it's intelligence information, then we both should know about it, right?"

Pop smiled and shook his head: "Rocco it's not intelligence, and I'm sorry you saw what you saw, but I guess you have a right to know what is going on. I allow those men to gamble at the tables. The games are high stakes games, and they are organized through the local crime family. I collect from each table and then from the mob guy who oversees the action. Now that you know, I guess you want your fare share."

Pop was very matter of fact as he explained the whole operation to his partner. They started driving away from the park, and finally, Rocco fully digested what he was just told. He looked at Pop with disbelief and started asking questions: "What do you mean, Pop? You're taking money from the mob to allow them to run an illegal gambling operation? What are you doing? You are as corrupt as they are. Is everybody in on the whole thing? Do the other guys in the unit know what's going on? Is the sergeant in on it too?"

Pop realized that Rocco was having a hard time accepting what was going on. So, he pulled to the curb and tried to explain the situation while he answered the barrage of questions that Rocco threw at him: "Rocco, no one is getting hurt by what we do. It's a live and let live philosophy where everyone benefits, including you. The other guys get their share as well as the sergeant. It is more or less just a way of doing business. The extra money comes in handy for a whole lot of things. You'll see. It's not something new, Rocco. It's be going on for a very long time, and it will continue long after we are gone."

"Pop, I can't believe what I'm hearing. It may have gone on for a long time, but it's going to stop right now. I am not going to be a part of something that is corrupt and goes against everything we stand for. It stops right now, or I will go to someone in the department who will make sure it stops. Do it on your own, Pop. Don't make me do something that will hurt a lot of people. And I am going to ask to work with a different partner. Maybe, someone new like myself, who hasn't yet been corrupted by you and the other corrupt individuals. I'm warning you, Pop. I will stop it if you don't."

"Hold on, Rocco. Think about what you are saying. I don't take to threats very well, and I'm sure no one else is going to appreciate them. You don't understand who you are dealing with. Do you really think that we are going to just sit back and let you ruin an operation that makes us all breathe financially a little easier? Let me answer that for you. No! You don't realize it, but you are putting yourself and others that you care about in jeopardy. Don't be foolish. If you can't handle it, get out. Go back to uniform patrol, or ask to be assigned to another precinct. You don't have to be a part of anything that you don't want to be, but keep your nose out of my business!"

Rocco just shook his head and got out of the car. As Pop drove off, Rocco couldn't believe how wrong he was about his partner, and for that matter, about the rest of the unit, and in particular, the sergeant. As he walked back to the precinct station house, his mind was flooded with the possibilities that were available to him. However, some of those possibilities had the potential to bring harm to him and maybe his family. He needed to bounce the situation off of someone who was level headed and outside of the situation.

===

As a result of arrests, overtime and court appearances, Rocco hadn't spent as much time as he would have liked with his girlfriend, Janet. However, they had gotten closer and were seriously talking about engagement and marriage. Janet was the ideal person with whom Rocco could discuss his next move. She knew the people involved and the nature of the police work in which Rocco was participating. Also, Rocco wanted to let her know that Pop had threatened that people who Rocco cared about could be in danger if he went ahead with his plan to reveal all. Janet would be a great resource for a discussion about the situation, but she also had a right to know. He decided to take the rest of the day off and head over to Janet's house. He was sure that she would be able to offer great insight into a complex problem.

Before he headed to Janet's house, however, he wanted to make a quick stop and ask someone else for whatever help that individual could offer. He left the precinct and drove directly to St. Boniface Church to seek advice. He didn't speak to a priest but petitioned Jesus directly to guide him in the serious decision that he was about to make. He entered the church, knelt down, and prayed.

Chapter Ten

A Blazing Message

Janet left work later than usual, and by the time she arrived home, night had fallen. She parked her car and headed toward the house. She only had a short walk before she would be at the front door, but as she walked, she heard steps behind her. The steps came closer and closer, and when she turned around, she saw two men in ski masks. One of the men slapped her across the face, and the other one went behind her and had his arm wrapped around her neck in a threatening choke hold. Recovering from the immediate shock of the situation, she heard the assailant behind her whisper: "Tell your boyfriend to back off or there will be a lot more than just a cut on the neck." The attacker then took the knife that he had in his hand and cut a two-inch incision into Janet's neck. As she immediately started bleeding, the knife wielding assailant threw her to the sidewalk, and the two individuals fled into the night.

Janet Commings held her neck and struggled to her feet. There was blood on her neck and on her hands. She was dizzy and hurt, but she was able to stumble to her front door. She rang the bell, and her mother opened the door to a shocking sight: "Janet, my God! What happened? Here, let me help you." Janet's mom ushered her into the house, and helped her to a chair. Janet's father came into the room and had the same reaction as his wife: "My God, Janet! What happened?"

As Janet tried to explain how she was attacked, her mother carefully examined the cut on her daughter's neck and prepared to clean and bandage it. Janet explained that two men approached her as she walked to the house. She further told her parents that the men threatened further harm "if her boyfriend didn't back off." Her parents questioned Janet as to what the statement meant. Janet responded that she had no idea, but that she would definitely ask Rocco when she saw him. Just as she finished telling her parents what had occurred, the front door bell rang again. Mr. Commings carefully approached the door and was relieved to see Rocco standing there.

Rocco immediately realized that something was wrong and went directly to Janet who was still shaking from her encounter. Rocco looked at her and saw the blood on her neck. Just as her mother and father had done, he caringly asked: "Janet, what happened?" Janet repeated her story again and when she was through, she asked Rocco what was going on:

"Rocco, the guy said that you should 'back off' or else. What does he mean? Back off from what?" Rocco knew what the two men were talking about. It had to be connected to the conversation he had with his partner regarding the corrupt activity in which the unit was involved. It seemed that they were really worried, and would do whatever they had to do to prevent Rocco from becoming a "Frank Serpico."

Rocco sat down and went through the whole story. He mentioned that he had decided to visit with her because he wanted to discuss the situation and get her personal perspective on what she thought he should do: "Janet, you now know the whole story. I am so sorry that they involved you in this thing. I had no idea to what level they would sink in order to keep the corrupt activity a secret. Apparently, I am, no we are, dealing with very desperate individuals. However, I am telling you that they will pay for what they did to you tonight. It may not be through the department, but they will rue the day that they caused you to bleed."

"No, Rocco, don't lower yourself to their level. Then, you become just as bad as they are. Also, they seem so desperate that they might not hesitate to really hurt you. It's not worth it. Rocco, I know how you feel about what they did and are doing, but you can't save the world. Sooner or later, they will get caught and justice will be done. I don't know if you should put yourself at risk, and you can't unofficially confide in any one in the department. Maybe, you should transfer out of the plainclothes unit and go back to patrol. Or maybe, you should even think about asking for a transfer to another precinct."

“It’s ironic, Janet, because those are the two options that I was given. However, it makes me feel that I am complicit in what the unit is doing. I know the problem, and I am just running away from it.”

“Rocco, you have seen what they would do just as a warning. Could you imagine what would happen if you actually went ahead and officially reported their corrupt activity. You, me and our families would be at risk. I believe, that at least for the present, you have to divorce yourself from any connection with the unit and apply for a different position. If the time comes when they are caught, and it comes to light that you knew about their activity and did nothing about it, you can always tell them that you feared for my safety and that of our families. I will have the scar on my neck to prove it.”

“Janet, you do realize that if they are involved with the mob in the park connection, then they are probably involved in other corrupt activities. How do I just let that continue?”

“How do you do it? For now, you just walk away. Let someone else take that first step. Sooner or later, they will mess up, and it will all come out. Rocco, I am scared not only for myself, but definitely for you. You don’t know what they will do, and you don’t even know how high the corruption goes. Ask for a transfer and make up whatever excuse you want, but get out of that unit.”

“I understand how you feel, Janet, but it is very hard for me to just walk away. However, I can’t be with you all of the time, and, apparently, they are not afraid to inflict pain. I will ask for a temporary transfer to patrol while awaiting a transfer to another precinct. That should allay their fears regarding my reporting the corruption. I am just so disappointed in the guys, and especially in Pop, who I trusted and admired. It is such a letdown. I don't know if I can even look at them; however, I promise you that it may not be today or tomorrow, but one day they will pay for harming you. I am sure that by now, all the guys in the unit, including the sergeant, are aware about what has occurred. Maybe, it might be best for me to ask for a leave of absence or an extended sick leave. This way, I won't have to interact with any one of them. At this point, I don't know who the enemy is, and what actions they are willing to take."

"Rocco, I disagree with your not going in at all. That shows out-and-out fear, and that is what people like Pop thrive on. No, go into work and meet controversy face-to-face. Understand that you have 'right' on your side, and no one can take that away from you."

"Janet, I think you missed your calling, you could have been a motivational speaker." They both smiled, and at least for the moment, they were both relieved. However, in the back of his mind, Rocco was plagued with the thought of returning to work. Since his request for a transfer back to patrol might take a little while, he decided that he was going to ask the plainclothes sergeant if, until his transfer came through, he could be assigned to data collection for the monthly unit activity report. Also, since the sergeant surely knew what had transpired between Pop and him, the supervisor would probably prefer that Rocco stay in the station house anyway. That way, he was away from the street activity, and his activities could be more closely monitored. Rocco was sure that his request would be granted.

The next day Rocco was back at work and was collecting data and numbers for the monthly unit activity report. He had no trouble convincing the sergeant to assign him to the office. In fact, the sergeant looked relieved that Rocco wanted to stay inside. The supervisor knew that Rocco had also put in for a transfer to another precinct. With the sergeant's endorsement, it should come about quickly.

When Pop and the rest of the plainclothes officers came in from the street, they all went about their business as if nothing had happened. All of them except for Pop who slowly moseyed over to where Rocco was sitting and directed some comments to him: "Hello, Rocco. How's it going? I understand that you interviewed for the unit secretary. I think that's a great decision on your part. Why put yourself in an uncomfortable position? If you need anything, don't hesitate to ask."

In a voice that only Pop could hear, Rocco responded: "You think you won? Sooner or later, you'll get caught, and I will have the last laugh when I add my testimony to the already damaging information that the district attorney will have. You will all get what you rightly deserve. Lastly, if you ever threaten or touch my girlfriend again, all bets are off. I will immediately go to the D.A. and file an official report of corruption, and at that point, I wouldn't care who it takes down. Additionally, I will inflict ten times the pain that you have caused my girlfriend, and you will never know when it is coming. You mentioned that I didn't know who I was dealing with. No, John (Rocco intentionally didn't use the nick name that he had given his partner), it is you who don't know!"

Pop responded: "You know, Rocco, you are not a very good listener. I told you once before that I do not react well to threats. I guess you forgot that." Pop just sneered, shook his head and went back over to his desk.

Since it was close to the end of the tour, the guys in the unit started preparing to leave. Rocco noticed, however, that two of the officers weren't at their desks. Rocco needed their activity sheets for the day, so he inquired as to their whereabouts. No one responded. As Rocco was about to let the sergeant know that he couldn't complete the day's activity sheet, he was distracted by the sound of horns and sirens. The plainclothes office was on the second floor, so the officers went to the front windows to see what was happening. They observed firemen fighting a blaze that had engulfed a car which was parked right across the street from the station house.

As Rocco looked more closely from his vantage point at the window, he recognized that it was his car that was ablaze. Rocco shouted a number of expletives and turned to run down the stairs to his engulfed auto.

Pop had been standing next to him and before Rocco started his run, Pop grabbed him by the arm and whispered: "I told you that I don't react well to threats."

Rocco got to his car just as the gas tank exploded. His car was totaled.

Chapter Eleven

The Replacement

Seeing his car totally destroyed, Rocco turned toward the stationhouse and looked up at the second-floor window where Pop was standing. Pop nodded and walked out of sight. With his anger reaching its limit, and his rage taking over his logical thinking, Police Officer Deloberti ran with reckless abandon across the street to confront his nemesis as quickly as possible. He didn't care what happened, but Rocco was not going to let John Hallerin get away with anything else. Unfortunately, that was the final thought Rocco had as an oncoming van crashed into him and sent him airborne. He landed unconscious in the middle of the street.

When the ambulance arrived, Rocco was still non responsive. However, after the initial treatment by the EMTs, Rocco opened his eyes. He didn't move, and the paramedics did not want him to move not knowing the degree of damage. With the help of some of the officers who came to Rocco's aid, the EMTs lifted Rocco onto a gurney and placed him inside of the ambulance. None of the officers who were in the plainclothes unit responded to assist their fellow officer. They just watched from their second story perches and were inwardly glad that the threat to their job security and possibly to their freedom was no longer as imminent as it could have been.

Rocco Deloberti laid in the hospital with broken ribs, a punctured lung, and a concussion. He was surrounded by his family, his girlfriend and her family, and the attending doctor and nurse. The doctor informed Rocco just how lucky he was, and that he should be making a total recovery. He also let Rocco know that he had to take it easy to allow the concussion to fade and the ribs to heal. Rocco understood and thanked the doctor who left the patient in the company of his visitors.

When it came time for everyone to leave, Rocco asked Janet to stay behind for a few more minutes. She told her parents that she would be with them shortly, and then asked Rocco what was on his mind. He started to tell her the whole story about what led up to his being in the hospital, but then he thought better of it. He did not want Janet to try and talk him out of any plan that he was going develop to seek his justified revenge. Janet realized that Rocco was holding back, and so she encouraged him: “Rocco, tell me. Don’t keep me in the dark. We are in this together. What is it?”

After a few moments of hesitation, Rocco told her exactly what had occurred. She listened intently without interruption and then responded to her boyfriend with a surprising comment: “I won’t deny that it is an awful lot to take in, and I truly understand how you feel. You know my feelings about getting back or seeking satisfaction, and ideally, I still hold to those commitments. However, this is not an ideal situation, so whatever you decide to do, count me in!”

One could have knocked Rocco over with a feather. He couldn’t believe what he had just heard. In fact, he couldn’t even speak. He just looked at Janet with bewilderment. She had, apparently, reached her wits end. She now wanted to dole out some of what others had been inflicting on both Rocco and her.

Rocco came out of the shock from what was just said: “Babe, I have mixed feelings about what I just heard. I am really happy that you support me, but you have to realize that we are dealing with desperate people, and desperate people do desperate things. I don’t know if I want you to take that risk. They have already shown you what they are capable of doing, and we have not even done anything yet. You can imagine what they would do if their lives actually became complicated with a whole lot of negative elements that we introduce. If they have any idea that I, or we, have anything to do with their problems, I am certain that Pop and his cronies would seek to make our lives miserable, or even dangerous. I don’t know if I want to put you in that position.”

"Rocco, you are not putting me anywhere. I am putting myself there, and I have made up my mind. I not only want to be a part of your plan; I need to be. The scar on my neck has still not fully healed."

Rocco knew that at this point, he was not going to convince his girlfriend to reconsider. Outwardly, he showed worried concern, but inwardly, he was actually happy to have her on board. It was going to be a while, however, before he could develop a plan and exact his revenge. The stay in the hospital and his recuperation period at home would give him plenty of time to devise a scenario that his corrupt comrades would not soon forget. That was all he could think about.

Rocco agreed to let his girlfriend partake in the upcoming plans, and he thanked her for being so supportive. She smiled and said that she would be back later to visit with him. Rocco was finally alone, and the impact of what his fellow officers did to him was sinking in. He thought of them now as no less than the criminals that they were sworn to stop. For the almighty dollar, they stooped to the levels occupied by the street thugs. As Rocco continued to ponder their corrupt actions, he not only came to totally disrespect them, but actually despise them. They were not cops. They were criminals, and he would deal with them as such.

His body having gone through heavy trauma from the automobile accident, and his mind working overtime on possible vindictive activities, the resulting physical and mental fatigue that plagued his existence slowly moved him into the arms of deep sleep. As the doctor had said, his body needed down time to recover, and sleep was the best way to foster that down time. Rocco slept through the visiting hours that evening and through the night. He only awakened for a few short moments when he turned, and his ribs let him know that they were still not yet mended. The pain startled him, but the fatigue won out, and he drifted back into that deep and much-needed slumber.

When Rocco finally awoke the next morning, he opened his eyes to doctors and nurses attending to him. They welcomed him to the day, and then started taking his blood pressure, his temperature, the percent of oxygen in his bloodstream and undertaking other hospital routine procedures. When they completed the initial examination, the doctor started poking around at his rib cage. With each touch, Rocco grimaced in pain. The doctor told him that the pain was to be expected, and that ribs take a while to heal. He also mentioned that "they have to heal by themselves." Rocco acknowledged the doctor's comments and forced a smile.

The final thing that the doctor wanted Rocco to do was to blow into a device to make certain that his lungs were working at full capacity. Rocco took the device and blew into it, but the ball that was supposed to rise moved just a little. At the doctor's insistence, Rocco did it again, and through the pain Rocco was able to move the ball a little bit more. It was difficult to really exert a lot of pressure to make the ball rise because the pain in his ribs also restricted the ability to take a deep breath. However, the doctor was insistent on Rocco repeating the exercise, especially since he came to the hospital with a collapsed lung.

So, Rocco bit his lip and continued to work through the pain. When the doctor finally told Rocco to stop, he also told him that he would have to breathe into this device at least three times a day. It was not what Rocco wanted to hear, but if it was going to get him out of the hospital any quicker, he would make sure to do it.

===

Janet was able to get off from work and come to the hospital in the afternoon. She was glad to see that her boyfriend was up and feeling a little better. They discussed a number of things, and Rocco told her that he had gotten visits from a lot of the cops in the precinct. He was even visited by the commanding officer, who was in the company of the plainclothes sergeant. They only stayed for a short while when Captain Geskasco told Rocco that if there was anything that he needed to just let the sergeant know, and he would take care of it. Rocco was so tempted to reveal all at that time, but he held his tongue and thanked the captain. Rocco never once looked at the sergeant. Rocco also mentioned to his girlfriend that not one of the officers in the plainclothes unit came to visit him. He pointed out that it was a clear indication that they were all in on the corruption scheme.

Just as he finished his diatribe about the corrupt cops, a young guy who Rocco had never seen before interrupted the conversation with: "Excuse me. I am Officer Bobby Santiago, and I heard that you had been hurt and taken to the hospital. I have just been transferred into the plainclothes unit, and I felt that I wanted you to know that I and the other officers are thinking about you."

"Well, thank you for coming, Bobby. However, I didn't know that there was an opening in the unit."

"Yes, the sergeant said that there will be an opening very shortly, and he wanted me to become familiar with the operation. So, here I am. I worked in patrol for about two years, and then was transferred to this command. I stayed in patrol here for a year when the sergeant approached me and offered me a position in the unit. I'm really excited to start, but I am really sorry to meet you under these circumstances."

"Thanks a lot, Bobby. I really appreciate your coming by. Good luck in the unit, and I'm sure we will be talking." Janet also thanked the officer, and Bobby Santiago left.

Janet looked at Rocco and said: "Wow, you're not even gone yet, and they already have a replacement."

Rocco looked at her and responded: "Yeah, a replacement who didn't have to interview for the position, and I bet an officer with no-where-near the needed activity to join the unit. He must know someone. He just might be the person that we are looking for. His 'contract' person might be the vehicle for us to use for the unit's demise. God works in strange ways!"

Chapter Twelve

The Cop Killer

Following his deadly encounter with Police Officer Joey Lelan, Austin Jones went into hiding, knowing full well that the entire police department would be looking for him. He had killed one of their own, and Jones knew that they would never give up looking for him. He never left the area, but hid in plain sight. He had many associates who had no strong liking for the police, so Austin had a number of locations where he could hide out. In fact, to ensure that no one would give him up, he regularly relocated to different friendly locations.

Knowing that a description of his car had been transmitted to every cop on patrol, and that they were probably still looking for it, Austin decided that the smart thing to do was to have his 2-door coupe repainted. Ultimately, he would have to leave his hideouts and get back into circulation, so he had to change the look of his wheels. One of the places where he spent some time keeping out of sight was the back-room apartment of a mechanic shop that often dealt with stolen car resurfacing. A stolen car ring utilized the shop, and when a "hot" car was delivered to the shop, the workers immediately began the process of changing its color and overall look. This was just the place Austin needed to help change the look of his car. His 2-door silver/gray coupe would be transformed into an all-black sports vehicle. This change would definitely facilitate his reentry into the criminal operations in which he thrived.

The police department had received a squeal from a confidential informant that, indeed, the mechanic shop where Jones brought his car had been involved with a major stolen car ring. Wanting to get as much as they could from the information that the department received, the local investigations team slowly worked the case with an eye on capturing the mob bosses who dictated the operation from the top. The police had eye-balled the shop for at least six months during which time they were able to get an undercover cop into the shop as another person who worked on the stolen vehicles.

Before long the undercover officer became a trusted member of the team and got involved with a variety of different tasks from painting the cars to changing the vehicle identification numbers (V.I.N.). Officer Jamie Weston had infiltrated the operation and was working on getting information on the "guys-at-the-top." As soon as he finished developing the profile on the mob bosses, the mechanic shop would be raided and the investigators would squeeze the workers for additional information. It was anticipated that the new information would lead to even a greater number of arrests. Jamie had come a long way from the pursuit he had shared with Officer Rocco Deloberti. With a successful conclusion to this undercover assignment, he could possibly become "Detective" Jamie Weston.

It was Jamie who was privy to a conversation regarding a paint job for a guy who had to hide from the cops. In the shop, Austin Jones explained to his friend and boss, Freddie, that he had to change the color of his car because the cops were looking for him, and they had a description of the car. When he was asked why the police were looking for him, he grinned and explained that "unfortunately" he had decreased the number of "pigs" by one. Since no one in the shop was crazy about cops, Austin's friend wanted all the details, and Jones was all too happy to tell the entire story, a story that Jamie Weston also heard.

As Austin Jones and Freddie laughed about the whole situation, Jamie wanted to kill them both. However, he outwardly maintained his cool and realized that soon these people would get their due. But now he wasn't just dealing with a stolen car ring, he was dealing with a cop killer. After what he heard, Jamie was going to get a lot of satisfaction in bringing this murderer to justice. Austin was bragging about how the officer flew over the car, and how he was able to drive right over the cop, hearing bones crushing. Undercover cop Jamie Weston couldn't wait until it was time to place the metal bracelets around Austin James' wrists.

Irony plays a huge part in everyday life, and it showed its face again when Jamie was given the task of redoing Austin James' vehicle. Jamie spoke directly to Jones and asked him what he was looking for. Austin told him that the main concern was changing the color of the car. He said that every "fucking" cop would still be looking for a silver/gray coupe. He was hoping that a black coupe would slide under the radar. Jamie told him that he understood, and that he would start on the project in a few days. Austin balked at Jamie's statement and told him that he needed it done as quickly as possible. Jones explained that he planned on leaving the area for a while and needed his car to expedite his escape. He didn't want to risk even the slightest possibility that someone would give away his location and facilitate his capture. After all, the police were offering a substantial reward for any information that would lead to his capture and arrest. In his criminal world, he knew that money talks. Sooner or later, somebody was going to give in to the temptation of easy money. Austin was not going to allow that to happen. He was smarter than that. He needed to get away as soon as possible.

Jamie wanted to delay the Austin Jones project for as long as he could, so he went to the boss and told him that he was behind on some of the other tasks that he had been assigned. If Jamie was going to be able to comply with the demand that the stolen car ring placed on him, the Jones' project would have to wait. He explained that he could possibly get to it in about three or four days. Since the doctoring of stolen vehicles was his business, and the Jones' car was a favor, the boss told Jamie to continue with his previous tasks. Making money and being on the good side of the mob was more important than taking care of a non-emergency favor for a friend. Austin Jones would just have to understand.

Freddie, the boss, walked over to where Austin was standing and explained to him that other priorities had to come before his sports car: "Austin, I only have one guy who will be available for your paint job, and that is Jamie. However, he has a number of different things that he has to complete before he can get to your car. You know who we are dealing with, and you know that you can't disappoint them. We will get to your car as soon as we can. It may take three or four days, but we will get to it. If you want to remain in the back room for a few more days, you are more than welcome to hide out there. Jamie will work as quickly as he can, but he has to finish with the cars that were delivered to us."

"Freddie, I appreciate your dilemma, but you know as well as I that sooner or later someone is going to reach out for the reward, and I will get fucked. I don't want to take that risk."

"Austin, I'm afraid that you don't have much of a choice. I have to do what I have to do."

Jamie couldn't be more pleased with Freddie's dictate to his friend. It was going to take at least three or four more days, and maybe longer. The time line fit in well with Jamie's plan.

When Freddie made his final comments to Austin, the disappointed cop killer started reaching under his shirt toward the weapon that he had secreted there. Freddie saw what Austin was about to do and warned him: "You don't want to do that, Austin. Don't even think about it." Austin stopped and looked directly at Freddie who pointed to the men in Austin's immediate vicinity. There were four individuals with semi-automatic weapons pointed directly at Austin Jones. Using his better judgement, Austin removed his hand from under his shirt and just nodded to Freddie. The boss was no fool, so he told Austin to hand over his weapon which he would get back when he left. Jones reluctantly gave Freddie his weapon and retired to the back room.

When Police Officer Jamie Weston finally finished for the day, he communicated with his police department contact, Inspector Warren Gillespie: "Hello, Inspector. I just wanted to give you some new information about the stolen car ring. I know you are ready to execute the raid, but I think it might be better if we waited just a few more days."

"Jamie, why do you think we should put it off? Do you have any new developments?"

"Yes, Inspector. Not so much regarding the ring, but about a person that the department has been looking for. Austin Jones is staying in the backroom of the shop. He brought his car into the shop and asked his friend, the boss, Freddie, to repaint it for him since he knew that the cops were looking for a silver/gray sport coupe. Inspector, that job was assigned to me. However, I was able to convince the boss that I had other jobs to complete before I got to Austin's car, and he agreed. One other thing: everyone, including Austin, is armed in that place. Just give me a couple more days to see if I can get any other useful information. I'm sure that Jones is not going anywhere. He's afraid that he might be captured, and if he attempts to leave without his renewed vehicle, he's concerned that someone might make a call and want to cash in on the reward that is being offered. When Jones gets his repainted car, he plans to skip out of the area and lay low for a while. If that happens, we lose him. However, I will make sure that we have plenty of time to nab him."

The inspector responded: "Okay, Jamie, but I will have your ass if this guy gets away. I want to break the car ring, but we have a cop killer in our sights. Do not lose him!"

"Inspector, I guarantee that he will never hurt another cop again, even if I have to permanently eliminate him."

Chapter Thirteen

No Valid Reason

It had been a number of weeks that Officer Rocco Deloberti was out of circulation; however, he recently had been given a clean bill of health. His request to go back to uniformed patrol had been granted, but he was still waiting for his application for a transfer to another precinct to be approved. Precinct transfers always took a while and sometimes were not even granted. Rocco wanted out of his present command as soon as possible. Hopefully with the endorsement of the plainclothes sergeant, who was close to the commanding officer, his request for transfer would be approved.

Since his present command was a high-crime precinct, most of the sector cars were a two-officer assignment. As fate would have it, the only sector car that was lacking a two-officer contingent was the one that Police Officer Jake Prathers routinely drove. So, Rocco Deloberti and his one-time competitor for a plainclothes position, Jake Prathers, were assigned together as partners, at least until such time as Rocco's precinct transfer application was approved.

Jake held no grudges and welcomed Rocco as his partner. To say that Jake was surprised to see Rocco back in uniform would be an understatement. Although they spoke of many things, the burning curiosity of why Rocco was back in uniform, plagued Jake. He finally worked up enough courage to ask Rocco the obvious question: "Rocco, I hope you don't mind, but it's really bothering me. Why in the world would you want to come back to uniform patrol?"

"No, Jake. I don't mind at all. Although plainclothes is definitely different, it wasn't all that I hoped it would be."

"Rocco, that doesn't say much. What were you hoping for?"

"Well, Jake. Without getting into the specifics, let's just say that the plainclothes officers do things in a way to which I couldn't become accustomed. I wasn't comfortable with some of the choices they made, and how they chose to enforce certain violations. They have also been working together for a long while, and I had a tough time breaking into their circle of trust. I guess that would be the same for anyone who just came into the unit. My comfort level suffered and instead of constantly trying to break through their closed circle, I decided to come back to patrol where I am more than comfortable with the daily routine of answering calls."

"Rocco, I am sorry to hear all that. I do think that we will get along just fine, but if there is anything that bothers you, don't hesitate to tell me."

"Thanks, Jake. That's a breath of fresh air."

Jake wasn't finished: "I don't want to beat a dead horse, but I have just one more question for you, if that's all right."

"Sure, Jake. Hit me."

"I don't know if you can answer this, but do you know the reason why I wasn't asked to join the unit once they knew that there was going to be a vacancy."

"Jake, I can't tell you why they didn't ask you, but I can tell you why this guy, Santiago, got the position. He walked into the unit as a relatively unknown and probably without any activity record to speak of. He was also recruited into the unit without any substantial interview. What does that tell you? Let me answer. It means that Officer Bobby Santiago has a 'hook,' and he got into plainclothes through a 'contract.' And, Jake, no matter how good your interview is, or how active your record, you are not going to beat a 'contract'."

"I guess I figured it was something like that. I just wanted to hear it from someone else. I imagine that his 'hook' has to be someone really up there. I don't know if I would want to be working with someone who got the job on a phone call. That would make me a bit nervous. I guess all things happen for the best."

Rocco agreed: "Take my word for it, Jake, it definitely happened for the best. Nothing against Santiago, but I'm sure that everyone in the unit knows how he got the position, and I'm sure that the sergeant and our commanding officer are not happy with appointing someone who is not their immediate choice. However, that's politics for you."

===

Rocco and Jake had been partners on patrol for about two months when they got a call to respond to a residence where a mother was screaming that her baby was not responsive. The mother was yelling for help, and when Rocco and Jake got to the scene, the mother was out in front of the home frantically signaling for someone to come and help her baby. The officers rushed inside with the mother and entered a room where the infant was lying in her crib. The baby was not moving and her complexion showed a trace of blue tint. Both officers understood that the signs did not look good, but Rocco picked up the baby and began to perform Cardio Pulmonary Resuscitation (C.P.R.) on her. However, both Rocco and Jake both surmised that their efforts would probably fall short as the infant had probably expired.

Even though the officers fully realized the situation, they rushed back to their police vehicle with Rocco continuing to administer C.P.R., and Jake getting behind the wheel heading toward the hospital. The child's mother was in the back seat still pleading with the officers to save her child. As soon as they arrived at the hospital, Rocco gave the infant to a responding nurse, and she took the child into the emergency treatment room. Rocco was somewhat certain that the nurse surely shared the same hopeless feeling that it might be too late to save the infant's life, but she treated the situation as if it was still a potential life-saving effort.

Shortly after the nurse took the child, a doctor came out of the treatment room and explained to the desperate mother that her baby had expired. This was not a surprise to either Rocco or Jake. They had believed all along that they were transporting a dead infant to the hospital. In fact, they both figured that the child was dead as soon as they saw her in the crib. However, in their good judgement, they were not going to leave a dead child in the crib for her mother to see and grieve over. If the child was left in the crib, she would have to stay there until agents from the Medical Examiner's Office came to the home and ultimately released the body. That could take forever! Therefore, to relieve some of the anguish and grief that the mother was feeling, they removed the child from the house. In so doing, the baby's mother did not have to endlessly watch and hope that her child would ultimately take a breath.

This unfortunate call to the home of an expired infant was not an isolated incident. No, in fact, Rocco and Jake and other patrol officers responded to a number of very similar calls. This heart-wrenching phenomenon known as Sudden Infant Death Syndrome (S.I.D.S.) had become one of the more frequent ways that infants throughout the city were dying. Although there were many reasons given for this apparently mysterious death, there was no definitive explanation as to why infants were dying in their sleep as they lay in the crib through the night. The possible causes varied from the child sleeping on its back and suffocating to the type of formula the infant was given. No one, including medical experts, could give a reasonable and valid explanation as to why this deadly phenomenon was occurring.

Being as compassionate as they could, responding police officers were not leaving the infants in their cribs. They were transporting them to hospitals so that tearful and desperate parents did not have to stare at a crib that held their motionless and unresponsive babies.

The calls involving S.I.D.S. were ones that the police officers dreaded. Not only were they concerned for the grieving parents, but the morbid experience initiated concerns regarding their own families. Many of the officers had young families, and as they responded to these catastrophic calls, they worried regarding their own infants and young children. What would they find in their own homes when their tour of duty was over? Many of the officers had sleepless nights, tiptoeing into the baby's room and over to the crib to make sure that their child was still breathing. Officers are told not to bring the job home with them, but when circumstances at work could possibly parallel what they might see at home, that dictum becomes an impossibility.

The calls for response to possible Sudden Infant Death Syndrome situations slowly diminished. Most of the doctors were now recommending that the child be placed on its side while it slept. Although this may not have been the main or only reason for S.I.D.S., the calls did decrease. As inexplicably as it had started and much to the relief of parents and police officers, the incidence of Sudden Infant Death Syndrome mysteriously slowed to a significantly lower number. With the impact and personal penetrating experience of S.I.D.S. fading, police officers found it easier, now, not to bring that aspect of the job home.

However, one officer still thought about a specific, disheartening and dangerous work encounter, and how he was going to balance the scales. For this officer, the job had boiled over into his personal life. His girlfriend had the scar to prove it, and his car was a blackened, burned-out heap of twisted metal. Rocco Deloberti thought about his circumstances every day, but thus far, hadn't come up with a plan that satisfied his thirst for revenge. His strategic move had to be so subtle that although it would be impactfully unforgettable to John Hallerin and the rest of the corrupt cops, it could never be traced back to him. The more he thought about it, the more he saw newly-appointed plainclothes officer Bobby Santiago as a key player in his potentially clandestine plan of attack.

Chapter Fourteen

The Mechanic Shop

Undercover Police Officer Jamie Weston was able to delay the work on Austin Jones' car for just about four days, but the time had come for Jamie to let Inspector Gillespie know that, unfortunately, there was no more information to garner. A day and time for the police raid was set. On the day of the raid, the Inspector had eight police vehicles and sixteen uniformed police officers ready to bring down the mechanic shop that supported the stolen car ring. Included in the uniformed ranks were Police Officers Rocco Deloberti and his partner, Jake Prathers. The officers were divided into specific entry sections. Rocco and his partner were entering through the side door and instructed to focus on the rear of the mechanic shop. In order for Jamie

Weston not to be mistaken as a "bad guy," he was instructed to make sure that he was outside of the shop when the uniformed police officers entered.

The back room of the mechanic shop did not have an exit door. In an emergency, the only way out was through a rear window in the room. Just as Jamie was about to leave the shop, he heard noises in the back room. He went back to the room to make certain that Austin Jones was still there. As Jamie went to the door of the back room, he saw Jones, who was apparently spooked or who had seen the approaching officers, attempting to exit the room through the window. As Jamie drew his weapon and ordered Jones down from the window, the uniformed police officers burst into the mechanic shop. Simultaneously, Austin Jones, with his gun in hand, turned menacingly toward Officer Weston. Jones, apparently, did not heed the verbal warnings from Jamie, and by his actions, put Officer Weston's life in jeopardy. Officer Jamie Weston fired two rounds at the gun wielding criminal. The rounds found Austin Jones' chest, and he was dead before he fell to the floor.

Uniformed Police Officer Jake Prathers was about ten feet away from undercover Officer Weston. Prathers ordered the undercover officer to drop his gun. Weston, still with gun in hand, was surprised by the order and attempted to turn to the officer to let him know that he was also a cop. Rocco Deloberti, who was right behind his partner, saw that Weston was about to make a fatal mistake that all plainclothes police officers are warned against. Weston, still armed with his weapon, was turning toward a uniformed officer. Rocco, who recognized

Weston, yelled to his partner not to shoot, but because of the perceived danger of the moment, Rocco's plea fell on deaf ears, and Police Officer Jamie Weston became the victim of fatal, friendly fire.

Rocco ran to assist Weston, but the officer was already unresponsive. Police Officer Jamie Weston was dead. Rocco called for assistance and yelled to get the ambulance team who was assigned to the scene. The EMTs rushed to assist Jamie Weston, but as Rocco had assumed, Jamie had expired. Police Officer Jamie Weston was pronounced dead by the EMTs at the scene. Jake Prathers, still with his gun in hand, hadn't moved. He just stood there in shock. He had just killed another police officer.

The operation having been completed, Inspector Gillespie approached Jake and tried to console him. However, there was nothing that anyone could say that would make Jake Prathers feel better. Police Officer Jake Prathers collapsed to the ground and began crying. Inspector Gillespie ordered the EMTs to attend to Jake who was apparently in shock. As the other uniformed officers bowed their heads in regret, the EMTs escorted Jake to the ambulance and drove away to the hospital. Jake Prathers was going to need a lot of time and help to get over the fact that he had killed one of their own, and there was no guarantee that he would ever recover from it.

It is very difficult for a supervisor to lose one of his officers. In this case, the Inspector lost an officer with whom he had worked very closely. Also, he lost an officer through an accident of routine procedure or the absence of it. Gillespie had bent over the body of his undercover officer and was visibly shaken. With tears in his eyes, he was overheard to say how sorry he was. He would also have to recover from the shock of being responsible for another officer's death. It was the inspector's decision to assign Jamie Weston to the undercover mission, and although the inspector warned the uniformed police officers that the possibility existed that an undercover officer would be on the scene, there was no way to guarantee that plainclothes officer's safety. Inspector Gillespie started scapegoating for some sort of consolation. He focused on the fact that Officer Jamie Weston violated the fundamental rule that applies to plainclothes officers when confronted by a uniformed officer: "Do not move, and follow the directions of the uniformed police officer." Had Weston followed that rule, he would probably still be alive.

Police Officer Jamie Weston died in the line of duty and was given an Inspector's Funeral by the police department. He had also reached his goal of becoming a detective; however, that rank was awarded to him posthumously. In addition to the many New York City Police Officers who lined the streets, there were hundreds of police officers from departments throughout the country and outside of the country. They all stood at attention out of respect for a fallen comrade. However, there was one officer who was conspicuously absent. Police Officer Jake Prathers was still under a doctor's care and had even, in his deepening state of depression, mentioned that suicide might be a welcomed solution to what he was feeling.

The entire department is affected when a brother officer is killed. However, Rocco Deloberti had lost two police officers with whom he had worked. Jamie Weston was gone, and Officer Jake Prathers might never return. Rocco also needed time to recover. He was granted sick time and sought consolation from his family and in the arms of his best friend, Janet. Although he definitely needed time off to recover, he also needed to get back to work to keep his mind busy. His getting back to work, however, was a problem for Janet. She was having second thoughts about her boyfriend, now her fiancé (Rocco proposed to her while he had been off), continuing with police work. The recent deadly incidents struck a sharp chord of concern with her that hadn't been there before. She approached the subject carefully, but strongly suggested that maybe he should look for a different line of work.

Rocco wouldn't hear of it. He was a police officer and would continue to be one. He understood Janet's concern, but he reminded her that she was the one who said that he should face his problems and not run from them. He also explained that he realized a positive from what had occurred. Scooter cop Joey Lelan could finally rest in peace. His murderer was no longer breathing and hopefully in hell. It took a while, but Joey's death was finally avenged, and Rocco was a part of that. He also reminded her that he had unfinished business with certain members of the department, and he could not complete that business from outside of the department. Janet knew that she wasn't going to be able to convince him to leave police work, but she had to try. She told Rocco that she understood but made him promise to be extra careful at work. He laughingly agreed.

When Rocco returned to work after his stay at home, he was now faced with the aspect of finding another partner. His request for transfer had not yet been approved, so he still had to work on patrol in the same precinct. For a while, he would be filling in for officers who were on vacation or out sick. That meant, for the most part, that he would be working with a number of different officers. Getting used to a new partner every few days is no easy task. Constantly working with new partners also presented a problem for the officers to get to know how each one would react in different urgent or emergency situations. Fortunately for Rocco, Jake Prathers returned to work a lot sooner than anyone expected. Two weeks and he was back at work; however, he just didn't seem right to Rocco. But Jake being back was a big relief for Rocco since he, once again, had a steady partner.

Although they had both been through a lot, they didn't speak about the incident. They didn't have to be reminded about the disaster that had taken place, but it was like the elephant in the room. So, one day while they were on patrol, Rocco brought the subject up: "Hey, Jake. How are you doing? I know we haven't discussed it, but you and I both know that it is always there in front of us. Instead of constantly trying to avoid the subject, why don't we bring it to light and put it behind us once and for all."

Jake responded: "That's a good idea, but it's really hard to face the fact that I am responsible for another cop's death."

"No, Jake. You are just one of the officers who was involved in an accident, an accident that unfortunately took a life. There was no way that you could have avoided it. And I don't want to talk ill of the dead, but Jamie violated a basic rule of plainclothes work. He, unfortunately, forced you into a position where you had to defend yourself. Anyone of us would have done the same thing. I am just glad that you are back and hopefully we can put this behind us, partner."

"Thanks a lot, Rocco. You are real good guy, and I appreciate what you said, but it will take a long time before the memory of that day fades even a little. Having said that, I am glad to be back with you."

Rocco nodded and said: "Okay, let's go get some bad guys."

They smiled and acknowledged their commitment to serve and protect. They continued on their patrol. The day was relatively uneventful, but it was busy enough for them to keep their minds engaged. Unfortunately, the last call of the day brought them past the mechanic shop where the disastrous incident occurred. They passed the mechanic shop in silence. Each knowing, however, that the other was cognizant of where they were.

Rocco and Jake turned in their equipment at the end of the tour, and they went to the locker room to change out of uniform. Jake was slow to remove his uniform and told Rocco that he had to make a bathroom call. Before Jack visited the bathroom, he thanked his partner for everything. Rocco nodded and said that he would wait for him. That was the last time that Rocco saw his partner.

Following the unmistakable sound of a gunshot, Rocco and other officers ran to the bathroom where they found Police Officer Jake Prathers in full uniform lying in a pool of blood from a self-inflicted gunshot wound to the head. The mechanic shop raid had claimed another life!

Chapter Fifteen

The New Partner

Rocco Deloberti had been dealing with one catastrophe after another. To the objective observer, it seemed as though there was a black cloud hovering over Rocco's head. In fact, that was the way Rocco felt. How many other negatives were just waiting around the bend. Other officers began looking at Rocco as a person to avoid. They were just waiting for lightening to strike again, and they didn't want to be a part of the collateral damage. It became more and more difficult for Rocco to get a partner to work with him. He still hadn't been approved for a transfer to another precinct, and all of the officers in his command were aware of the negatives affecting Rocco's existence.

===

Police Officer Bobby Santiago saw what was happening and decided to delay his appointment to the plainclothes unit. He took exception to the way the other officers were looking at Rocco and told Captain Geskasco that he would volunteer for the open position in patrol. He explained to both the captain and the plainclothes sergeant that he would wait for the next opening in the plainclothes unit and apply again for it. Both the captain and the sergeant welcomed Santiago's decision. They could now assign an officer of their own choice to the unit. Without much hesitation, Bobby Santiago was assigned to patrol as Rocco Deloberti's partner.

At first, Rocco was leery of Santiago. He couldn't figure out why someone would want to voluntarily leave plainclothes to become his partner in patrol. Rocco had left because of a specific reason. Bobby Santiago wasn't in plainclothes long enough to develop a distaste for what was going on. So, Bobby's decision was a mystery to Rocco and to most of the other officers in the precinct.

Quickly enough, however, Bobby and Rocco became close partners and friends. They were very much alike, and Bobby had adopted the same ideals that Rocco held dear. After about a month together, Rocco thought that it was time to finally find out the truth. He had originally accepted the lame excuse from Bobby that he felt he was not quite ready for a plainclothes assignment, and that he wanted to get more street experience before he entered the unit. Now, however, Rocco and Bobby were close enough for Rocco to say: "Okay, Bobby. What's the real reason you volunteered to come back to patrol and be my partner? No one voluntarily leaves a plainclothes assignment to come back to routine patrol. Level with me. Why are you here?"

"I'm surprised it took you this long to push me into a corner. So, let me explain. There are some things that you haven't been privy to, but there has been an internal operation going on for quite a while. I am here to make sure that your good intentions do not destroy a plan that has been going on for a long time. I am also here to ensure that you don't do anything that would further endanger you or anyone close to you."

"I'm not sure I understand, Bobby. You have to be more explicit."

"I will be, Rocco, but I need your word that you not mention to anyone what I'm about to tell you. Do I have your word?"

"You certainly are making it more mysterious than it probably is, but sure, you have my word."

"Great! I know that you have come across certain activities by the plainclothes team that go against many of the principles that are sacred to you. The guys in that team, however, aren't what you believe they are. John Hallerin or "Pop" as you call him, is not the bad guy. He is, in fact, working with a special operations task force to take down a very powerful arm of an organized crime family. He is on our side, and although you have seen him do things that go against everything we stand for, he and the team are very close to ending their assignment. I am here to make sure that you do not blow the whole operation that we've been steadily working on and are close to successfully completing."

"Wait a minute, Bobby. You're telling me that Pop and the others are the good guys. Well, those good guys cut my fiancée and destroyed my car. Good guys don't do that."

"You're right, Rocco. Good guys don't do that, but it was not them who did it. Pop explained to his mob contact about what you saw and your attitude toward it. They took it upon themselves to act. Pop didn't even know that it was going to happen."

"Bobby, I noticed two of the plainclothes guys standing by my car when it was burning. They set it ablaze."

"No, Rocco. You're wrong. They ran down to your car to stop mob members from torching your car. Pop got a call right before they all came back to the station house. Although Pop disagreed with the caller, the mob wanted to show you that they can get to you no matter where you are. They struck right across from the station house to prove a point. Unfortunately, our guys were too late to stop it. The department will make good for your loss, and we have already assigned twenty-four-hour clandestine protection for your fiancée. The mob definitely went too far when they threatened Janet. When we contacted her, we made sure that she knew what was going on. She agreed to cooperate with us and help us with you."

"Wait a minute! Are you telling me that Janet, my fiancée, knows what is going on and I don't?"

“Rocco, now you do. We need your cooperation, and rest assured that they will pay for what they did to both you and Janet.”

“You guys have some pair of balls. You intentionally put me, Janet, and our families in jeopardy so that you could continue with a police operation. Are you fucking kidding me?”

“Rocco, this operation is far more serious and complicated than you think. In addition to a myriad of crimes that they committed, we are pretty sure that the organization has been involved in the past murders of police officers. We need additional time to sure-up our case. I understand how you feel, but understand how the widows of those other police officers also feel. Please help us. We need your cooperation, and I am way out on a limb even discussing this with you, but I feel that you have a right to know. I can almost guarantee that big mob bosses will be going down for a number of crimes including the murder of police officers. We are that close!”

Rocco Deloberti just stared out of the window of the police vehicle. He kept shaking his head in apparent disbelief as to what he was hearing. The silence in the car was deafening and was only broken when Bobby spoke again: “Rocco help us. Is there anything else that you need to know? I have to let the department bosses know that you are now aware of everything. In the same sentence, however, I would like to tell them that we have your full cooperation. Do not think of it as a betrayal, but better as a judgement decision that was mandated by the situation.”

“Bobby, you sound like a politician who is running for office. Don’t try to sugar coat the arrogance and disconcern that you and the others have shown by blaming your actions on a situation. It boils down to a distrust that you and everyone else were harboring until something outside of your control occurred and mandated a revelation. Then you were forced to expose the elements of an undercover operation. How do I know that it won’t happen again?”

“Rocco, you don’t. I can only tell you that we are all on hyper-alert to prevent further injury or loss to you or Janet. It might not be a bad idea to speak to Janet about the entire situation.”

“Did you think that I wasn’t?”

Rocco pulled into the station house parking area, and left Bobby sitting in the car. Rocco went to the desk sergeant and told him that he needed the rest of the day off. The Sergeant granted Rocco’s request. Rocco went to the locker room and changed quickly. It was near the time that Janet would be getting off from work, so he decided to go directly to Janet’s house and meet with her. He left the station house without any acknowledgment to Bobby Santiago who was standing at the exit door and who tried to speak to him: “Are you okay, partner?”

Rocco abruptly stopped, turned toward him and said: “Partners don’t do what you did. They don’t keep secrets, and they surely wouldn’t put me and others in harm’s way. It seems that you have a lot to learn about being a partner, and maybe you should start looking for someone else to teach you.”

Police Officer Bobby Santiago had no comeback for Rocco, and he was not about to tell him that he was sorry. He worked within the guidelines that were given to him and followed direct orders. It was orders that highlighted the fact that the more people who knew about the operation, the greater the risk of it not succeeding. Failure of the entire operation was not going to come about because of his inability to maintain a mandated code of strict confidentiality. He was a good soldier, and success had to come before personal feelings. Bobby now had to inform his bosses that the confidentiality that was so strongly emphasized had been breached by the influence of his recurring and overwhelming personal feelings.

Chapter Sixteen

Two Predicaments

Rocco went directly to Janet's home and waited in his car for Janet to arrive. As he mentally reviewed his conversation with Bobby Santiago, he couldn't believe that his fiancée had joined ranks with the investigators without telling him. As far as he was concerned, no matter what the situation, there should be no secrets between him and Janet. He was most interested in what Janet would say regarding the whole situation. Would she offer lame excuses? Would she tell him that she did it for him? Would she lie?

Rocco did not have to wait very long before he saw Janet approaching the house. He jumped out of his rental car and quickly approached his fiancée. However, before he actually reached her, he was tackled to the floor by two individuals who were, apparently, surveilling Janet Commings. The men held Rocco down and had him in cuffs before he could tell them anything. It was Janet who recognized Rocco and yelled to the aggressors that the person they had captured was her fiancée and a police officer. It was obvious that the protection team did not know Rocco, and in his haste to approach Janet put the team in a response mode. It also became quite obvious to Rocco that Bobby Santiago was not exaggerating when he said that Janet was getting clandestine protection.

After a bit of a scuffle, Rocco was able to identify himself and gain his freedom. The officers who were assigned to Janet apologized to Rocco but explained that his approach seemed threatening to them. Rocco understood, and the entire situation was settled amicably. Janet hugged Rocco and told him how sorry she was that he had to get involved with the other officers. Rocco nodded and immediately turned the conversation toward her involvement with the police department: "Janet, none of this would be happening if you didn't strike a deal with Bobby Santiago and his allies. What the heck is going on, and why haven't you said anything to me? You've put me in a very compromising position, and I don't appreciate it."

Janet saw how angry Rocco was, and she knew that no matter what she told him, he wasn't going to accept the fact that one, she was working with the police department without his knowledge, and two, she never mentioned anything about Bobby Santiago or his involvement. Janet felt that she was in a "no win" situation, and regretted ever agreeing to Santiago's proposition. She carefully constructed her response to Rocco: "First of all, I am sorry that I caused you any problems. I thought that my involvement would ultimately help you. I regret my decision, and you're right. There should be no secrets between us. I am really sorry."

"Janet, I don't know if just 'sorry' cuts it. There are a number of repercussions that are going to result from what has occurred here. I have been put in a very embarrassing position. I have to face the rest of the officers who are involved in the operation in addition to those officers in the precinct who have no knowledge of what is taking place but will surely have heard what transpired here today. I do not know who is involved or to what extent, and I realize that no one is going to enlighten me. I would guess that I am on a 'need-to-know' basis. You really socked it to me, Janet!"

"Rocco, that was not my intention. I didn't plan on 'socking it to you,' and I don't appreciate your implying that I didn't care what happened to you. In fact, it was my intention to protect you as much as possible, and I was assured by Officer Santiago that everything would turn out better for you if I cooperated as much as possible with them. So, I did."

"Janet, let me ask you a question. Do you think that the officers who tackled me will be there all of the time? There is no way that they, Bobby Santiago or anyone else would be able to protect you all of the time. You have put yourself in a very vulnerable position. No matter what Santiago has told you, he cannot guarantee your safety. And I don't want to be put in a position where I have to say, 'I told you so'."

"Rocco, stop it! You're beginning to scare me."

"You should be scared. The more fear you have, the more careful you will be."

"Rocco, can we put this behind us. I don't want this to come between us, and it seems the more we discuss the worse it gets."

"No, Janet. We can't put it behind us. We are living it every day. I really need some time to think things over. I almost feel that I've been betrayed. It's not a very good feeling, and I don't know where I go from here."

Janet was really taken aback by Rocco's last statement. She heard what he said, and the inference that she drew was not a good one. She understood him to say that he wasn't sure about a number of things, including their relationship. She was not going to be left in limbo. She reached for her left hand, pulled the engagement ring from her finger and held it out to Rocco. At first, he hesitated, but then, he took it from her hand. Janet had thought that the extreme measure of offering the ring back would shock Rocco into a more conciliatory frame of mind. Unfortunately, and to her shocking amazement, he took the ring. With tears in her eyes, she chokingly said: "You, apparently, have a lot to think about. I do not want to cloud your thinking. When and if you arrive at a decision, you can contact me. And at that time, it will be my turn to make a decision." Janet, with tears rolling down her face, turned and walked into her house.

As Janet walked away, Rocco Deloberti began to realize what he had just done. He loved Janet, but found it so hard to accept the fact that what she did bordered on betrayal. This thought prevented him from stopping Janet's retreat. He looked as she entered her house without ever turning around. For all intents and purposes, she had just walked out of his life, and he definitely didn't know if she would ever again be a part of it. It was a great loss for him, and he wanted to run into the house and tell her that he was sorry, but his strong personality and ego created a barrier that he couldn't negotiate. One could say that he cut off his nose to spite his face.

Rocco decided that he had to work quickly and make a calculated decision one way or the other. Was his pride and ego more important than saving a relationship with someone with whom he had planned to spend the rest of his life? Unfortunately, accepting the ring and allowing her to walk away created a scenario where one could say that the damage was already done. No matter how quickly he contacted her and tried to smooth over their rift, he realized that the damage couldn't be erased. Had his inflexibility eliminated any possibility of returning to the positive relationship they once enjoyed? Unfortunately, even if he was able to reconnect with her, the black cloud of distrust and possible betrayal would always be floating above their heads. He felt that he really blew it this time, but it was her actions that brought the situation to a head. Logically, that was how he was justifying his obstinance.

Rocco, who really wasn't a drinker, decided to go to the local bar and drown his sorrows in the muse of alcohol. He went to the gin mill that many of the cops in his command frequented. He was among friends, and felt comfortable in the confines of a cop's place. He didn't order beer. He hated the way it tasted. Therefore, he was forced into ordering a stronger concoction.

Police Officer Rocco Deloberti spent approximately two hours in the bar, and at this point, he was feeling no pain. As he consumed his fourth or fifth drink, he thought he heard the accented voice of Police Officer Bobby Santiago. He turned from on his bar stool and saw Santiago sitting at a table with some other officers, including the plainclothes sergeant who worked in the precinct.

With alcohol affecting his better judgement, and alcoholic courage streaming through his veins, he went over to the table and addressed the group: "You guys should be careful about who you drink with. This scumbag (pointing to Santiago) has just ruined my life. He did things behind my back, and I trust him as far as I could throw him. He deserves a beating." Santiago rose from his chair and tried to talk some sense to Rocco. Rocco took Santiago's rising as an offensive action, so he reared back and attempted to "clock" him. However, Rocco's aim and speed were both negatively affected by the heavy consumption of alcohol, so Santiago had no problem ducking the punch.

The other officers got up and pulled Rocco away from Santiago and the table. They brought him back to his bar stool and told him that it was time for him to leave. He resisted their suggestion and tried to push his way back to the table. The guys held him at bay and called for a taxi. The cab arrived quickly, and they attempted to usher him into the waiting vehicle. However, before he left the bar, he was able to pick up a bottle from the bar counter and fling it at Santiago. The bottle missed the intended target, but landed on the side of the sergeant's head. The sergeant was bleeding, and he yelled after Rocco that he was going to regret what he did.

Instead of Rocco's visit to the bar helping to ease the pain of the predicament that he was in with his former fiancée, it created another situation that was even more detrimental to his existence. It wasn't a good day for Police Officer Deloberti, and the upcoming ones were about to get even worse.

Chapter Seventeen

The Captain's Office

In the short time that Rocco Deloberti had been on the job, he had witnessed too many police officer deaths. The black cloud reputation that Rocco had was growing with time. Finding another partner was no easy task, but Rocco had even greater problems to face. He knew that the plainclothes sergeant who got hit with the bottle that Rocco had thrown was going to bring official charges against him. Rocco figured that he would be charged with "Unfit for Duty" and "Conduct Unbecoming a Police Officer." These were the least of the charges. He could also be charged with "Disorderly Conduct" and "Assault." These are violations of the law. However, it was his belief and hope that the sergeant would keep the charges relative to violations of the department's rules and procedures.

When Rocco came in for his next tour of duty, he was ordered to report to the commanding officer's office forthwith. He was aware that Captain Geskasco would want to see him, but it was still difficult to prepare for whatever was about to come. Rocco knew that the captain was going to read the "riot act" to him, but he wasn't sure what would follow on a precinct level. He wondered how far the captain would go with restrictions. He even wondered if the charges and specifications that were coming down through channels would force him off of the job. Rocco knew he was totally wrong with what he had done, and he only hoped it didn't amount to his termination. His record wasn't a clean one, and now with additional charges, it could very well mean his looking for another job. He was hoping against hope that this wouldn't be the case.

Police Officer Deloberti gingerly approached the captain's door. He knocked and waited for the commanding officer to give him the okay to enter: "Come in."

"Police Officer Deloberti present as ordered, sir."

"Great! Just the way that I wanted to start my day with a cop who thinks he can continue to do as he pleases and not suffer the consequences. Take a seat!"

Rocco knew that it was not going to be pleasant, but he didn't think that the captain would open up with pointed unpleasantries. Apparently, he was wrong.

"Deloberti, I have had many officers come under my supervision, but I can truly say that you take the cake. I have never seen someone who totally disregards the future as long as the present is satisfied. You are that person. It seems that you continuously throw caution to the wind no matter the consequences, and the sad part is that you are not the worst cop with whom I have ever worked. But your activity and good work ethic go by the wayside when you are constantly involved in situations that do not fare well for you. You were drunk and you assaulted a ranking officer. What were you thinking?"

"Captain, that's the point. I wasn't thinking. I know you might have your doubts, but I am not a drinker. I don't even like the taste of alcohol, but I had a very bad interaction with my fiancée that day, and I decided to drown my sorrows in the numbing flow of alcohol. Of course, I am not offering my personal problems as an excuse for what I did to the sergeant, but they did play a part in my overall actions. My engagement was over, and my fiancée's interaction with Officer Santiago was a big part of our separation. So, when I saw Bobby at the bar, I became incensed and all I could see was the person who was responsible for my immediate problems. Certainly, I overreacted when I tossed the bottle at him; however, my aim was terrible, and I hit the sergeant by mistake."

"Rocco, whether you were aiming at Santiago or the sergeant, you threw a bottle at a fellow officer. Let me ask you. Would it have been better if you hit your target?"

"No, sir. I was wrong no matter who got hit."

The captain continued: "That brings me to another specific point. In our 'Policy and Procedures' manual, it specifically states that an officer has to be fit for duty at all times. Were you fit for duty, Rocco?"

Before Rocco could answer, there was a knock on the door and the police officers' union representative barged in: "Excuse me, captain, but you are questioning a police officer without giving him the benefit of union representation. That is a specific violation of our contract. I must ask you to stop with the questioning and give me time to speak with the officer. I am also advising the officer to refrain from answering any other questions that you may have until I can confer with him."

Rocco knew that he had the option of entering the captain's office with union representation, but he chose not to avail himself of that benefit. He rose from his chair and directed his comments to the union representative: "Hold on a minute. I know that I have a right to representation, but I chose to see the captain on my own without the union. Thanks for your help, but I don't need the union right now."

The representative continued: "Let me ask. Did the captain tell you that you have the right to union representation before he started asking questions and discussing the situation in which you are involved?"

Rocco looked directly at the captain and then turned to the officer and said: "He didn't have to advise me. I opened my comments with the fact that I knew that I had the right to union representation, and that I didn't see the need to opt for that benefit. So, thank you for intervening on my behalf, but I would like to speak to the captain on a one-to-one basis."

The union rep was shocked that an officer was refusing representation, so he asked: "Are you sure that you want to do that?"

"Yes, I am absolutely sure. Thank you." The union rep shook his head and left the office.

"To answer your previous question, captain. No, I was not fit for duty. I was wrong with what I did, and no matter the determination. I fully admit that my actions were not those befitting a police officer."

Captain Geskasco was surprised by what Rocco told the union rep and even more shocked by his unsolicited admission of guilt. Once again, he had seen many officers violate some specific rule or regulation, but he had never seen an officer throw himself so unabashedly on the "mercy of the court." It was both unique and refreshing, but it did not erase the seriousness of the situation.

"Officer Deloberti, I appreciate your candor and honesty, but I have to inform you that you are suspended without pay until the final determination at your department hearing. Unfortunately, that determination could include loss of vacation days, an extended period of suspension, or even termination. You are not to speak to anyone except your union representative regarding this case, and you are not allowed to enter the stationhouse without specific permission from me or the administrative lieutenant. Do you understand what I have just said?"

"Yes, sir. I understand, and I am sorry for embarrassing you and the department. Here is my gun and shield."

The captain accepted Rocco's equipment and on a friendlier note commented: "I am sorry it has come to this, Rocco, but you brought this on yourself. I don't know what the future holds for you, but you have to remember that good deeds and actions are quickly erased by the results of one poor judgement move."

"Thank you, sir." Rocco got up to leave, and as he approached the office door, Captain Geskasco said one last thing: "By the way, thank you for your support with the union rep and your explanation of how you opened your comments."

"No thanks necessary, Captain. When I first came into your office, I was nervous, and so I probably spoke in a very low tone. It was probably so low that you didn't hear me acknowledge that I knew I had a right to representation but refused it." The captain nodded affirmatively, and suspended Police Officer Rocco Deloberti left the commanding officer's office.

Rocco knew that the union representative would be waiting for him as soon as he left the office. He was right. The rep grabbed Rocco by the arm and ushered him into a vacant office: "Rocco, what the hell are you doing? Do you not want to be a police officer anymore? Is that it? Nobody refuses representation when they are speaking to a boss about potential 'charges and specifications.' You could have said things in there that ruined any chances of your ever returning to work. Additionally, you set a very bad precedent for officers who are involved in similar circumstances. Tell me. Why did you refuse my help?"

"I didn't refuse your help. I just refused to exacerbate a situation that could only tend to hurt my representation when we go to trial. Cooperation smooths the path to determination. Your presence in the office could only be interpreted, even if it was not, as adversarial at the time. I laid the ground work for humility and accountability, and you, although good-intentioned, would have lessened the objectivity I need for any kind of re-instatement. That is more important to me than justifying my union dues."

"You, apparently, do not know how the process works."

"I may not know the process, but I know human nature. And that is more predictable and dependable than any argument the union could offer. I will need your help to maneuver through the procedural steps, but I have to trust in my own judgement and the groundwork that I laid."

After hearing Rocco's comments, the union representative just shook his head and walked away.

Chapter Eighteen

The Hearing

Police Officer John Hallerin (Pop) was putting pressure on his mob contact in the park. He told the guy that he needed more of a cut so that he could distribute more money to his own guys. The news was not welcomed, and the contact person did not have the authority to grant additional monies. Pop mentioned that he noticed an increase in the number of card gambling members. He also mentioned that he saw a marked increase in the dollar amount that was being bet. Pop told him that with the betting amount rising, his cut should also increase. The thug who oversaw the gambling operation in the park emphasized again that he could not authorize any increase. Pop was glad to hear that because it left the door open for him to meet the next guy up on the mob ladder who could make the monetary decision.

Pop kept up the pressure, and the park mobster said that he would relay the message regarding the increase. Pop said that a message relay wasn't good enough, and that he wanted to speak directly to the boss so he could negotiate a fair amount. Once again, the low level thug said that he would relay the message and arrange for a meeting. Pop felt that he had the thug on the run, so he emphasized that he wanted the meeting as soon as possible, or gambling in the park would come to an immediate halt. Pop could tell by the guy's facial expressions that he didn't like being threatened. The mobster would now have to relay the threat which he knew wouldn't be well received. He told Pop that he would see the boss that same evening and try to arrange for a meet.

As far as Pop was concerned, he scored a victory. He was about to meet one of the operational bosses of the family. That's just what he wanted, and he was sure that Santiago and his handlers would be happy with the progress. However, this was just the first step. The goal was to get the organized crime bosses who sat at the top of the ladder. Pop wasn't sure how far up he would be able to go, but he was going to give it his best try. He had the advantage. If the mob wanted to continue with the gambling operation in the park, which seemed to be growing, they would have to deal with John Hallerin. It seemed as though Pop was in the driver's seat. The park thug said that he would get back to Pop the next day with information on where and when the meeting might take place.

Early the next day, Pop made his usual stop at the park. He was anxious to hear what had been arranged. When Hallerin arrived at the park, he looked for his contact but didn't see him anywhere. As he surveyed the area looking for the park mobster, he was approached by two individuals who undoubtedly were mob connected. Pop preempted their opening comments: "Hey, I'm looking for Tony. He is supposed to have some information for me."

One of the two individuals answered: "Tony won't be here. He has been sent to handle some other matters. We are here to escort you to a location where you can meet with our boss."

This wasn't exactly the way Pop had thought it would go down, and he was sure that Tony, his original contact, was being punished for allowing Pop to get to the point where more money was being demanded. Pop knew that he would never see Tony again. Maybe, no one would. Pop got what he wanted, a meeting with the boss, but he wasn't sure that he would ever return from the meeting. The approach of the two individuals with whom he was now speaking had all the earmarks of the mob's way of eliminating a potential problem. However, he wasn't certain, and he didn't want to risk the fact that he could actually meet with the boss.

Knowing that a situation like this could develop, the department took additional precautions to guarantee Pop's safety. Not only was he wired, but his movement was being monitored by a police department drone and officers who were riding in a non-descript vehicle. With the deployment of the increased safety net, Pop agreed to accompany the two individuals to a waiting vehicle. As pictured in most organized crime movies, the driver sat alone in the front while Pop sat in the back seat between the two family envoys. Pop was not happy with the situation and was becoming more concerned about his safety. To break the deafening and threatening silence, Pop asked: "Where are we going? I am still on duty, and I can't be gone for that long a period of time. How long before we get there?"

Pop's inquiries were ignored by the two escorts. To show that he wasn't going to be intimidated, although he was quickly feeling the sweat rolling down his back, he spoke in a more demanding manner: "Hey, I'm speaking to the two of you. Where are we going? Are you deaf? Do you hear me? Answer me!"

One of the two men answered swiftly and accurately with a sharp and well-placed blow to Pop's abdomen. He bent over in pain trying to catch his breath. His worst fears were now realized. Even if there was a meeting, he was not going to return from it. Hallerin's innermost thoughts pointed to the possibility that he was heading for an execution, his own.

The black sedan that was now serving as Pop's last ride headed out of town and toward a sanitation dumping station, a potential burial site for John (Pop) Hallerin. The drone and the following surveillance vehicle were well aware of what was about to happen, and so they stepped up their safety procedures. The sedan stopped at the entrance gate to the dump, and the driver nodded to the gate keeper who electronically opened the gate barrier. The gate keeper was well aware of who these people were, and he never even looked to see where the vehicle was going. He knew better. The vehicle proceeded on a dirt road heading toward the rear of the site.

When the surveillance vehicle realized where the black sedan was heading and what the apparent intentions of the thugs were, the officers quickly set up a sniper position on one of the hills overlooking the dump. The officers were closely monitoring the activities. When the sedan stopped and John Hallerin was pushed out of the vehicle, the mob guy closest to him pulled out his weapon and pointed it directly at Pop. The very next thing that Pop heard was the sound of two faint gun shots.

Because of the immediate threat, Pop's horror led him to believe that the sound he heard was the mobster's gun discharging a round into his chest. In fact, he even winced. But what he saw was the collapse of the two men who had been guarding him during his death ride. The driver, having assessed the failed mission, quickly turned the car around and headed toward the exit gate where, unfortunately for him, two police vehicles were waiting. He was taken into custody without incident. The other two henchmen, who were the targets of the police sniper, were pronounced dead at the scene.

Although the entire police operation concluded with a certain amount of success and without injury to any of the officers, the results were not nearly close to what the police department investigators had hoped to accomplish. Even though they had the driver of the death vehicle in custody, he was a lower level member of the crime family and had very little useful information to disclose.

The gambling operation in the park was quickly shut down, and James Hallerin was re-assigned to "Special Operations." He had wanted to speak with Rocco Deloberti before he left, but unfortunately, Rocco was still suspended and awaiting the results of the department trial. There were still a number of loose ends that Pop felt had to be tied up; however, that task would have to wait until Pop could make arrangements to see Rocco. In the interim, Pop felt that he owed Rocco because of what he had put him through. So, he decided to try and intercede with the complaining sergeant to go lightly on Rocco. Pop wasn't sure that he would be able to convince the sergeant, but he was going to give his best shot.

===

The trial date had arrived and suspended Police Officer Rocco Deloberti was listening to the detailed testimony of what occurred on the day in question. It was the sworn testimony by the plainclothes sergeant who was the recipient of Rocco's errant bottle toss. Although the statements were as accurate as they could be, they weren't given with anger or malice. They were brief and to the point. Other officers who testified, including Bobby Santiago, also did it with no hint of outrage. Police Officer Deloberti knew that he was definitely going to be found "guilty" of the charges against him, but he had hope that the final determination would not be dismissal from the job.

Before the hearing officer pronounced final judgement, the plainclothes sergeant, who was the main complainant in the case, asked to make an additional comment. He was granted the request and the sergeant began his statement: "It is my feeling that Police Officer Deloberti intentionally violated the rules and procedures of this department, and that he acted in a manner that not only compromised his oath of office but also demeaned the very mission of a police officer."

As the sergeant was, apparently, further indicting Police Officer Deloberti's actions, Rocco now felt that he was doomed to termination. He felt that the sergeant was ensuring that Rocco would never wear the uniform again. He was just piling it on, and it was sounding worse and worse, if that was possible. Rocco couldn't slouch any lower in his chair.

The sergeant continued: "There is no way that I encourage these actions or actions like these; however, I believe that one has to investigate the reason for these actions."

Rocco rose in his chair and began to listen more intently. It sounded like the sergeant was about to offer an excuse for what Rocco had done. Deloberti continued to look and listen with amazement and shock.

The sergeant continued: "The officer had just learned that his fiancée had betrayed him by not letting him know about her cooperation with the department. The ensuing discussion resulted in their engagement ending, and Rocco not trusting anyone. He also learned that it had been Officer Bobby Santiago who had approached his fiancée and had indirectly affected his future with Janet. With the officer having nowhere else to turn, he went to the local gin mill to drown his sorrows. It is my understanding that Rocco Deloberti is not a drinker, but knowing the potential effects of alcohol, he felt that he needed it to numb the immediate pain of betrayal and distrust."

Rocco couldn't believe what he was hearing. It wasn't the fact that the sergeant was relaying what had occurred, but doing it in a way as to lessen the immediate impact of his actions.

The sergeant continued: "As a novice drinker, alcohol quickly took hold of his emotions and logical thinking, and it was at this point that Officer Deloberti heard the familiar voice of Officer Bobby Santiago. What Rocco heard was the voice that, in his mind, was responsible for his present state of despair and distress. Deloberti reacted, as most of us would, in a manner which caused him to land in his present position. With the influence of alcohol-induced courage and rage, Rocco lashed out. The bottle landing on the side of my head was a result of his anger; however, his target was not me but that of Bobby Santiago. No matter the target, his action was definitely wrong, and I don't condone it. What I am asking of this hearing is to weigh the fact that Police Officer Rocco Deloberti has been an asset to this department, and his termination would negatively affect the overall operation of our cooperative law enforcement mandate. The department would lose a valuable advantage."

One could have knocked Rocco over with a feather. Instead of totally sinking him, the sergeant sounded like he was endorsing Rocco for a promotion. Coming from the main complainant, his statement had to have some effect on the hearing officer. Rocco hoped that it would take "termination" off of the table. The hearing officer told the group that he would return in a short time with a determination. The next forty minutes were the longest in Rocco's life.

When the hearing officer returned, one could hear a pin drop in the room. Rocco stood up with his counsel to hear the verdict: "Officer Deloberti, you are suspended for an additional two months without pay, you will lose ten vacation days, and the loss of one year's seniority. This hearing is adjourned."

Rocco had been severely disciplined, but he still had his job, which by all accounts and measures, was precariously on the edge. As the hearing went on, Rocco had felt that he was doomed. He just couldn't explain the unexpected supportive comments that he had previously heard. He immediately went to the sergeant and thanked him for his support. The sergeant looked at him and said: "Don't thank me. If it was up to me, you would be on the unemployment line. You should be thanking him." The sergeant pointed to the back of the room where John (Pop) Hallerin was standing.

Rocco went to Pop and thanked him for what he did. Pop just nodded and said: "I guess you finally got your 'fair share.' See you around." Pop smiled and left. Rocco finally realized what a good cop and friend John (Pop) Hallerin really was.

Chapter Nineteen

The Hospital

It had been quite a while now that Janet and Rocco had not been in touch, and although things had quieted down a lot with the gambling operation coming to a conclusion, there was still a rift between the formerly engaged couple. Rocco decided that it was time to get together with Janet to discuss the possibility of rejuvenating their relationship. He felt that the longer it took for them to communicate, the less chance of mending fences. He knew that he didn't want to forfeit the opportunity of starting over. Janet was a pretty and intelligent young woman who would have no problem in attracting another partner. He also knew that he should have contacted her before now just to keep the lines of communication open. However, there were so many things going on in his life with the department charges, the hearing, and the suspension that he unintentionally put the romantic relationship on the back burner. Because it had been such a long while, he didn't know what kind of relationship, if any, still existed between the two of them.

Rocco threw caution to the wind and swallowed a huge slice of humble pie. He proceeded to contact his one-time fiancée. Janet's cell phone rang until it went into voicemail, but Rocco decided that leaving a message wasn't what he wanted to do. He thought about it, and decided that he would go to her house and wait for her to come home from work. He would have the element of surprise on his side which he hoped would elicit a positive response form Janet. Although it was a bit early, he got into his car and headed toward Janet's house. Being early would give him some time to build up the courage that he needed to actually meet with her after their hiatus.

Rocco waited and time dragged on. It was way past the time that Janet usually walked down the block to her home. Rocco began to make excuses like she had to work overtime or that there were train delays, or even that she stopped off to do a little shopping. However, he was now waiting for just about two hours, and was about to leave when he noticed a blue sports car pull up in front of Janet's house. Rocco couldn't see who was in the car, but he was able to make out the outlines of two people. He waited patiently to see who had arrived. As one of the figures exited the car, the illumination from the street light showed that Janet had come home. The other person in the car didn't exit but waited for Janet to open the front door of her house where she waved a "goodbye" to the occupant in the car. The driver then made a U-turn and proceeded on his way. As the car passed by Rocco, who was now slouched down in the front seat of his vehicle, he was able to clearly see who the driver was. Upon recognizing the operator of the vehicle, Rocco shouted out an ear-splitting expletive to himself and pounded his fist on the not-so-soft dashboard.

Rocco Deloberti was beside himself. He had waited too long to contact Janet, and a wolf circled the prey and caught her attention. He was disgusted because he had only himself to blame. He guessed that Janet had been seeking some consolation after their break-up, and who better to go to than someone who knew the whole situation. Bobby Santiago was the one who drove the blue sports car that chauffeured Janet to her residence. This guy continued to be a thorn in Rocco's side, but now it was more like a knife in his back. His idea of a surprise had been a good one, but he was the only one who was ultimately surprised.

Rocco tried to calm down and logically think of his next move. He had a couple of options: one, he could march into Janet's house and demand to know what was going on; two, he could find out where Santiago lived and beat the hell out of him; or three, he could just drive away and accept what fate had dealt him. Unfortunately, Rocco Deloberti was not happy with any of his choices. Also, he had to be careful because he was still on suspension and any questionable behavior in which he was involved would result in his immediate termination from the job.

He was behind the eight ball, so to speak. He didn't know what to do or how to rectify the situation.

Rocco felt like a fool for letting the lack of communication go on for such a long period of time. Because of the "no-contact" situation, Janet had to assume that Rocco had decided against trying to work out their differences. If his foot could have reached it, Rocco would have kicked himself in the ass. However, there was another option. If he could control himself, he could just ring the front door bell and surprise her anyway. He could let her know that he had come to his senses and that he wanted to renew their relationship. He would then be able to tell by her body language as to whether or not the possibility existed. He was fearful, though, that he might react as a lion who had not been fed if the possibility didn't exist. His apprehension and curiosity was overwhelming, so he had to find out. He decided to ring the bell.

Rocco Deloberti pulled himself up by the bootstraps, took a deep breath and walked to Janet's front door. He hesitated and held his hand above the bell. He still had time to retreat, but he manned up and rang the bell. It was Janet's voice that answered in response to the doorbell: "Come in! Come in!" Rocco heard a harrowing almost desperate yell and quickly opened the door. Janet turned and with a disappointingly concerned face explained: "Rocco. It's you. What are you doing here? I am waiting for an ambulance. I think my father is having a heart attack." As Janet finished speaking, she heard knocking at the door, and once again she yelled to come in. This time it was the EMTs who were responding to Janet's call.

===

The EMTs triaged Janet's dad and prepared him for the trip to the hospital. It was also their opinion that Mr. Commings had suffered a heart attack. They wheeled him out to the ambulance and took off to the hospital. Seeing that Janet and her mom were visibly shaken up, Rocco volunteered to take them to the emergency room. They quickly accepted Rocco's invitation, and the three of them sped off in Rocco's car. Other than the sobbing and emotional trauma, the ride to the hospital was a quiet and uneventful one. Each of them weighing the unknown seriousness of the attack, and how it might affect the rest of Mr. Commings' life. Even though they knew that they would have to be patient for any diagnosis from the doctor, they couldn't wait to get to the hospital. There was never any parking spaces in the hospital lot, but in this instance, they were able to park in the emergency room parking area where there were a few available parking spots.

Mr. David Commings was rushed into the emergency treatment room where doctors were attending to him and trying to stop the possibility of him getting another more serious attack. Sitting in the waiting room and having one's imagination run wild is the unintended punishment that all hospitals levy. Unfortunately, very few people escape this sentencing. Janet, her mom, and Rocco were now part of that group who had to sit and wait.

Rocco tried to alleviate some of the tension: "Your dad got to the hospital very quickly. I'm sure that the doctors will be able to stabilize him and prevent any permanent damage. He's a strong individual, and he'll hopefully come through this with flying colors."

Janet responded: "Thanks, Rocco. I appreciate your saying that." There was a pause, and Janet, once again, addressed Rocco: "It was fortuitous that you arrived just when we needed you. However, I was wondering why you came to the house. I haven't seen you in such a long time, and we really haven't spoken, so I just can't believe that you showed up when you did. What's up?"

Although he knew it would come up sooner or later, Rocco was still taken by surprise when the question rose to the surface. He hesitated and tried to figure out a way to carefully broach the subject of their relationship. It was definitely the wrong time to start negotiating a comeback, but Janet had put it to him, so he had no other choice. Just as he was about to start his response to Janet's question, a voice from behind him interrupted: "Hi Janet. I came as soon as I could. Is everything okay? Have you heard anything from the doctors?" Rocco couldn't believe it. It was that same familiar voice that had plagued him for what seemed like forever, but now, it really raised his blood pressure.

Janet turned to Santago: "Hi, Bobby. Thank you for coming so quickly. I really appreciate it. No, we haven't heard anything yet, but it's somewhat definite that my dad has had a heart attack. However, we got him to the hospital quickly, so we are hoping that the doctors will be able to prevent any serious damage."

"Well, that sounds good. Hey, Hi Rocco. How are you doing?" In addition to being shocked that Bobby Santiago was there, he now had to speak to him as if there was nothing wrong. Rocco was incensed that Santiago was there, but it added to the seriousness of the fact that there was definitely more than just a friendship evolving between Janet and Rocco's nemesis.

"I'm doing okay, Bobby. I had no idea that you would be here. How did you find out about Mr. Commings?"

"Oh, Janet texted me when it happened, and I had just left the house, so I wasn't that far away. I just turned around and headed for the hospital."

"I didn't realize that you and Janet had gotten so close."

"Yeah, we just hit it off after that whole undercover operation concluded. She's a great girl, but I'm sure you know that."

Rocco had to calm down, because his blood was beginning to boil, and all he wanted to do was to smash Santiago in the face. However, he took the high road and with a lot of difficulty said: "Well, since you are here now, I guess I can leave Janet and her mom in your hands."

"Yeah, thanks. I appreciate your being there when they needed you."

Everything that Bobby Santiago said irritated Rocco even more. Santiago was so presumptuous and confident that although Rocco wanted to stay, he just couldn't deal with the whole situation. Janet had overheard the entire conversation and turned to Rocco: "Yes, Rocco thanks for all of your help, but you still didn't tell me why you were at the house."

Rocco dejectedly responded: "It really doesn't matter now. I am just glad that I was there to help. I hope everything turns out okay with your dad." Rocco didn't want to leave, but Janet was definitely not insisting that he stay, so he said "goodbye" and turned to go. Before he left, he faced Bobby and whispered: "Would you jump into my grave that quickly?" Rocco didn't wait for any response to his rhetorical question. He continued on with his depressing exit.

Rocco Deloberti was a beaten and saddened individual. However, he was also very angry and uptight that the individual who was apparently going to take his place in the romantic relationship that he once enjoyed with Janet Commings was the last person he would have ever imagined, Bobby Santiago. This guy was instrumental in ruining his professional life, but now he even slithered into his personal life, and it seemed that he had been successful in both maneuvers.

Chapter Twenty

The Comeback

As Rocco was walking out of the hospital, his mood was depressed and filled with the regret of not acting sooner. He realized that he had lost someone who was very dear to him and with whom he had wanted to share the rest of his life. He was unaware of the fact that he was involuntarily shaking his head from side to side in a negative manner. He was talking aloud to himself and didn't care about what the people around him thought. He was totally involved in his own pity party when he came face-to-face with the revolving exit door which almost slammed him against its frame.

Just about the time that Rocco reached his car, he thought he heard his name being called, but quickly connected it with wishful thinking. He didn't even turn around. As he placed his hand on the car door release, he heard his name again. This time it was louder and seemed to be much closer. He gave in to his curiosity and turned to see Janet running toward him. His first thought was that something disastrous had happened, and her father had suffered complications. He would help with whatever Janet needed. When she finally got to him, she was out of breath and had to take a moment before she spoke: "Rocco, I'm glad that I caught up with you. You never answered my question about why you came to my house tonight. Why were you there?"

Rocco was shocked that she came after him just to find out why he was at her house. He took her inquiry as a positive. Maybe, this was an opening, a chance to begin again. It must mean something for her to leave the waiting room just to have her question answered.

He anxiously, but cautiously responded: "Well, Janet, I was coming to see you to talk about us and the possibility of reconnecting. However, I saw you with Santiago, and when I finally managed enough courage to come to your front door, you were yelling for help. Everything else went on the back burner. After what happened with your dad, I didn't think that it was the right time to discuss anything about us. When Bobby arrived at the hospital in response to your text, I knew that my idea about discussing anything with you was too little too late. So, yeah, the reason I came to your house was to tell you how foolish I was to have waited so long to make things right. However, I didn't realize that it was more than foolish, it was disastrous. Does that answer your question?"

"It sure does, Rocco. I couldn't believe that I hadn't heard from you for such a long time, so I contacted Bobby to find out if everything was okay. He told me about the job and what you were going through with the sergeant. He also offered to meet with me to discuss the entire situation. I agreed, and I met him after work tonight. He told me the whole thing, and that with the help of Pop you were able to keep your job. I know that you are suspended, but we both know that it could have been worse.

After speaking with Bobby, I realized that he wanted to be more than just a messenger. I told him that I wasn't ready to date other people yet, and he understood. I texted him tonight, because at that point, I had no one else on whom I could depend. As you can see, he responded as quickly as he could. I am sure he took my text as a positive, but I only did it out of desperation and help. I explained that to him just a little while ago. If you could, I would prefer for you to stay for a while. If that's okay."

Rocco was beside himself: "Janet, it's more than 'okay,' it's something that I thought I had lost for good. Sure, I'll stay for as long as you want me to, but what about Bobby? The two of us being there isn't the best of scenarios, and I do not want to get into any sticky situation with him. Since you did text him to come to the hospital, I don't know how he will take my staying and his going."

"Don't worry about that. He knows where I stand. I appreciate the fact that he came to the hospital, of course, but I am sure he will leave when you come back in with me."

The more Rocco thought about it, he didn't care how Bobby took it. Rocco was going to let him know that things were back to normal between him and Janet, and that his "help" was no longer needed. Santiago hadn't fooled anyone, especially Janet. She knew from the get-go that his help and good intentions came with conditions and other attachments. So, as soon as he tried to open the door to more than just a "friends" relationship, she quickly put her hand out and stopped the door from opening any more than necessary.

Rocco walked back to the emergency room with Janet, and when they got there, she immediately asked her mom if the doctor had spoken to her. Mrs. Commings just shook her head, and continued staring into space. Before Janet could say anything to Bobby, he turned his attention to Rocco: "Hey, I thought you were departing and leaving things in my hands. Did you have second thoughts?"

Rocco was quick to respond: "No, Bobby. I didn't have any second thoughts, but thank goodness, Janet did."

Janet saw that things were getting a little too "hot," so she intervened: "Bobby, I really appreciate your coming to the hospital. You're a good friend, but Rocco has decided to stay with us, so if you want to go, you can."

Santiago knew that he was getting the old heave-ho, and he was not happy about it. He had taken Janet's text as a positive sign that something could possibly develop between him and her. However, his bubble had just burst and furthermore, he had faced defeat in front of Rocco Deloberti. It was a hard pill to swallow, and he wanted to make sure that Janet was certain about her decision: "Janet, are you sure you want me to go? I really don't have anything else planned, and it would be no problem for me to stay."

Janet realized that Bobby was giving it his last ditch effort, and she was sure that it was antagonizing Rocco. She decided that she had to be more demonstrative: "Thanks again, Bobby, but since Rocco is staying, I really don't need any other help. I hope you understand. Really, Bobby, thanks for everything, but Rocco will take care of anything that we may need."

Not only did Bobby understand that she was telling him that all she needed was Rocco to be there, but he felt that he was unceremoniously being kicked to the curb. He had no reason to feel that way. Janet had not given him any signs that their relationship could go any farther than a friendship, but his imagination had worked overtime in forming a fantasy that now was never going to develop into any form of reality.

Bobby Santiago rose from his chair and said nothing. However, as he turned to leave, he faced Rocco. Bobby whispered so that only Rocco could hear: "You may have won the battle, but the war is mine!" Without saying anything to anyone else, Bobby Santiago just turned toward the exit and left. He hadn't given Rocco a chance to respond, and maybe for Rocco that was a good thing.

Janet felt the cold as Bobby left, and she had heard him whisper something to Rocco upon leaving: "Wow, I didn't think that Bobby would take it so poorly. He was never given any indication that our relationship could develop into anything but friends. He really seemed angry. He didn't even say 'goodbye,' but I thought I heard him whisper something to you when he left. What did he say?"

"It was really nothing, Janet. He just told me that if I needed anything that I should just contact him."

"Rocco, you were never a good liar, but I'm not going to press the issue. I am sure you will take everything in stride."

===

The emergency room treatment door opened, and a doctor approached Mrs. Commings and Janet. He told them that the heart attack was more severe than they had anticipated, but he was hopeful that Mr. Commings would fully recuperate. He also mentioned that the patient's lifestyle was going to have to change to avoid any further complications. The doctor mentioned a change of diet, an exercise program and certain medications that Mr. Commings would have to take for the rest of his life.

Janet and her mom listened carefully to what the doctor was saying, but for the entire time, they were mentally celebrating that dad was still alive. Yes, he hadn't gotten another attack, and all they wanted to hear was that he was okay for now. They could care less about what he would have to do in the future, but they would both make sure that he followed the doctor's orders. They asked if they could see him, and the doctor told them a nurse would come out and tell them when they could go in and visit with their relative. Janet and her mom hugged each other with the celebration of the good news. Included in the hug, however, was Rocco Deloberti. It seemed as though he was back.

From a distance and out of sight, Bobby Santiago witnessed the joyful celebration and what amounted to total relief for the family. He also witnessed the hug that included Rocco. Like a witch over her caldron, Bobby had to brew a solution that would deteriorate the bond that allowed Janet and Rocco to remain close even though they had been so distant. It was not so much that Bobby Santiago had lost Janet, who he never really had, but it was just the fact that he had lost. Bobby Santiago was not used to losing, and one could be sure that he would make every effort to turn his temporary negative situation into a positive and permanent win.

Chapter Twenty-One

Strange Seems Normal

The days passed slowly as Rocco waited for his suspension to end. He was chomping at the bit to get back to work. A lot had happened during his separation from the job, and he was ready to get back to work. For the most part, things had worked out well for him, and he took his discipline as well as could be expected. However, he was quite surprised at the fact that his punishment did not include a transfer to another command. In fact, he thought that a transfer would be the first on the list of changes for him, but up until now, nothing had come down to change his assigned precinct. There were only two days left before he would report for active duty again, and as of the present, he was going back to his former command.

The police department worked in strange ways and gave very little notice regarding personnel changes that had to be made. So, the day before Rocco was to report to his precinct, he received a phone call from the administrative lieutenant who was assigned to his command: "Hello this is Lieutenant Jansen. Am I speaking to Officer Rocco Deloberti?"

"Yes, Lieutenant. I am Police Officer Rocco Deloberti."

"Well, Officer, a phone message has just come down to the command, and as of 0001 hours tomorrow morning you are assigned to the five four precinct in the Bronx. You will report for duty at the precinct at 0800 hours. Do you understand the message?"

"Yes sir. Although I am a bit surprised and a bit taken aback, I guess I should be grateful that I still have a job."

"You got that right, son. No one believed that you would be coming back, but some people have a lot of sway. You are officially notified, and good luck."

The lieutenant didn't wait for Rocco to say "goodbye." He just hung up. To Rocco, it sounded like Jansen was pissed that Rocco was getting another chance, even though that chance brought him to the far reaches of the Bronx. The five four precinct was the northern most precinct in the city. It bordered Westchester County and the town of Yonkers. It was also the farthest location from Rocco's residence, and it served as a message that the department really didn't want Rocco Deloberti to remain a police officer. He was sure that the traveling and the tolls were meant to persuade Rocco to look for employment elsewhere. However, Rocco was determined to make things right and get back on track.

Unfortunately for Rocco, and for that matter, for any police officer who is transferred for disciplinary reasons, your reputation not only followed you, but most of the time, arrived before you did. This was the case with Rocco. He was assigned to a command where he knew no one, and no one knew him. Unfortunately for Police Officer Deloberti, no one wanted to get to know him. His reputation was a story about an officer who seems to get into trouble. He did not have to look for it; in most cases, it found him. Other officers did not need that kind of stressful condition to weigh them down. They all had enough to deal with, and they didn't need an additional burden to carry around.

===

The way that other officers viewed someone like Rocco was that he traveled on the "trouble highway." No matter where or when he traveled, the highway always brought "trouble" his way. Working with someone like that always put whatever officer was working with him at the time also at risk. Therefore, it was not going to be easy for Rocco to find a steady partner. Officers were going to avoid him like the plague. However, this was all included as part of the discipline that was handed down. If the department made it as difficult as possible for the officer to exist, then maybe the officer would resign. Rocco knew this, and he was determined to beat the system. In fact, by still having a job, in his mind, he had already beat it.

Without traffic, the ride to the Bronx took about forty-five minutes to an hour. Unfortunately, Rocco was assigned to the day tour which meant that he would be traveling during rush hour. He was sure that this assignment was also planned. So, getting to work on the day tour took about ninety minutes and a lot of aggravation. And to boot, all this came with the caveat that he had to pay a toll for the Throgs Neck Bridge. It was an expense that truly cut into his take home pay. However, traveling over a bridge was the only way that he could get to the Bronx from where he resided. Rocco just took it in stride because there was nothing he could do about it. He hoped, in time, that things would change, but right now he had to play with the hand he was dealt.

===

Commanding Officers speak to one another, and he was sure that one of the first items on his agenda was a scheduled introductory meeting with the commanding officer of the five four precinct. As soon as he walked through the station house doors and reported to the desk officer, he was told to see the commanding officer. Rocco knew it was coming, but he thought that he would at least be allowed to stow his gear in a locker before he met with the Captain. That was not to be the case.

Rocco had done a little of his own research and inquired through different sources as to the character and management style of his new boss. Captain Ellis Bracken was known to be somewhat of a rebel, but he ran a very tight ship. It was his thinking outside the company box, and his "locking horns" with his immediate supervisors that apparently delayed his promotion to deputy inspector. However, Bracken was not going to change, so he remained in his present rank which was not the usual supervisory level for a commanding officer of a Bronx precinct. Rocco didn't know if the commanding officer's out-of-the-norm management style would help or hurt him. He was about to find out.

Rocco put his gear in an unoccupied office and proceeded to the commanding officer's room. As he approached Captain Bracken's office, he was intercepted by the precinct administrative lieutenant: "Are you Officer Deloberti?"

"Yes. Lieutenant. I am Police Officer Rocco Deloberti. I was told to report directly to the captain's office. Is there a problem, sir."

"There will be a problem if you don't just take a second and listen to what I have to say."

Apparently, the lieutenant took Rocco's unintended tone as argumentative, and he shut Rocco down quickly.

Rocco realized this and tried to smooth things: "Sorry lieutenant. I guess I'm just a bit nervous and trying to get used to a brand new command."

"Understood, Rocco. I am not the enemy, but you have to know that your arrival has caused a lot of angst among the other officers. Before you go in to see the captain, come into my office so I can give you a little rundown about the precinct and Captain Ellis Bracken."

"Sure, Lieutenant, but I was told to report to him immediately."

"Don't worry about that. I'll take care of it, and I will be going into the captain's office with you anyway."

Rocco followed the lieutenant into his office. Before the lieutenant sat behind his desk, he reached out his hand and said: "Rocco, I am Lieutenant Joseph Calabrese. I am the administrative lieutenant." He shook Rocco's hand and proceeded to his chair behind the desk and motioned to Rocco to take a seat. So far, Rocco was impressed with the lieutenant's actions. The lieutenant was Italian, and Rocco thought that maybe he was trying to help another Italian police officer. However, by the lieutenant's next comments, Rocco couldn't be more wrong: "Rocco, you know that everyone here knows about you and why you've been transferred to this command. I also realize that it is hardship for you to travel here, but you still have a job, and you are lucky to still be a police officer. You have to make the best of a shitty situation. If you don't, that man in the commanding officer's office will hasten your unemployment, and I will cut your legs right out from under you. Do you understand that?"

"Absolutely, sir. I know things will be difficult, and I also know that my reputation has preceded me. I am lucky to still be a police officer, and I won't forget it."

"Rocco, luck has nothing to do with it. Your friend, Hallerin, knows many people, and he convinced Sergeant Shanahan not to persist with pressing for your termination. My own opinion, and I will deny that I ever said it, your bottle couldn't have landed on a more worthy target. I know Shanahan, and I know that he could have stopped the incident, but he allowed it to continue. I can't stand this ethnic shit, but understand that if you were a McDonald or a Collins, the incident might not have exploded into what it became. Don't misunderstand me. It is my contention that the ethnic associations: the Irish club, the Italian club, the Spanish club, etc. are a necessary evil. Is there ethnic prejudice still existing in this department? Absolutely! Do these clubs come to the aid of those officers who are members of a specific club? Yes, they do. However, in my opinion, these associations only tend to divide the officers. Before anything else, we are all police officers, and we belong to only one club, the Blue Club. Do you get where I'm coming from?"

"Understood, lieutenant."

"Fine. Now, before we go into the captain's office, let me explain a few things to you. This is an outpost precinct. It means that many of the officers here are not exactly what one would call the ideal police officer. Having said that, however, they would not hesitate to help anyone of us, if we needed it. The major problem you will have is getting a partner. No one wants trouble, and to many of the officers, you spell trouble. Bide your time, and ultimately someone will decide to give you a shot. The captain will harp on the same subject. Just listen and agree with what he's telling you. Other than that, you are a big boy, and you will have to find your way around. Any questions?"

"No, sir, and thank you for taking the time to speak with me."

"No thanks necessary. Now, let's go see the captain. By the way, take this for what it's worth. It's nice to have another Italian around, but if you fuck up, I will be the first to run a stake right through your heart."

Rocco knew that the captain was supposed to be a little strange, but if the lieutenant was "normal," he couldn't imagine what the captain was going to be like. Rocco and the lieutenant proceeded to the captain's office. Much to the chagrin of the lieutenant, instead of the lieutenant announcing himself and entering, Rocco knocked on the captain's door, and they were both greeted with: "Enter if you dare!"

The odd adventure and mystery of the five four precinct had begun, but Rocco Deloberti couldn't wait to face any and all of the challenges in an effort to make things right and save his wounded reputation. In contradiction to what the lieutenant had just said, he worried that the officers of the five four precinct would not afford him any opportunity to demonstrate that he was a good cop, no matter how much time he gave them. He could do nothing but wait and see.

Chapter Twenty-Two

Finally, a Partner

Administrative Lieutenant Joseph Calabrese was absolutely right. Not only was it difficult to find a partner, but the other cops treated Rocco as if he had the plague. His meeting with Captain Bracken was what he had expected and what the lieutenant had told him to expect. The captain emphasized exactly what the lieutenant had told Rocco, and also informed him that as the commanding officer, unfortunately, he had no say in who was transferred to his command. Bracken spoke about a number of different things that Rocco could expect and gave Rocco the "low-down" regarding the demographics of the command. Although Ellis Bracken definitely had a strange way about him, Rocco took to him. To

Rocco, Captain Bracken seemed like a no-nonsense type of supervisor who just wanted everyone to do their job. If an officer did something that was praiseworthy, the captain would be the first person to applaud the action. However, if an officer screwed up because of indifference or laziness, well, in Rocco's opinion, Commanding Officer Captain Ellis Bracken would come down on that officer like the hammers of hell. Rocco was going to give his time in the five four a real targeted effort even if he had to overcome his reputation and the rumors that had spread about him.

For the first few months, Police Officer Rocco Deloberti found himself riding mostly in a "one-man" car. This occurred for a number of reasons: one - the obvious decision by others that they did not want to ride with "trouble," two – Rocco was being assigned to the part of the precinct that wasn't as active as other parts; therefore, lessening the possibility of his getting into trouble, and three – it was easier to supervise Rocco, without a partner, in an area that was less busy. Rocco was aware of all these reasons and just accepted his fate.

===

On a number of occasions, officers were forced to ride with Rocco or were forced to work alongside him. Absences, unavailability of vehicles, or necessary back-up, many times, dictated the cooperative working arrangements. One of the officers who found herself working with Rocco was Police Officer Kathleen Dancer. When a dispatched call is assigned to a "one-man" car, but more than one officer might be needed, an additional "one-man" car also responds to the call. So, it was on a certain day tour when the call came in for an elderly missing person. It was Officer Dancer's call, and Rocco was assigned to assist as the backup officer. He had worked with her on a few other calls, and they had gotten along well.

There were a number of high rise apartment buildings in the five four precinct, and the call for a missing person originated in one of these buildings. Kathleen Dancer was the first to respond, and Rocco arrived shortly afterward. They responded to an apartment on the fifteenth floor where they were greeted by an elderly woman who was concerned about her husband.

Mrs. Gertrude Rosen's concern was centered around the fact that her husband went to the building's outdoor parking lot to retrieve her jacket that she had previously left in the car. Gertrude was worried that her husband had not yet returned. After getting the jacket, her husband, Stanley, was supposed to come back to the apartment to escort his not-so-stable wife down to the car. Gertrude explained to the officers that her husband had been gone for over thirty minutes, and that he should have been back long before that. Officer Dancer stayed with Gertrude in the apartment to gather information for the report while Rocco headed to the parking lot to find Stanley. Mrs. Rosen was visibly nervous and her hands began to shake. Dancer consoled her and let her know that Officer Deloberti would find Stanley and bring him back to the apartment.

When Rocco left the Rosen apartment, he did not have a good feeling about the whole situation. Gertrude was up in years, and she had mentioned that her husband was a few years older than she. She gave Rocco a description of the car, and he began his search in the rather large parking lot. The Rosen family car was one that was popular, and therefore, there were a number of vehicles that matched the description that Gertrude had given to Rocco. He examined two or three vehicles with no positive results. Rocco was coming to the end of the parking area when he spotted another car that matched the description. As he approached the vehicle, he saw a figure sitting behind the steering wheel. As he got closer, the figure was not sitting but was slumped down in the driver's seat. When Rocco opened the car door, it became apparent to him that Stanley Rosen had expired. Rocco checked for vital signs, but Mr. Rosen had been dead for a while. Police Officer Deloberti called for a supervisor and an ambulance.

Both the supervisor and the ambulance arrived in short order, and Rocco proceeded back into the apartment building to deliver the very sad news to Mrs. Rosen. Department procedures suggested that officers responding to such a situation should try to get neighbors to help break the news and ultimately console the remaining partner. Rocco did just that. He knocked on doors and explained that he needed support for Mrs. Rosen. He was able to get three neighbors to accompany him to Mrs. Rosen's apartment. When Rocco returned to the apartment, he knocked on the door and entered. Kathleen saw the group who was with her partner, and she knew immediately that Mr. Stanley Rosen had passed. Gertrude was apprehensive as Kathleen and Rocco approached her with the neighbors in tow. Police Officer Kathleen Dancer was the one who broke the news to Gertrude. Mrs. Rosen immediately broke into uncontrollable sobbing. The police officers backed away and allowed Gertrude's neighbors to, as much as possible, help diminish some of the pain that the death of a loved one always initiates.

After allowing the neighbors to offer some consolation, Officer Deloberti asked Mrs. Rosen if there were any relatives that she wanted him to contact for her. Gertrude told Rocco that she had three children, but two of them lived out-of-state. However, she had a son who lived locally, and she gave Rocco his number. Rocco proceeded to contact Mrs. Rosen's son who took the news of his father's death more painfully than expected. He said that he would leave immediately and come to his mother's apartment. Kathleen told Gertrude that her son was notified, and that he was on his way.

The paper work was completed, the body was removed, and Gertrude's son was now with her. It was time for the police officers to resume patrol. The Rosen's had been married for fifty years, so their permanent separation pulled at the heart strings of everyone who had been involved in the sad experience. Both Kathleen and Rocco were not immune to those feelings, and at times, one could see tears welling up in the officers' eyes. When they reached their respective vehicles, Kathleen stopped Rocco from entering his car: "Can I speak to you for a minute?"

"Sure, Kathleen. What's on your mind?"

"First of all, if you are to be my partner, you'd better start calling me 'Kate' like everyone else. Secondly, we've ridden together a few times, and I think we approach the job in a very similar way. However, you showed your true compassion when you handled Mrs. Rosen the way you did. I appreciate how you reacted and I'm certain that we could get along well as partners. Unless you've made other arrangements, I'd like to let the captain know that we want to be partners. What do you think?"

Rocco jokingly smiled and said: "Well, Kate, I have to give some serious thought to the subject. There are a lot of other officers who also approached me with the very same offer. I might need some time to decide." Rocco put his finger to the side of his head simulating the thinking process, and then he quickly removed it and said: "Absolutely, Kate. I appreciate your offer. Thanks."

"No thanks necessary, Rocco. Although I am a good cop, and I can hold my own, guys are not knocking down my door with offers to be their partner. I guess the insecurity and prejudice of having a female partner still lingers with a number of officers. So, our partnership will have a mutually beneficial effect. I will go in to see Captain Bracken at the end of our tour."

"Hey, Kate. Would you mind if I came with you to see the captain?"

"Our partnership is definitely starting out on the right foot. I was hoping that you would want to be a part of the request. See you when we finish."

Kate and Rocco got into their vehicles and resumed patrol. Rocco Deloberti had a smile on his face that went from ear to ear. He not only had a partner, but he had one who was well respected in the precinct, and one who the commanding officer had previously recommended for outstanding police service.

===

Rocco and Janet had resumed their serious relationship, and they were once again engaged to be married. Janet was an understanding woman, and for the most part, took things in stride. There was one negative to the partnership that Rocco and Kate had agreed upon. Kate was a single, very good looking female. Rocco, Janet's fiancée, was about to spend eight hours a day, five days a week with a young woman who half of the precinct wanted to date. Even though Janet was an even-minded individual, the new partnership was not going to be an easy sell. It is said that cops spend more time with their partners than they do with their wives or girlfriends. For the most part, that is a true statement. Although the time inequalities between wife and partner were a problem for most cops, in Rocco's case, the problem was compounded by the fact that his partner was a "knockout." Rocco wanted a steady partner to normalize his police routine, but there was an old adage that unfortunately applied to Rocco's new situation: "Be careful what you wish for, you just might get it." With a steady partner, he might normalize his police routine, but with this particular officer, he just might jeopardize his personal interactions with his fiancée.

If the situation were reversed, Rocco would have no part of it. He hoped that Janet would be more understanding and possess a lot more self-confidence than he had. The road back into Janet's heart had been a rocky one, and Rocco did not want to put any additional speed bumps in the way.

Chapter Twenty-Three

Meeting the Other Half

Rocco told Janet the good news about having a steady partner, and she was very happy for her fiancée. He mentioned how his partner was well respected in the precinct and how the job would be even more appealing now. Rocco broke the news about having a female partner by casually referring to his partner as "she." He explained that Kathleen Dancer was a good cop, but most of the guys in the precinct did not want to ride with a female partner. He further explained that the partnership was mutually benefit for both Kate and him.

Janet sat stoically and listened as Rocco tried to justify the fact that he was going to have a female partner. She realized that he felt almost guilty in accepting a female as his partner. She also knew that he was attempting to allay any of her fears regarding a mixed partnership. Janet let him go on for a while, and when she decided that he suffered enough, she interrupted his justification diatribe: “Rocco, you don’t have to continue to explain that you will be working with a female. I know that you are up against the wall in finding a partner, so I am glad that you finally were able to get one. The fact that she is a female only bothers me with respect to the idea of whether she can protect you as well as a male partner could. If you have confidence in her abilities, then I have no problem with her working as your partner. I am sure that Kate already knows that you are engaged, and it would be unfair of me to assume that just because she is a female that her being your partner would present a problem for us. I am happy for you.”

Rocco almost couldn’t believe his ears. He hadn’t known how he was going to approach Janet with the idea that he was working with a female, but Janet took all the worry and angst out of the situation. This just reaffirmed to Rocco that she was a very special woman. He breathed a strong sigh of relief, and he was going to make sure that Janet didn’t regret the attitude that she had. It was going to be all business with Kate, no matter the circumstances.

===

Even though they had worked together before, their first tour of duty as permanent partners was a little awkward. They both were at a loss for words and there was very little conversation for the first part of the tour. However, after responding to a number of jobs, the mood became a more opened one, and they both began speaking a lot more.

Although they were getting along fine, a month had passed, and Kate just felt that there was something that was bothering her partner. She had an inclination as to what it might be so she asked: “Hey Rocco, I meant to ask you. How did your fiancée take to the fact that you are riding with a female partner, or did you not tell her yet?”

“No Kate. I told her as soon as I found out that we were going to be partners. I didn’t want to keep anything from her.”

Kate responded: “So, tell me. How did she react to the fact that you are riding with a single female who has been categorized by some as a “knockout?”

“To tell you the truth, she took it really well, at least outwardly. I don’t know if it is bothering her, but she hasn’t shown it.”

“That’s really good, Rocco. She seems to be a stand-up person. I can’t wait to meet her.”

Rocco was taken aback by Kate’s last comment. He really didn’t know how Janet was going to respond to the fact that Kate not only was a single female, but a very pretty one who half of the precinct wanted to date. He was actually dreading the time when his partner and his fiancée would meet. Kate was quite attuned to the dilemma that Rocco was facing, and she knew how much Rocco was avoiding the inevitable meeting. So, she cut to the chase and decided to relieve some of the pressure that her partner was obviously feeling: “Rocco, I’m going to make things a lot easier for you. It's obvious that you are concerned about the time when I actually meet Janet, and sooner or later you know that I will. Maybe, I can help out a little." Kate looked at her watch and spoke again: "Do you mind if we stray a little from our sector and eat at the diner in the south end of the precinct?"

"No problem, if that is where you want to go."

Kate took out her cell phone and began texting. It seemed a little odd to Rocco, but he didn't say anything. Kate started driving in the direction of the diner. The parking lot of the diner was pretty full because Kate and Rocco were arriving during the usual lunch hour period. Kate found a spot and they went inside. As usual, when uniformed cops enter a location, everyone stops and stares. After a while, police officers get used to it and take it in stride.

Apparently, Kate knew the manager of the diner, and he escorted the officers to a table in the rear. When they reached the table that Rocco assumed was going to be theirs, he saw that someone was already sitting there. He was confused and turned to the manager who turned to Kate. Kate nodded and said: "Rocco Deloberti meet Gloria Santiago, my better half."

To the objective observer, one would have thought that Rocco was frozen in time. He just stared at Gloria and then back at Kate. He acted like he didn't hear correctly. Kate saw the shock and eased him into the present: "Hey Rocco. Are you okay? I told you that I was going to make your life easier. I'm sure the fact that I am gay will relieve some of the concern that Janet may have. Understand Rocco, that you are one of the few who actually know about my sexual preference. I would like to keep it that way. I am sure that Gloria would also like to keep her private life- private. She is a police officer in Queens, and we met when we were assigned to an overtime detail in Manhattan."

Rocco came to his senses and finally addressed Gloria: "Very glad to meet you, Gloria. Sorry for the rude entrance, but I just assumed that Kate was one of the guys, so to speak. Silly me!"

Gloria graciously responded: "No problem, Rocco. Kate has told me about you, and I'm glad to finally meet you. Apparently, there are a lot of snakes who work in the five four, and I'm glad that Kate was able to find a good guy."

Rocco was relieved: "I'm the lucky one, Gloria. Not too many guys want to work with me. It seems that I've earned the nickname, 'trouble,' and not too many cops want to associate with 'trouble.' We've only worked together for about a month or so, but Kate is one hell of a cop, as far as I am concerned. And please don't take this the wrong way, but I am really glad that she is gay. She is right. It makes my personal life so much easier."

"I totally understand. And I'm not telling tales out of school, but she also thinks that she has found a really good partner."

Rocco's mood had totally changed and he said: "That's good to hear. I didn't have too much of an appetite before, but I can eat up a storm now. Why don't we order?"

It was like an anchor had been lifted from Rocco's shoulders. He was of the mind that things were looking up. He had his girlfriend back; he had his job back; and even had a steady partner. Rocco was feeling really good about life for a change. He got along well with Kate's life partner, and they discussed past assignments and different situations that they had experienced. This impromptu meeting with Gloria and Kate served to break down any secretive or bothersome barriers that might have existed.

After listening to background stories from both Kate and Gloria, Rocco felt comfortable enough to rehash some of the problems that he had in his last command. He was speaking about his experiences with the precinct scooter patrol and the death of Police Officer Joey Lelan when Gloria interrupted and mentioned that she was at the funeral. She stated that she was amazed at the turnout for the officer and the many different departments that were represented. Rocco told her that the attendance was not unique to the Lelan funeral: "Unfortunately, I have been to a few funerals and the attendance from outside departments is always overwhelming. Police officers line the streets for blocks to offer their last respects to a fallen brother or sister. There are times when you cannot see the end of the police line. However, it is reciprocal. We also send our officers to funerals of police officers who have been killed in the line of duty and who are attached to other departments. When you think about it, it is the least that we can do."

Gloria continued the conversation: "Yes, my cousin had mentioned that same thing. He has gone to a number of funerals for police officers who were from other departments. Unfortunately, I guess the longer that one is on the job, the number of police funerals increases. It is definitely a sad commentary on the current risk for law enforcement. In fact, my cousin tried to persuade me to look for another job. He was not happy about my becoming a police officer. He is more like my older brother than my cousin. I don't know what I would do without him."

As Rocco listened to Gloria tell her story, a bell went off in Rocco's head. He believed that it was just a coincidence that she shared the same last name as someone who remained a thorn in Rocco's side. He was almost certain that it couldn't be the same person. After all, "Santiago" was a relatively common Spanish name, but with his bad luck, it probably would be the same guy. He had to find out for sure.

"Gloria, you mentioned your cousin. Does he have a long time on the job? And where does he work?"

Kate was a seasoned cop. She knew all about the previous bottle-throwing incident, and she even knew about Rocco's engagement problems. She was hoping that this subject would not come up, but to her dismay, she felt that the newly tied bonds of a partnership might very well strain and possibly rupture. She had known all about Gloria's cousin, and when the time was right, she would have mentioned it to Rocco. This was not the time, however.

Gloria innocently answered Rocco's question: "Oh, Bobby has been on the job for a while now, and he works in some sort of special unit, but at the time of Officer Lelan's death, he was working out of the five four."

With a burning red face, Rocco inquired: "Your cousin is Bobby Santiago?"

"Yeah, that's him. Why do you know him?"

Rocco didn't answer but gave Kate a disgusted "why didn't you tell me" stare, and he got up, turned his back on his fellow officers, and just left the diner.

Since they were riding in the same police vehicle, Kate and Rocco had to endure each other's presence. It was quite uncomfortable, and not a word was said as they drove back to the station house. Rocco let Kate know that didn't want to hear anything from her, and it was obvious by his actions that he had nothing to say. All Rocco could think about now was how he would have to start all over again looking for another partner, one that wouldn't stab him in the back!

Chapter Twenty-Four

The Reluctant Spy

When Rocco saw his fiancée, he couldn't wait to tell her what happened. He originally had great news for her, but that news had deteriorated into him looking for another partner. As it was before, that was not going to be an easy task. He felt betrayed by Kate, and that feeling of betrayal was not an easy one to dismiss. He didn't know what Kate had been waiting for to tell him about Gloria's relationship with Bobby Santiago, and as he thought about it, he didn't know why she also waited so long to let him know that she was a lesbian. He guessed that one thing depended on the other, and since Gloria had not come up in conversation, there was no reason for her to let him know about Bobby.

Things were really messed up, and as he explained the whole situation to Janet, he became more and more incensed over Kate's secrecy. Janet sat quietly and attentively as Rocco rambled on about the event and his feelings. When he took a breath, she took the opportunity to weigh in: "Okay, Rocco. Why don't we look at the whole scenario without an emotional influence. It seems that Kate felt that she had no reason to let you know that she was gay. She hadn't known you for any length of time, and apparently, she wanted to keep her sexual preference protected. There could be many reasons why she didn't tell you right away, but that is one of them. When she finally did tell you, she didn't waste time in introducing you to her partner, Gloria. It just so happened that Gloria is related to someone who you do not like. That is not Kate's fault, and what difference would it have made if you found out sooner regarding the relationship between Gloria and Bobby?"

"The difference is the fact that I don't want Bobby knowing about anything I do or say. He's a bad guy who is looking for a way to screw me. Gloria could easily be the vehicle by which he knows my every move."

"Rocco, do you really think that every time Kate and Gloria get together that you are the topic of discussion?"

"No, I'm sure that they do not just speak about me, but Bobby could easily use his cousin to ask questions and keep tabs on me. You seem to forget that I told you that, in his mind, we are at war. He feels that he lost an initial battle with me, but in his words 'I will win the war.' Why would I want to be involved with someone whose wife or whatever has a direct line to someone who doesn't have my well-being at heart? All I would be doing would be revealing information that he could possibly use against me. You may not see it the way I do, but Bobby Santiago is not a nice guy. He is an egotistical, selfish individual who doesn't like to lose, and right now, he feels that he lost."

"I understand what you are saying, but from what you told me about Kate, I don't think she would intentionally want to hurt you. Rocco, you have to weigh what you have with her against how difficult it will be for you to find another partner who is willing to ride with a guy who others have deemed 'trouble'."

There was a pause in the action. Rocco said nothing, and Janet looked at him waiting for some kind of response. She knew that her fiancée was mulling things over and considering what she had said, but she didn't think that it would take this long. She couldn't take the silence any longer, so she said: "Well, Rocco. What do you think? I am sure that if you sat down with Kate and explained your concerns to her over the situation, that she would probably allay some of the fears that you may have. Why don't you give her a chance? She gave you a chance when no one else in the precinct seemed to give a damn."

Rocco finally gave in: "Okay, okay. As always, you make a lot of sense. Am I happy with the relationship? Absolutely not, but I can at least give Kate a chance to speak about it. I may have jumped too quickly. I will speak to Kate and let her know how concerned I am. And I will have to depend on her to let Gloria know that I should not be a subject of conversation with her cousin. If we can get that settled, I think Kate and I can continue to work together; however, my guard will still stay up."

===

When Rocco left the diner without saying a word to anyone, Gloria was left wondering what had happened. Although Kate had done her research, Gloria really was unaware of what had occurred in the past. Kate ultimately explained everything to Gloria, and she understood why Rocco had been so abrupt at the diner. Gloria assured Kate that she had no intention of discussing anything about Rocco with her cousin. She was sorry that Rocco thought that she was going to act as a pipeline for Bobby. She even asked Kate whether or not she wanted her to speak directly to Rocco. Kate thanked her for the offer but told her that Rocco was overreacting and that she was sure that when Rocco calmed down, she would hear from him.

Gloria had been trying to contact her cousin, Bobby, but her calls went unanswered. She wanted to set things straight with Bobby and find out what his side of the story was. She felt bad about putting her other half, Kate, in such a compromising position, but blood is thicker than water as the saying goes. As Gloria pondered her next move, her cell phone rang and Bobby's name appeared on the screen.

"Hello, Bobby. I've been trying to reach you to let you know about my meeting with Kate and Rocco. I'm a little confused, and I need you to tell me what's going on."

"Calm down, Gloria. You sound like you're all in a huff. Did you do what I asked you to do?"

"Yeah, Bobby. I made like I didn't know anything, and that I was surprised that Rocco knew you. When Rocco figured out that we were related, his whole attitude changed, and he looked at Kate with eyes that could kill. In fact, I think that he no longer wants to work with her. I don't like what's going on, Bobby. I need to know the whole story."

"Gloria, are you forgetting who you're talking to? You only need to know what I tell you, and that's all. I want you to keep close tabs on Rocco and keep pumping Kate about what's going on between the two of them. Rocco will be on his guard now that he knows that we are related. And even if Kate and him get back together again, which I believe they will because neither one of them can find a partner, Rocco will be very careful what he tells Kate. That's okay, but sooner or later, he'll slip up and let her know something that I will be able to use against him. That's why you have to continue to bring him up in conversation. Kate will confide in you. I'm counting on that."

"Bobby, it sounds like you're out for blood. I love Kate, and I don't like using her as a pawn. She would not do that to me, and I don't want to jeopardize my relationship with her. Rocco seems like a nice guy, and according to Kate, he is a nice guy. Why are you so intent on hurting him?"

"You want to know the story, let me give you a little piece of it. When I was out sick for a bit, Rocco offered to chauffer the girl that I was seeing since she didn't drive. He picked her up and drove her where she wanted to go, which, most of the time, was to see me. It seemed that he was doing the right thing by me; however, what his offer did was to allow him to spend a lot more time with my girl. They became very close and before I knew it, they were dating. Justifiably, that all came to an end when Rocco was transferred to the five four in the Bronx. Their relationship ended and mine had already been terminated. That's what 'mister good guy,' Rocco Deloberti, did, and that's a big part of the reason why he's going to pay. Is that enough for you?"

"Bobby, I can't believe that. He seems like a good guy, and now he is engaged. I guess it's all water under the bridge for him."

Bobby made like he was incensed: "You got that right, Gloria. He's engaged, and I sit here alone holding my pecker."

"Easy, Bobby. I didn't know what happened. I'll take care of things with him and Kate. I wonder if I should let Kate know what kind of a guy he really is."

"No, don't say anything to Kate. Once she finds out, she will act differently toward him, and he'll see the change and just clam up. Just continue with what you're doing, and sooner or later, we'll get him good. Don't say anything to Kate!"

"Okay, Bobby. I have to go. Kate is calling me."

"Gloria, remember what I said. Don't say a word. You know if the tables were reversed, I would do the same for you. I'll talk to you soon."

Gloria answered the call from Kate who seemed to be in a good mood. Kate explained to her spouse that Rocco approached her and said that he reconsidered. He said that he had a conversation with his fiancée, and she convinced him to see the light. It was ironic for Gloria. After just speaking about the broken relationship between Kate and Rocco, she gets a call telling her that things are back on track. Bobby would be glad to hear that, and now she had to start the unobtrusive inquisition regarding Rocco's activities. Gloria did not like the position she was in, but she also knew that Bobby was depending on her, and it really wasn't right what Rocco had done to her cousin. Gloria looked at herself as the reluctant spy, and she realized that spying could wind up to be a very dangerous game.

Chapter Twenty-Five

The Fickle Finger of Fate

Things were going relatively well between Kate and Rocco. They had gotten their fair share of calls, and they were looked upon now as a team that others could depend upon. Even though they were in a quieter part of the precinct, the Bronx is just not a quiet borough. When calls for service in their sector were not demanding their attention, they would handle calls in other sectors that were overflowing with waiting jobs. This willingness to help out strengthened the bond that they had forged with the other cops in the precinct. They were looked upon as a team that would not shirk their responsibilities, and one which complimented the response time of other busier radio car teams. The overall attitude towards Kate and Rocco had become a friendly and appreciative one that permeated their interactions with their fellow officers. Things couldn't be better.

Helping out one of the adjacent busy sectors, Kate and Rocco answered a call for "shots fired." Unfortunately, in the Bronx this was not an uncommon call. Assuming that it was going to be another one of those calls that resulted in a "gone-on-arrival" disposition, they handled the call in a cautious but routine manner. However, this call was anything but routine. When they arrived on the Grand Concourse (a multi-lane large major thoroughfare in the Bronx), they not only heard shots being fired, but they witnessed a man in his forties parading in the middle of the Concourse firing shots into the air. They also saw a woman standing on the sidewalk frantically yelling to the man she called "Louis" to stop.

When Rocco stopped his police vehicle, he opened the driver's side door as cover while Kate ran to take the woman out of harm's way. From behind the cover of the car door, Rocco yelled to Louis: "Louis, put down the gun and get down on the floor."

Louis turned his head to Rocco with the gun still pointing in the air. He smiled and continued to discharge rounds skyward. Once again, Rocco yelled to Louis to put the gun down and to get down on the floor. Louis disregarded Rocco's remarks and turned toward the police car. Louis's gun was still pointed skyward as he now walked toward Rocco and fired shots in the air. From the top of his lungs, Rocco yelled to the man to drop his weapon and get down on the floor. Louis just kept coming, but now, only twenty yards away, Louis pointed his weapon in Rocco's direction. This put Rocco in a very compromising situation. If Louis did not surrender his weapon, Rocco would have no other choice but to fire at the oncoming aggressor. Rocco desperately shouted one last time for Louis to drop his gun, but Louis brought the gun up to eye level and aimed directly at Rocco's position behind the car door. That was the last thing that Louis ever did.

From her vantage point, Kate determined that her partner was in a dangerous position, and so, she fired at the threatening man and brought him down. Rocco was stunned that Kate had fired, but she felt that the threat was imminent and had to be eliminated. So, she discharged two rounds which squarely hit Louis in the chest. He was probably dead before he hit the ground. The woman who was now being held back by other police officers, broke the restrictive hold and ran to the fatally wounded man. She screamed with the realization that her husband had died. She lifted his head and brought him close to her chest. With the help of the other officers who responded, they were able take the woman away from the scene.

===

The subsequent investigation revealed that Louis Triano had been diagnosed with non-treatable terminal cancer. By all indications, it seemed that Louis Triano decided to end his life at the hands of the New York City Police Department. His actions were not unique because "suicide-by-cop" had become one of the options for those who wanted to end their lives but could not work up the courage to do it themselves. The scene was now swarming with police officers and bosses. It was always this way when there was a police-involved shooting.

Firing one's weapon at another human being is a traumatic event. Some police offices never recover from it. In this instance, not only did a police officer fire her weapon, but she discharged rounds that caused the death of another. Kate Dancer was shaking from the experience, and responding Emergency Medical Technicians were treating her for shock. As is the procedure when an officer is involved in a shooting, the duty captain also responded to the scene. It is his responsibility to put the pieces together and interview the officers involved. In this case however, he would have to wait to interview the shooter. She was in the ambulance and being taken to a nearby hospital for treatment. Kate was very poorly facing the results of her actions. She had taken another human life, and that seemed to be very difficult for her to accept.

Although Rocco wanted to be with his partner, the duty captain ordered him to stay at the scene so that the captain could get some facts. While the duty captain was interviewing Rocco, the precinct patrol lieutenant, who had also responded to the scene, was with the Mrs. Triano inquiring about what had led up to the deadly scenario. It was then that the police department officials found out that not only was Louis Triano diagnosed with terminal cancer, but he was a retired member of the New York City Police Department. Louis had been killed by a brother officer.

When Rocco found out that the dead man was a retired cop, his thoughts immediately went to his partner, Kate. She was having difficulty dealing with the fact that she took someone's life, but when she found out that it was the life of another City police officer, she would be devastated. Rocco knew that it was going to take a very long time for her to deal with her actions, and he wasn't sure that she ever would. At the very least, Police Officer Kathleen Dancer was going to be out for an extended period of time. Selfishly, he thought about his own circumstances. If he didn't have a steady partner, he would once again have to fill in for those officers who were out sick or on vacation. That was a drag. Although he and Kate were now considered "good" cops, he would still have to work with a number of different partners. However, because of the fact that he and Kate had built up a good reputation and rapport with other cops in the command, there would be a lot less reluctance to partner up with Police Officer Rocco Deloberti.

===

It took a while, but the investigation was completed and closed as a "good shoot." Kate was still out on leave and seeing the department psychologist. No one knew how long Kate was going to be out, and that was wearing on Rocco's work routine. Working with different partners wasn't as bad this time as it had been before. Rocco was accepted more readily and even though his tag, "trouble," was still floating above his head, officers were more willing to work with him.

It had already been a month since Kate was out. She was on extended sick leave dealing with the demons that the shooting had unleashed in her mind. The way things looked, it was going to be quite a while before Kate was ready for duty.

More so, the rumor was spreading that Kate might not want to come back at all. She had never voiced that to Rocco whenever he visited her, but he had heard the rumor from a number of other officers. So, Rocco was still bouncing around working with different partners every other day.

===

One afternoon, just as Rocco was getting ready to exit the station house, he bumped into another officer who was backing into the building with all his gear in tow. Rocco moved to get out of the way, and when the officer looked up and saw him, she immediately recognized him: "Hey Rocco, guess who's coming to town?" Rocco recognized the voice, but couldn't believe that it was her.

"Gloria, what are you doing here?"

"Wow, that's some welcome. It's nice to see you too!"

"Sorry, Gloria. I was just surprised to see you here. Really, what are you doing in the five four?"

"Well, Rocco. This is my new command. I put in for a transfer so that I could be closer to Kate. Apparently, the bosses knew about our relationship and the problems that Kate was having, so they expedited my transfer. I am now assigned to the five four. Aren't you glad to see me?"

Sarcastically, Rocco answered: "I couldn't be happier."

"Rocco, I thought all that stuff in the past was settled between the two of us. Didn't Kate explain where I was coming from."

"Yeah, you're right. Kate did explain, and I shouldn't be jumping the gun. Well, if you're here, welcome aboard."

"Thanks, Rocco. I hope we can work together and be friends."

"Okay, Gloria. Now, you're jumping the gun. I am sure we can be friendly; however, I don't know if we'll be working together. Let's take one step at a time."

"Sure, I understand, Rocco. We'll take things as they come."

Rocco couldn't believe what fate had dealt him. He was the only one without a partner, and now there was someone new in the command who also didn't have a partner. He knew that the natural course of events would see him partnered with the new officer. He recalled what Kate had said, and he trusted her judgement. But Gloria was still related to that scumbag, Bobby. Rocco was going to have to keep his guard up even higher than it had been before. Both Kate and Gloria had reinforced the idea that no one was conspiring with Bobby against Rocco, but all Rocco could think about was that hackneyed adage that echoed: "blood is thicker than water."

Chapter Twenty-Six

One Unknown Fact

Rocco had calculated his situation correctly. In short order, Police Officer Gloria Santiago was assigned as Rocco Deloberti's partner, at least until such time as Kate Dancer returned to precinct patrol work. In Rocco's opinion, Gloria was not the cop that Kate was, but he recognized that Gloria was serious about the job and tried hard to erase the awkwardness that was apparent in their situation. Where Kate spoke very infrequently and addressed most of her comments toward job-related activities, Gloria spoke incessantly and about everything. It came to the point where Rocco was having a hard time hearing the police radio. He hinted to Gloria that it was difficult, at times, to understand what the dispatcher was saying. Gloria acknowledged his concern but continued with her non-stop oration. Since his subtle hint didn't work, Rocco had to be more direct. He reached down to the radio and increased the volume to the point where it easily drowned out Gloria's comments. She finally got the hint: "Oh sorry, Rocco. I guess I'm speaking a little too much. When I am nervous, I constantly speak."

Rocco answered: "We've been riding together for a while now. I am surprised that you are still nervous. I thought we got over the initial shock of the new partnership, albeit a temporary one. What are you still nervous about?"

"I keep thinking that, in the back of your mind, you still harbor the thought about my relationship with Bobby. I don't know how to allay those fears, and because of that, I'm continuously trying to keep your mind off of that subject. Even though this partnership arrangement between us may only be a temporary one, I would like it to be a smooth and pleasant one."

"Gloria, I just can't erase the fact that you and Bobby are related, but I don't constantly think about it. I'm impressed with how well we work together, and I have no regrets at all having you as a partner. You're a good cop, and I am comfortable riding with you. Also understand, that although my mind is on the present, I constantly think about Kate and how she is doing. There's nothing to be nervous about because your relationship to Bobby Santiago takes up very little space in my stream of consciousness."

Rocco said what he had to say in order to bring about a relaxed mood, but Bobby Santiago and his threat to "win the war" was always on Rocco's mind. Although the distrust he first felt toward Gloria was slowly diminishing, it was still lodged in the back of his mind. Her actions did not demonstrate anything but cooperation and loyalty toward Rocco, but he had been burned before, and it was difficult to completely let his guard down. He was certain that as time went on, he would feel even better about Gloria.

Gloria responded to Rocco's remarks: "That's so good to hear, Rocco. I also think about Kate a lot. She is just a different person, and I don't know if I'll ever see the old Kate again. I am working with her and the psychologist to try to expedite her mental recovery. So, I also have Kate on my mind."

"Gloria, in your opinion, is she progressing? Do you think that she will be coming back to work in the near future?"

"I really can't say one way or the other. She has her good and bad days; however, on her bad ones, it is very difficult to penetrate her thought process as she focuses on what occurred on that terrible day. I know you don't want to hear this, but I am not sure whether or not she will ever return to police work. I hope she does, but she has taken the results of her actions very poorly. She sometimes talks to me about it, but finds it very difficult to finish her comments as she breaks down and cries at the thought of having killed a fellow officer."

Rocco felt the anguish that Gloria was relating: "That's so sad to hear, Gloria. I wish that I was the one who had fired the shots, so that she wouldn't be suffering the way she is."

"Now that you brought it up, Rocco, how come you didn't fire?"

"You know, Gloria, I thought about that many times, and I have never come to a concrete reason other than I perceived the threat as less imminent than Kate. Maybe, I froze, and if that's the case, Kate saved my life."

===

Gloria felt the need to reveal something further to Rocco: "Rocco, since the whole event involved my life partner, I wanted to find out more about it. I knew one of the detectives who was working with the duty captain on the investigation of the shooting. I learned some very interesting facts about the case. You mentioned that Kate may have saved your life, and it's advantageous to believe that when she fired, she saved you. Since you are not as devastated as Kate, and it seems that you have recovered from the effects of the shooting, I can tell you that Kate could never have saved your life."

Rocco was stunned, and wasn't sure that he correctly heard what Gloria had said: "What are you talking about, Gloria. That guy was only about fifteen feet away from me when Kate fired; and furthermore, he was pointing his weapon directly at me. I should have been the one to take him down, and I should be grateful that Kate reacted the way she did."

Gloria was insistent: "Listen to me, and understand why I can never tell Kate what I am about to tell you. Kate must never know this. Do you understand?"

"What are you talking about, Gloria. What can't we tell Kate."

"Kate did not save your life. She couldn't have. The investigation showed that Louis Triano came at you and pointed an empty weapon in your direction. At that time, he was incapable of hurting anyone. He deliberately emptied his gun before he turned toward you. He knew that sooner or later one of you was going to eliminate the threat, and therefore, he would have completed his "suicide-by-cop" mission. Unfortunately, Kate was the instrument he used to complete his task."

"Gloria, are you telling me that Triano came at me with a weapon that he knew was empty?"

"Yes, that's what I am telling you."

"I don't believe that. The investigating detective told you that?"

"Yeah, Rocco. He told me in confidence that the irony of the whole situation was the fact that Kate is suffering from an action that she never had to take. She fired and killed a man who, at the time, was wielding an empty weapon. Of course, Monday morning quarterbacking is one hundred percent, and, at the time, no one knew the facts."

Rocco was floored. He couldn't believe, no he didn't want to believe, what Gloria was saying. He was totally devasted, and he couldn't imagine how Kate would feel if she knew. He understood, now, why Gloria had said that Kate could never know what the investigation revealed. He felt even worse about the situation and how his partner, Kate, was reacting to it. The knowledge that the man's gun was empty would definitely put

Kate over the edge. Rocco was certain that If Kate ever found out about the empty weapon, she would never return. She was having a tough enough time, now, as it was.

Rocco finally collected his thoughts: “Although I am reeling from what you told me, I am glad that you had the confidence in me to let me know. I respect you for that, and you are right, Kate can never know about the empty weapon.”

They ended their tour that day with hardly a word being spoken. That was something new for Gloria, but she realized how concerned Rocco was after she told him about the empty weapon. He became very pensive and quiet, and Gloria thought it best to let him work things out without interruption. So, she kept her mouth shut.

After getting out of uniform, they met and left the station house together. On the way out, one of the officers stopped them and told them about a party that was being planned for one of the guys who was getting married. They both acknowledged the invitation and tried to make a mental note as to when it was scheduled. However, celebrating was the last thing on either one of their minds, so they would have to see the officer again and find out when the party was actually taking place.

Rocco thanked Gloria again for the confidence she had in him, and he told her that he was going to visit Kate. Gloria became instantly worried that Rocco might innocently reveal the damaging news. Rocco saw her troubled face, and allayed her concern: “I see you’re worried. Don’t worry. The last thing that I would want is to compound the suffering that Kate is going through. I will be extra careful not to divulge anything that I shouldn't. Kate is a good person, and she needs to recover. I only want to help."

Gloria was relieved: "Rocco, you're a good person too. I envy Kate for having a partner like you. I want her to recover also, but if she decides that she doesn't want to come back, I would more than welcome a partnership with you."

"Thanks, Gloria."

"No thanks necessary. I mean what I say."

For Gloria, it was getting harder and harder to accept the position that her cousin, Bobby, had put her in. She did mean what she said about Rocco, and unfortunately, it seemed that her cousin was burdening her with a task that was meant to bring down a good man. That was her quickly growing opinion of the situation, and it seemed to be getting stronger by the day.

Chapter Twenty-Seven

The Spoils of War

Rocco followed through with his intention to visit Kate. To Rocco's surprise and satisfaction, his partner seemed to be coming along well. She was alert and kept the conversation going. Rocco mentioned that Gloria and he were getting along well, but that he missed Kate sitting next to him. She smiled and said that she also missed riding with him. She also told Rocco that the psychologist said that she was coming along fine, and that hopefully, she would soon be able to return to work. That was music to Rocco's ears. He told her that he couldn't wait to see her back in uniform. He repeated the fact that Gloria was working out well, but he again emphasized that she was no Kate

Dancer. Kate patted him on the arm and thanked him for the compliment.

As they continued talking, the doorbell rang. Kate told Rocco that she was expecting her psychologist to be coming for another session. She answered the door, and the psychologist entered with a nod to Rocco. Kate introduced Rocco to her psychologist, and the therapist gave him a warm welcome with the caveat that at some time in the near future, she would like him to be present with Kate during a session. Without hesitation, Rocco agreed to the request. He would do anything if it meant that Kate would recover more quickly.

Rocco realized that Kate's session was about to begin, and that he had to leave. He was surprised that the psychologist visited Kate at her home and was told that this was the final session where the therapist would visit Kate. The subsequent therapy sessions would be held in the psychologist's office. It was explained to him that patients are more comfortable in their familiar surroundings. So, in situations like these, the therapist starts the sessions in the patient's home and gradually works with the patient to come to the therapist's office. This is also an indication that the patient is becoming more confident in dealing with the debilitating trauma that he or she had experienced.

Kate had asked Rocco how his fiancée, Janet, was doing. So, as he bid his farewell, he mentioned that Janet started finalizing plans for a wedding day. Kate couldn't be happier for her partner, and she told Rocco to let Janet know that she was available if Janet needed any help. Rocco thanked her and in that same vein, told her about the upcoming party for one of their fellow officers who was also tying the knot. Kate inquired as to the date and time, but Rocco couldn't recall. On his way out, he promised to let her know as soon as he found out. He said his goodbyes and left.

As Rocco walked to his car, he was happy and relieved that Kate seemed to be coming along so well. He wasn't sure if she was yet ready to return to work, but he was hopeful that it wouldn't be long before he would be riding with her again. Gloria had mentioned that she would be seeing Kate later in the evening since she was well aware of the therapy schedule. Maybe, Gloria, at that time, could remember the date that they were given regarding the planned pre-wedding party for their fellow officer. Kate really seemed like she wanted to be a part of that celebration. As far as Rocco was concerned, this was another good sign.

===

In her weekly report to her cousin, Gloria really had nothing new to relate. She mentioned, again, how well she was getting along with Rocco, but Bobby immediately lashed out at her, and, in no uncertain terms, reminded her that Rocco was a "wolf-in-sheep's-clothing." He also reminded her that they were "blood," and that they have to look out for each other. Although it was only over the phone, he spoke in a tone that actually made Gloria take a step back. Bobby frightened her with how determined he was to seek some sort of revenge. Once again, she didn't like being a part of situation that seemed to have destruction as its only goal. It became obvious that Bobby

Santiago would not stop until he was successful in levying as much hurt as possible onto Rocco Deloberti's life. Unfortunately for Bobby, he was disappointed in the lack of content in Gloria's report. He didn't hear anything that would help him facilitate the development of a diabolical plan.

Gloria closed her conversation with what she thought was an inconsequential remark about a pre-wedding party for one of the guys in the precinct. She was about to say "goodbye" when Bobby asked her to repeat what she had just said. She thought nothing of it and told him about the planned party for one of the officers who was getting married. Bobby was elated: "That's it, Gloria. We got it!"

Gloria was confused: "What are you talking about? It's a precinct party for one of the cops. How is that going to help you?"

Santiago enthusiastically responded: "It is perfect. I am sure that although everyone is invited to the party, including the female officers, that at one point, the party will relocate and most likely evolve into a 'male only' event. It more-than-likely will become an impromptu bachelor party, and you know what that means, Gloria."

"Yeah, I know what it means, but I still don't see how it will help you. Am I missing something?"

"You surely are! What do you think Janet Commings would say or do if she found out that her innocent and loyal fiancée did nasty things with some strippers?"

“Bobby, you’re barking up the wrong tree. I think I know Rocco pretty well. He is not going to partake in anything like that. Hell, you don’t even know if something like that is even planned. Forget it, Bobby. You’ll just have to wait for the right time and the right circumstance.”

Bobby Santiago was insistent: “No, Gloria. Apparently you don’t know cops very well. I would bet my bottom dollar that there is going to be a party after the party, and you can be sure that there will be a lot of flesh being flashed around.”

“Bobby, you’re missing the point. I don’t care if those women are totally naked, you’re talking about Rocco Deloberti. He’s not going to get involved in anything like that. He’s not that kind of guy, and he’s surely not going to jeopardize his relationship with Janet. Bobby, you’re thinking is totally flawed.”

“Oh Gloria! You’re such a beautiful, naïve person. Sure, Rocco wouldn’t intentionally do anything to hurt Janet, and yeah, maybe he’s not into that bachelor party stuff. However, if he wasn’t himself and wasn’t able to stop the goings-on, he might be able to be put into a very compromising position. And if Janet becomes aware of that position, it might be one that he can’t talk himself out of. That situation just might put a tear in the bond that is holding their relationship so tightly together. Understand that if the bond breaks, and there is a strong possibility that it will, Bobby Santiago, once again, will be there to console the very disappointed and anguished former fiancée of one, Rocco Deloberti.”

Gloria was even more confused: “First of all, what do you mean ‘once again,’ and what do you mean when you say ‘if he wasn't himself'? I don't understand. Please explain it to me, Bobby."

"Well, I'll give you the entire explanation when I develop the whole plan. You just have to know that I will need your help. Also, you have to understand that the plan will involve a way to seemingly compromise Rocco's feelings about debauchery. His actions will almost be involuntary, but they will certainly portray him as a willing participant in some very nasty deeds. Let me know as soon as you find out the date and time of the party. Continue with all of your good work. Talk to you soon."

Before Gloria could ask him about the other question regarding the "consolation" that he had once before offered to Janet, Bobby hung up. She never heard him so excited and exhilarated as he thought about his devious "gotcha" plan. There were many things going through Gloria's mind, and none of them were good. It bothered her that Rocco was going to be put, as Bobby called it, into a compromising position. What did that mean? She immediately thought of some kind of drug, and with Bobby, that was not out of the question. She did not want to be involved in any plan that included the use of drugs. The more she thought about it, she didn't want to be involved in any plan at all.

What were her options? Well, she could just tell her cousin that she wanted out. That would go over like a lead ballon, and she feared the consequences of her non-participation. She pondered another option. Once she learned of the plan, she could tell Rocco to beware of certain situations. However, if Bobby ever found out that she betrayed him, he would make sure that she would never do that again. Lastly, she could make sure that she was there with Rocco so that he would not fall into any traps. Sure, she could be there for the first party, but if there was a party after the party, she was certain that she would not be welcomed to attend that event. Gloria was at a loss, and she didn't like the way things were developing. She accepted the fact, however, that she no longer wanted to be a part of any scheme that was directed at hurting Rocco or his fiancée. Unfortunately, the fear of what Bobby was capable of doing to her overshadowed her willingness to disengage.

Bobby Santiago was beside himself with joy. He now had the perfect opportunity to strike out at his nemesis, Rocco. Santiago had the rudiments of his plan already worked out, but the weak link in the operation, Gloria, bothered him. He had to make sure that Gloria was on board with everything, or all of his efforts would be in vain. If Gloria failed him, cousin or no cousin, she may never see the light of another day. That's how determined and vicious he was about his retaliation plan. The information that Gloria had related to him was better than he had anticipated. He was sure that when Janet saw the character of the individual she was planning to marry, she would run for the hills. He then would have an open invitation, as "victor," to collect the spoils of the war, Janet. He couldn't wait!

Chapter Twenty-Eight

A Future in Turmoil

Janet had called Rocco to meet with her to discuss some of the specifics regarding their wedding. So, he made it his business to put aside some time to meet and discuss this important matter. However, as she spoke about the location, the wedding party, the color of the gowns, etc., his mind went to other things. Although he openly didn't show it, he was still very concerned about Bobby Santiago and his ultimate plan to "win-the-war." Janet saw through his façade and tried to redirect his attention: "Rocco, are you listening. You look like you are a thousand miles away. I can't do this all by myself. I need your help. There are a lot of decisions to be made, and I don't want to make them alone. So, just for a little while could you concentrate on us?"

Rocco was chastised and he knew that Janet was right: "You're right, Janet. I'm sorry. I just have some things on my mind, and they are distracting. Okay, I'm all ears."

"I know that you are concerned about Kate, and you should be. I also know that Bobby Santiago and his devilish plan to get back at you, whatever that is, is concerning and distracting. Personally, I think that he is all talk, but you probably know him better than I. Having said all that, we have to concentrate on our future before it is here right in front of us. I will help you as much as I can, but you have got to help me too. Is it a deal?"

"Definitely, Janet, although I really don't know how much you will be able to help me. Kate is fighting a battle that only she alone can win, and until such time as Bobby shows his hand, I won't know what I am up against. On the same subject, I have had my doubts about Gloria, but she seems to be proving me wrong, and that is good. Okay, I am listening."

Janet took her cue and started to describe some of the concerns that she had. Rocco did his best to keep on track, and to show her that he was attentive. He demonstrated that attention by commenting and nodding every so often. But like most guys, wedding plans were something that they just accepted and went along with. To Janet, however, they were uppermost in her mind. The wedding was less that nine months away, and that was all that Janet could think about. Rocco, though, viewed the upcoming months as a period in which someone like Bobby Santiago could jam a stick into the spokes and tumble the whole bike. Rocco knew it was coming, but he didn't know when, where, or how the hammer would fall. So, although he gave his fiancée the guarantee that he would pay close attention, his nagging worries still disturbed his stream of consciousness.

During a break in the action, Rocco inquired as to how Janet's father was coming along. The doctors had mentioned that the previous attack was more severe than originally diagnosed, and that Mr. Commings' life style had to change. Janet said that her dad was not happy about many of the changes, but between her and her mother, they made sure that he stayed on track. She mentioned that the biggest change was his diet, and that was his biggest complaint. She said that he really didn't enjoy eating that much anymore because all of the dishes and snacks that he liked were not good for him, and therefore, were on the "can't have" list.

Rocco was pretty friendly with Janet's father, and he always spent time talking with him. Today, that conversation was a welcomed break in dealing with the arduous specifics of wedding planning. Rocco was a little taken aback by Mr. Commings' physical appearance. He just didn't look well. Apparently, it was more obvious to Rocco than to Janet and her mother since they saw him every day. In Rocco's opinion, Mr. Commings did not look good. His pallor was colorless, his movement was limited, and his breathing seemed labored. Rocco's initial thought was that he should be in the hospital under observation.

After a few moments with Janet's father, Rocco went to Janet and expressed his concern: "Janet, I know that you and your mom see your dad every day, and maybe because of that, you can't see what I believe is a deteriorating condition. His movement, breathing and complexion are disturbing, and I believe that before something happens, he should be under a doctor's care in the hospital. I know you don't want to hear that, and I'm sure that your mom won't be happy to hear it, but your dad has looked much better in the past. Pardon me for saying this, but he looks like he is ready to check out. I don't want to be so morbid, but it's better to be safe than sorry."

Janet listened carefully and responded: "Rocco, you don't realize what it means to bring him back to the hospital. It will be upsetting to him and definitely to my mother. I don't know if I want to do that to them."

"Janet, I understand that you and your mom might be upset, but would you be more upset if you wait and, God forbid, something drastic happens to your dad? Again, I don't want to be morbid, but in my line of work, you acquire a special feel for these sorts of things. To be very blunt about it, your dad could die!"

The last statement really upset Janet and she lashed out: "Rocco, please! I don't need to hear that. I'll discuss it with my mom, and we'll make a decision then. I guess we don't see him as bad as you do. I'm not saying that you're wrong, but going back to the hospital will destroy my dad."

"Janet, I am telling you that you can't take long in making your decision, and whether he likes it or not, being back in the hospital just might save your father's life."

Janet wasted no time, and she went into the kitchen to discuss the situation with her mom. Although she might not have been of the same opinion as Rocco, she apparently took Rocco's remarks very seriously. She explained the concerns that her fiancée had, and from Rocco's vantage point in the living room, he could see Mrs. Commings shaking her head in a negative manner. However, Janet continued speaking with her mother and informed her that maybe they were not seeing the forest for the trees. Rocco saw Mrs. Commings break down and start crying. He didn't know if it was because she reluctantly agreed with his recommendation or that she was overcome with the seriousness of the whole situation. She just sat down in a chair, put her head into her hands and stopped talking. Janet put her arm around her mom and tried in vain to console her.

Shortly after the kitchen meeting, Janet asked Rocco to come into a private room so that they could discuss the situation. She told him that her mother definitely did not want her father to go back into the hospital. She wanted to give him more time to naturally recover at home. Rocco didn't interrupt but visibly shook his head. He totally disagreed with Mrs. Commings' decision, and, in his opinion, it was a decision that could easily be detrimental to Mr. Commings' health. He didn't know how he was going to convince them of the urgency, but, as fate would dictate, he didn't have to.

From the other room, Janet and Rocco heard Mrs. Commings yell for them. They rushed into the living room to see Mr. Commings gasping for air and holding his chest. Without asking anyone, Rocco got on the phone and dialed 911 for an ambulance. While he was talking with the emergency operator, Janet ran to get her father's medicine. She quickly came back into the room and placed a nitro glycerin pill under her father's tongue. However, after that, all they could do was to wait for the emergency medical technicians to arrive with the ambulance.

What seemed like forever, but was only about seven minutes, the ambulance crew arrived. They administered oxygen and quickly found out from Janet what had occurred. They told the family to meet them at the hospital where the family could answer the deluge of questions that the hospital always had. The EMTs immediate concern was to get the patient to the hospital as quickly as possible. Rocco had let them know that he was a police officer, and that they could be straight with him. So, in a clandestine manner, they let him know that things did not look good for Mr. Commings. Unfortunately, Rocco, through his experience on the job, already knew that things were not looking good for Mr. Commings.

Mrs. Commings rode in the back of the ambulance with her husband, and Janet and Rocco followed closely behind. Janet broke down in tears repeating the fact that she should have realized sooner that her father was not doing well. She also repeated that if Rocco hadn't told them how bad her father looked, they would probably still be totally shocked that Mr. Commings was on his way back to the hospital. He was most likely suffering from the effects of another heart attack or even worse, possible heart failure.

===

Rocco took no satisfaction in the fact that he had been right about Mr. Commings' condition. His only thought was that if he had visited sooner, he might have been able to prevent Janet's father from being transported back to the hospital under emergency conditions. As far as Rocco was concerned, the present condition of her father was a touch-and-go situation. He looked bad and was suffering from a number of dangerous symptoms. If Rocco didn't know better, he would have said that Mr. Commings' chances of full recovery were slim to none. However, he was not going to share his feelings with Janet who was already overcome with guilt and concern. In fact, he felt that, at this time, it was better to say nothing other than that her father was in good hands.

When they arrived at the hospital, Janet ran from the car almost before it came to a stop. Rocco understood how she felt, but her hasty and dangerous exit leaving the car door ajar almost caused Rocco to hit another parked vehicle. He chalked it up to luck that he was not involved in filling out an accident report.

As soon as Rocco parked his vehicle in the emergency room parking area, he hurried into the emergency waiting room. He sat down next to Janet who was trying to console her mom. They were both teary-eyed and shaking their heads almost in a manner to say "why is this happening again?"

Rocco was able to speak with one of the technicians who transported Mr. Commings to the hospital. The EMT mentioned that the patient had experienced another heart attack in the ambulance, and that through the on-board communication with an emergency room doctor, the EMT was able to treat the patient sufficiently enough to deliver him to the hospital. Rocco interpreted the information as something he already knew. It was not a good sign. Another heart attack would have surely weakened Mr. Commings heart, and made him more vulnerable to additional attacks, any one of which could be fatal. Rocco was assuming the worst.

As usual, the wait in the Emergency Room sitting area was tortuous. However, it wasn't too long before a doctor called out the family name and came to speak with Janet and her mom. Although Rocco couldn't hear what was being said, looking at the somber face of the doctor and the whispered tones in which he spoke, Rocco knew exactly what the doctor was saying. Both Janet and her mom broke out into uncontrollable sobs. There was nothing that Rocco could do or say that would console either one of them now. Rocco just hugged Janet and held on.

What was supposed to be a meeting regarding upcoming wedding plans turned out to be a notification of the demise of a very much loved father and husband. It pulled at Rocco's heart strings to see his fiancée so distraught, and he not being able to lessen the pain. Unfortunately, everyone's thoughts were consumed with life's dictate regarding a permanent separation from a loved one.

Ironically, Rocco would have preferred directing his thoughts to the upcoming wedding celebration. However, the thoughts of a wedding were the farthest thing from everyone's mind, including the one who, just a very short time ago, was demanding that Rocco pay attention to their future, a future that was now uncertain and in turmoil.

Chapter Twenty-Nine

A Family Disagreement

To say the least, things had changed. Although there were still plans for a wedding, no one knew for sure when that would take place. However, the one thing that Janet knew for certain, and the thing that bothered her the most was the fact that her father was not going to be there to walk her down the aisle. Mrs. Commings had been devastated, and the very last thing that she was ready for was a celebration. Janet felt the same way, but she didn't want to delay the wedding indefinitely. She also was aware of the fact that everyone had to get over their initial grieving before anything like a wedding was going to take place. Janet discussed the situation with Rocco who let her know that he was agreeable to whatever she wanted to do.

Apparently, word got around regarding David Commings' death. As Rocco was visiting Janet and her mother, he happened to notice some of the consolation cards that were sent to the family and which were placed on the living room table. He briefly looked them over until he came to the one that was signed by Bobby Santiago. Santiago had written that he will always be there for her, and if she needed anything, including a shoulder to cry on, he was available. He wrote how sorry he was about her loss, and that if she wanted to talk about anything at all, he would listen.

As Rocco continued to read the long note on the card, his blood began to boil. Rocco knew that Santiago meant nothing that he wrote. He just wanted to be in Janet's life and leave the door open in case her immediate social plans collapsed. This made Rocco even more concerned about Bobby Santiago's revenge plan. Without thinking clearly, he took the card and tore it into pieces. His hatred, and more than likely, his jealousy prompted this knee-jerk reaction. Rocco hurriedly put the torn pieces of the card into his pocket and hoped that Janet would not remember that the card was ever there.

===

As a result of the cases that Bobby Santiago had closed with the rest of his unit, he was promoted to the rank of "Detective" and transferred to the Organized Crime Prevention Division. This was definitely a step up for him, and the prestigious move brought him in contact with high ranking department officials as well as other state and federal officers. Things were going exceptionally well for Bobby, but Rocco

Deloberti still weighed heavy on his mind. He was not going to give up his plans for an all-out assault and hopefully the social downfall of his competition. Bobby was obsessed with winning and ultimately getting another chance with Janet.

Gloria kept reporting to her cousin, and in their last conversation she told him the scheduled date of the congratulatory party for the-soon-to-be married police officer. The wait was finally over, and Bobby would soon get his chance to destroy Deloberti. Now was the time that the two cousins needed to meet. Bobby wanted to go over his plan with Gloria who would be an intricate part of its success. He arranged for a meeting date and time and would not take any excuse from Gloria regarding her not being able to make it. She agreed to the meet and became more intimidated each time she spoke to her cousin. He was so obsessed that she feared that he would do anything that he needed to do to ensure success. That included getting a guarantee for her participation. She did not think for a minute that he would not use physical persuasion to solidify her cooperation. He had mentioned on a number of occasions that blood was thicker than water, but she had no doubt that he wouldn't think twice about spilling some of her "thick" blood. So, in fear of physical harm, she met with her cousin on the day, date and time he suggested.

They met in a small Spanish restaurant in Queens. It was an area and a restaurant to which they were both familiar. Bobby had been going to this restaurant forever, and he was friends with the owner. It was a quiet out-of-the-way location, and one in which Bobby Santiago felt that confidentiality would not ever be compromised. Gloria, had gone to the restaurant a few times with Bobby, and so the owner also knew her. After a few brief words with the owner, Bobby ordered drinks and turned the conversation toward her: "Well, Gloria. It's good to see you. You're looking good, as usual. How are things going in the new precinct? How do you like the five four?"

Gloria answered all of her cousin's questions in a way that she was sure he didn't want to hear: "Everything is fine, Bobby. Rocco and I are getting along well, and we have made a number of good arrests. I know that's not what you want to hear, but that is the case. The rest of the guys in the precinct have come to respect me, and I'm feeling comfortable with my partner and the precinct as a whole."

"No, you're wrong, Gloria. I am glad that you are getting along so well with Rocco. Because of that, he will not suspect you of anything. It only helps with the execution of my plan."

Now Gloria was really curious about her participation in her cousin's scheme: "Okay, Bobby. Tell me what you want me to do. Just know that I am not comfortable with deceiving my partner, and yeah I know that blood is thicker than water. I don't need to hear that again."

Bobby was somewhat surprised by Gloria's attitude, but he didn't want to turn her off. He would rather that she voluntarily cooperate with him other than being threatened to do so. So, he said nothing about her remarks and started telling her about the plan: "I am sure that you will be attending the party for the cop who is getting married. It will probably be held in a local gin mill that also has a back room. It is in the back room where my plan will materialize. It is there that Rocco Deloberti will act like a buffoon and get involved with the strippers who I'm sure will do anything for the right amount of money."

Gloria interrupted: "I told you before, Bobby, that Rocco is not going to do anything that would jeopardize his relationship with Janet. And especially now that her father has passed, I'm sure he is even more sensitive to her needs. You are not going to get Rocco to do anything nasty with those women."

"You're right, Gloria. I am not going to get Rocco to interact with the strippers. You are!"

"What are you talking about, Bobby. Why would I want to convince him to get involved with them, and why do you think he would listen to me anyway?"

"Oh. Gloria. You are so naive. Usually toward the end of the first party, everyone will have one last toast to wish the honored guest the best of luck. It is that toast that will shortly cause Rocco to react in a manner that would seem totally out of character for him. That toast will put him over the edge."

Gloria was still confused: "You're wrong, Bobby. He won't let himself get to that point. In fact, he's not even a drinker."

"Gloria, whether he is a drinker or not, he will not insult his friend by not toasting him. The last round before the "after party" will do him in, and before you argue to the contrary, you will make sure it does."

At this point in the conversation, Bobby Santiago reached into his pocket and pulled out a round, white pill and showed it to Gloria. Finally, Gloria understood what her cousin was saying. He wanted her to spike Rocco's drink so that as the night progressed and Rocco attended the party in the back room, his mental acuity would be so negatively affected that he would become a pawn in the hands of the strippers. She also figured that Bobby would get to the strippers in advance of that night and pay them well to participate in his devious plan. To them, it would just be a way to make additional money, and they would have no problem cooperating. Gloria was now getting the whole idea, one which she definitely didn't like.

"Bobby, I told you before that I will not do anything that involves drugs. You know I can lose my job and possibly be arrested. How can you ask me to do something like that?"

"Gloria, have I ever let you down? Do you think I would put you in a position where you could lose your job or be arrested? I have it all covered."

"Do I think you would put me in a compromising position? Yes, as long as you get what you want. Bobby, I'm not going to do it!"

Santiago got up from the table, looked at her, and very softly said that he understood. He looked away, and then with the back of his hand, he slapped her so hard across the face that she had all to do to stay in her chair. She was in shock and bleeding from the mouth. He looked down at her and said: "What did you say? I thought I heard you say that you weren't going to help me. Is that what you said?"

Gloria didn't answer. So, he bent down even closer and repeated his question: "Did you say that you weren't going to help me?" Again, Gloria didn't answer, but this time to force an answer from her, he smacked her across the face one more time.

"Okay, okay! Yes, Bobby I will do want you want."

"Gloria, I thought you would see it my way. Take a napkin and blot your face. You seem to be bleeding. It's not a good look for you. I will be in touch, and we'll discuss our plans further. Take care. It was good seeing you."

Bobby turned, waved goodbye to his friend, and left the restaurant. The owner of the restaurant came over to Gloria and asked if she was okay. She told him that it was just a family disagreement. He looked at her and told her that it probably was more than just a disagreement since she still had her hand frozen on her off-duty weapon. She said nothing further and just left. Her hand never moved from her weapon.

Chapter Thirty

Timing is Everything

Gloria was incensed at what her cousin, Bobby, had done. The feeling carried over for days to the point that her partner, Rocco, realized that something was wrong. To him, Gloria seemed divorced from the present, and that was not like Gloria. Of course, he couldn't know that she was upset with the way her cousin had treated her, but more so, she felt the pangs of guilt each time she looked at Rocco. She was going to be the instrument that led to a disastrous fall for her partner. It was very difficult for her to take. There were so many times that she was tempted to tell Rocco what was about to happen, but she was sharply reminded of the sting that she felt from Bobby's wrath. Both the mental and the physical threat prevented her from saving Rocco from what would surely be a life-changing event for him. She needed to tell him and she wanted to tell him; however, self-preservation intervened and influenced her otherwise.

===

Rocco decided to find out what was on Gloria's mind and what was driving her to the point of distraction. She had been distant for a number of days, and that worried him on a couple of different levels. He worried that she did not have her full concentration on the job, and he also worried that she was suffering from some internal stress that could easily affect her overall health. Gloria's new condition manifested itself in a lack of conversation on her part. She was a chatterbox, and for her to remain silent for most of the time meant that she was thinking of other things. Apparently, her mind was not on him or the job, and that was troublesome for Rocco. He decided to come right out and ask her what was wrong. He would not take "nothing" for an answer. Just as he was about to question her, she turned to him and started a conversation: "Hey, Rocco. Did you get the information about the day and time of the wedding party for our friend? Are you going to be able to make it?"

Rocco was glad that his partner started talking, and he answered her quickly: "Yeah, Gloria. I already put it on my calendar. It should be a good time, and Freddie is a good guy. You're going to make it, right?"

"I've been thinking about it. Those parties are all the same. If you've been to one, you've been to all."

“Yeah, but Freddie is a good guy and a friend. You should try to make it. We’ll go together.”

Gloria saw that she wasn’t going to convince Rocco not to attend, so she gave in: “Okay, I guess you persuaded me. Are you going to go to the “after” party? You know. The one where you guys become degenerates and embarrass yourselves.”

Rocco answered: “I don’t want to be singled out as a prude, so I will probably just stay for a short time. I’m really not into that kind of debauchery.”

“I figured you wouldn’t be, but you know after a couple of drinks strange things can happen.”

“Gloria, you know that I am not a drinker. I never get to the point where I don’t know what’s happening or I can’t control my actions. When it starts getting really bad, I will slither my way out of the party and be gone. You sound like you’re worried that I might do something crazy or get into a situation that I might regret. I thought you knew me better than that.”

“I do, Rocco. I just wouldn’t want you to jeopardize anything with Janet. Your wedding is just around the corner, and you do not need to get bogged down with potential situations or complications that you might not be able to talk your way out of.”

Rocco started to get worried: “Hold on, Gloria. You’re talking like you know that there is something in the wind, and that I am going to be the one who is blown away. Do you have anything that you want to tell me?” Rocco smiled inquisitively.

He couldn't figure out why Gloria was so concerned about his attending the party, but he was actually getting a little up tight.

Gloria saw the look on Rocco's face, and she decided to bring it down a notch. Rocco was questioning if she knew something that might affect him. Even though he smiled, she could see a certain amount of concern on his face. She decided to allay his worries and just pawn it off as one friend's concern for another: "No, not at all, Rocco. The way things have been going with you: the death of Janet's father, the emotional problems with Kate, and having to deal with another crazy partner, I guess I just worry that you do not need any other stumbling blocks coming your way. I'm just a worry wart." She smiled as if to say "that's me. I worry for nothing."

Rocco shook his head in tacit agreement and said: "Okay, let's get back to being cops." Gloria acknowledged his comment and focused on the radio and the road.

===

While they were on patrol and not busy responding to specific calls for service, they received a message to call the precinct. This usually occurred when something that needed clarification or explanation came to the attention of the precinct supervisor. So, Rocco proceeded to call the supervisor. The message involved an incident that had occurred before Rocco was assigned to the precinct. Apparently, a male high school student had been shot as he participated in a practice session with the high school relay track team. The supervisor related the entire story to Rocco so that he would be prepared when he visited the high school principal.

The supervisor continued with the story and told Rocco that as the young student, who was the third runner in the relay, raised his hand to clutch the baton from his incoming team mate, he felt a strange pain just on the side of his chest under the arm pit. At the completion of the practice, the student approached the coach and complained about the pain. When the coach examined the young man, he saw a small hole that was slowly discharging blood. A call went out to the school nurse, and the athletic director, who was a former New York City detective. Having had a lot of experience with injuries and wounds, the former detective immediately recognized the small puncture wound as a bullet hole, apparently from a small caliber weapon.

The supervisor went on to tell Rocco that when the ambulance arrived, the young man was still talking and very much alive. However, as it was later learned, the student was slowly dying from the internal injuries caused by the ricocheting effect that the small caliber round had on the internal organs. The student died shortly after arriving at the hospital. The supervisor now got down to the meat of the message. He said that no one had heard a gunshot, and there were no witnesses to any one firing a weapon. However, the supervisor told Rocco that after a long period of inactivity on the case, an arrest had been made, and the supervisor wanted Rocco and his partner to notify the school authorities that charges had been filed.

Rocco was curious as to how an arrest was effected without the benefit of any useable evidence. The supervisor continued with his story: "The northeast corner of the high school field is bounded by an elevated train line. Apparently, there were two individuals riding on a motorized dirt bike in the street under the elevated structure. The passenger on the bike had his new, illegally-acquired 25 caliber semi-automatic hand gun with him, and as he passed the field, he fired a shot indiscriminately in the direction of the running track. Just as he fired, a train passed overhead and drowned out the sound of the gunshot. The discharged round found its unintended target, the chest of the male student. It was that reckless action that ultimately killed the young athlete."

Rocco was even more confused: "Boss, if there were no witnesses and no immediate evidence, how, after all this time, was an arrest made?"

The supervisor continued: "That is the unbelievable part of the whole story. It seems that the boy who was operating the motorized bike on that day moved to Georgia and ultimately applied for a law enforcement position. Georgia required a lie detector test. During the test, the boy was asked if he was ever involved in any incident connected to a possible crime. The boy hesitated, and he was further questioned. During that questioning, he told the investigator about the incident with the 25 caliber weapon, and he named his friend. The Georgia investigator followed up and contacted the New York City Police Department. Detectives found the friend who fired the weapon, and they were able to get a full confession from the shooter. That's the story in a nutshell. I want you to notify the principal of the school so that he can let the rest of the school community know that the case is finally closed."

Rocco couldn't believe what he had just heard. What seemed like a case that was going to remain "cold" forever was solved by good police work and cooperation between departments that were miles apart. He couldn't wait to tell Gloria the scoop. However, when Rocco turned toward his partner and was about to relay what the supervisor had told him, she spoke first: "Rocco, I don't want you to go to the party for Freddie."

Rocco was surprised and taken somewhat off-guard: "Gloria, what are you talking about? We're both going."

Gloria was determined to convince her partner not to go: "No, Rocco. It won't be good for you if you go."

"Gloria, what are you talking about? What's the matter?"

"I just have this premonition that something bad is going to happen. I really don't want you to go."

"Gloria, you're talking crazy. We all have bad thoughts at times. They mean nothing. We'll go and have a good time."

Now, Gloria was desperate and running out excuses: "I feel it, Rocco. You're putting yourself in a very dangerous position. Something could happen that will ruin your life. Please don't go."

"Okay, Gloria. I appreciate your concern, but I'll be extra careful and anyway, I have you there to watch my back."

That was the worst thing for Rocco to say. She already felt guilty about deceiving her partner, but now his trust in her just compounded the overwhelming feeling of betrayal. People say that timing is everything. Just when she was about to reveal all and throw caution and her personal safety to the wind, her cell phone rang and a picture of her cousin, Bobby, appeared on the screen. Her thought process stopped in its tracks, and she answered the call. The one time that she had worked up enough courage to save the day and her partner was destroyed by the same instrument that would ultimately be used to destroy Rocco Deloberti's future.

===

The enthusiasm that Rocco had in wanting to relay the unbelievable story that the patrol supervisor had just related to him was replaced by the persistent, nagging feeling that Gloria knew more than she was revealing. Her worried concern about his safety was over-the-top. It appeared that she not only knew that something might happen, but she knew exactly what it was.

Rocco never got a chance to tell Gloria what the supervisor had said, so when they arrived at the high school, he left his partner in the car, and he went in alone to give the good news to the principal.

The comfort and confidence that Rocco had been feeling about his partner had suffered a disheartening blow. She was hiding something, and partners don't hide things from each other. Rocco's guarded safety barrier that had been slowly coming down quickly stopped its descent and now rested, once again, on a level of uncertainty and doubt.

Chapter Thirty-One

She Reluctantly Agrees

Rocco's relationship with Janet was strong, but the death of her father slowed the wedding plans. It was originally Janet's idea to marry as soon as possible so that she would have her father to walk her down the aisle. However, fate had different plans, and David Commings succumbed to a fatal heart attack. This tragic event put the wedding plans on hold, and Rocco didn't press the matter. He wanted to marry Janet, but he was in no great rush to tie the knot. The delay allowed them both to save more money and better plan for their future together. It was obvious, however, that the wedding was not going to be the same without Janet's father being there. This fact became more obvious as the couple talked about the potentially new arrangements for their wedding ceremony. Janet was not filled with the same enthusiasm that she once displayed, and Rocco concentrated mostly on comments and expressions of emotion that were meant to ease some of the dismay that his fiancée was definitely feeling.

In an effort to steer Janet's mind in a different direction, Rocco spoke about work and how unexpectedly well he was getting along with Gloria. He also mentioned that his visits with Kate were not exactly encouraging, but that she was trying as hard as she could to get over the emotional trauma that she had experienced. Unfortunately, neither Kate nor Rocco knew for sure whether or not they would ever be partners again.

===

During the conversation about work, the wedding party for Freddie came up. Rocco mentioned that he was going to attend the party with Gloria, and that he would probably bow out of the after party that was usually attended by only the guys. Janet knew what Rocco was hinting at, and she responded accordingly: "Rocco, you can go to whatever party that you want. I know who you are, and I have unwavering trust in what you would do or not do. You should have a good time and just be yourself. Just remember, however, that you have a fiancée and that we are planning a wedding. I know that you will."

"No worries, Janet. Like I said, I will probably just slip away afterwards, and no one will even know that I was gone. You know that I am not any kind of drinker, and you also know that I am not a fan of those 'wild' bachelor parties. I'll toast to Freddie's future, and when the guys start moving to the back room, I'll make myself invisible as soon as we enter. I've waited for a long time to marry you, and we've had to negotiate some very rough waters; however, we are still able to arrange for our wedding. I am not going to jeopardize our future."

Janet could not be any happier: "I know you won't, and Gloria will be there anyway to make sure that you stay on track. She's a good person, and I know that she has your best interests at heart. She'll actually act as a spy for me!" Janet smiled and Rocco laughed knowing that Gloria and Janet were good friends.

===

Since the day of Freddie's pre-wedding party was very close, Bobby Santiago called his cousin and arranged for another meeting. They met in the same small Queen's restaurant where they had originally met. Gloria was even more nervous this time than she had been before. This was going to be the final meeting before Rocco's downfall. As a result of unexpected traffic, Gloria was late to the meeting, and Bobby let her know that he didn't appreciate having to wait for her. She tried to explain, but Bobby being Bobby, didn't want to hear it. He told her to sit down and pay attention to every word he said. Before he started his focused instructions, he ordered a drink for himself. He didn't want Gloria drinking for fear that alcohol would interfere with her thought process. However, she insisted on one drink. She needed it to calm her nerves. Bobby gave in and ordered her just one.

He began by warning her that if his plan failed, it would be her fault. He emphasized the fact that he didn't appreciate failures, and that someone would surely suffer if his efforts did not succeed. He didn't have to emphasize the point. Gloria knew that if she failed, she forfeited her safety. Cousin or no cousin, she would be held responsible for anything other than success.

"Gloria, you have a real easy job. I know that you can work a room, and I know that Rocco has a lot of faith in you. He trusts you. So, it should be quite simple for you to spike his drink before he goes into the after party. You have to be extra careful that no one sees you. That could be disastrous for both you and me. I'm sure you'll have plenty of time to pepper his drink."

"Bobby, what am I going to use?"

Santiago reached into his pocket and took out two white pills that were wrapped in aluminum foil. He explained that she only had to use one of the pills, but just in case she dropped or lost the first pill, she had an extra one to work with. He also explained that the pill was fast dissolving, and it would only take seconds to disappear.

"Bobby, what will the pill do to Rocco? Will he pass out, and how long before it affects him?"

"No Gloria, he won't pass out, but he won't have total control over his mind or body. He'll be conscious, but he will not be able to physically resist the advances of the beautiful and naked ladies."

"What does that mean, Bobby? I'm sure he will not want any part of the women you're talking about."

"Gloria, he won't have a choice. The women will be paid handsomely to interact with him whether he wants to or not, and their frolicking will be recorded for later use. To the untrained eye, it will seem like good old Rocco was encouraging the ladies to interact with him as they showed him their attributes."

"When you say 'recorded,' Bobby, who will be taking videos or photos, and who will you be showing them to?"

Santiago had no trouble in answering the questions: "The young ladies will be doing their job, interacting and recording. The results will ultimately be viewed by Rocco's fiancée. Let me ask you. Do you really believe that a good, wholesome, woman like Janet Commings would want to associate with someone who is entertained by the likes of the women at the bachelor party? Let me answer that. Absolutely not! She'll want nothing to do with Rocco Deloberti and the unsavory character that the photos will show him to be. When her disappointment and shock break the bond that was holding them together, I will be there to pick up the pieces and console the distraught damsel in distress."

Gloria hated the position that she was in: "So let me get this straight, Bobby. You are going to pay these women to set up Rocco, and then take photos of their activity to show to his fiancée. You have absolutely no scruples. I don't know if I can be a part of this. You are going to ruin his future and hurt Janet to the point that she may never recover. I can't be a part of it."

Santiago did not like what he was hearing: "Gloria, are you telling me that you're refusing to help me? Do you remember what occurred the last time that you had doubts?"

"I don't care what happens to me. Rocco is too good of a man to have me betray him like that. Threaten me all you like, but I am not going to change my mind!"

"No, Gloria. I will not threaten you, but I am certain that you would not want anything bad to happen to Kate. She is just an innocent person who is suffering from a traumatic event. I don't think she could take any more suffering. It's your choice."

"You wouldn't harm Kate. She's done nothing to you. Leave her out of this."

"I'm willing to do that, Gloria. As long as I have your total cooperation, no harm will come to Kate."

Gloria was in a terrible situation. She didn't care what happened to her, but she couldn't risk any harm coming to Kate. Unfortunately, she knew that Bobby would carry out his implied threats if she didn't cooperate. She had to make a choice between Rocco and Kate, and of course, Kate was going to win. She hated her cousin for putting her in such a compromising position, but he definitely had the upper hand.

Gloria reluctantly agreed to help her cousin: "Okay, I will help. Just make sure that you keep your word and leave Kate out of everything."

"Gloria, you're not telling me what to do, are you? I told you that Kate will not get hurt as long as you do what you have to do."

"Okay, Bobby. What is your plan, and what do I have to do?"

Bobby explained the plan again, in detail: “I mentioned it to you once before, but for the sake of clarity, I will go over it again. The white pill that you have will work wonders when it dissolves in Rocco’s drink. I already told you that there will be a final toast before the guys go into the back room. Just before Rocco raises his glass, you will drop the pill into his drink. It will take a little while before it starts working, but once it does, there will be no turning back. Unfortunately, you will not be able to see the results of your handiwork, but be assured that the pill and the women will do their job.”

Gloria despised her cousin, but for the sake of Kate’s safety, she had no choice but to comply with Bobby’s dictates: “I hate that I have to call you my cousin. You are a cold, egomaniac who can’t take ‘no’ for an answer. Karma is a bitch, and one day, it will be your turn in the hopper.”

===

Santiago saw the reluctance that his cousin was displaying, and he informed her that he was going to guarantee her cooperation: “That’s not the way it works, Gloria. I’m too smart for that. You have two days before the party, and I’m sure you will not do anything to jeopardize my plan. However, just to make sure and to give you some moral support, I am going to have my people looking after you. Unfortunately, I’m thinking that there may come a time when you weaken in your resolve. However, my friends will be there to make sure you don’t weaken to the point that you destroy my surprise. Once again, if you do anything to jeopardize the success of my expert plan, you will risk the safety and security of your dear life-partner. I’m sure that you do not want to put her in harm's way. So, before you do anything stupid, think about Kate's future."

Bobby looked at her with threatening determination and continued: " Do you have any questions?"

Gloria just stared at him. She said nothing, but got up and walked out of the restaurant. She never looked back. Out of her cousin's sight, she hurried to a space between two parked cars and expelled the entire contents of her stomach. She was actually sick over what she had to do, and even with the threat of harm coming to Kate, she wasn't sure that she could carry out her cousin's mandate. Gloria Santiago was in a compromising position. However, it could probably be better described as a "no-win" situation!

Chapter Thirty-Two

The Plan Takes Effect

The day of the wedding party for Freddie was a quiet one for patrol officers. None of the officers wanted to make arrests or get involved in anything that might deter their attendance at the party. Gloria and Rocco were no exceptions. Although they never steered away from their responsibility, they tapered their responses to warnings and suggestions. The two of them talked about the party and what might take place as the party progressed. Gloria was searching for the opportunity to surreptitiously discourage Rocco from attending the "after party." She couldn't come right out and tell him, but she really didn't want him to be the subject of her cousin's vindictive plan. However, the threat of harm coming to the love of her life, Kate, loomed heavy in the back of her mind. She had never felt so helpless and compromised. When she thought of Kate, Gloria knew that Kate would tell her to warn Rocco because that's who Kate was. She always worried about the other person with total disregard for her own safety. However, this time Kate wasn't going to know about the situation, so she could have no say in the matter.

===

Since there wasn't much activity on the tour, it seemed to drag by. Eight hours felt like sixteen, but before long, Gloria and Rocco were turning in their equipment and changing out of uniform. They headed over to the local bar with a number of other officers to get a jump on the party. Of all people, Freddie was delayed with a report that he had to submit at the end of the tour. Apparently, that didn't matter to the other officers who were at the bar already. They were going to start the celebration even if the guest of honor wasn't there yet. It didn't affect them. Alcohol was alcohol no matter who was present. In fact, no one seemed to care whether Freddie was there or not. They were going to have a good time regardless.

Rocco and Gloria were in no rush to start drinking, but they were in the midst of a crowd who gulped their drinks as if they were seeing their first glass of water after being stranded in a desert for days. Rocco hardly drank and Gloria usually had a limit of only two or three drinks. However, because of the weight of her cousin's assigned task, she felt that she could finish off an entire bottle. She was on edge, and it was apparent to Rocco that she seemed out-of-sorts.

Rocco voiced his concerns to his partner: "Gloria, are you okay. You seem to be fidgety and uncomfortable. Is something bothering you? Are you feeling okay? Let me know if anything is bothering you."

"Oh, I'm fine Rocco. I guess I just don't do well in crowds. I'm okay. I just don't like to be with a lot of people in a confined area."

"We only just got here, but if you want to go outside and get some fresh air, just let me know. I don't have a problem with that."

"No, I'm okay, Rocco. I'll get used to it, and before you know it, the party will be coming to an end. That's when you guys start retreating to the back room where the debauchery begins. Rocco be careful, please!"

"Nothing to worry about, Gloria. I'm not into that stuff. Unless you're setting a trap for me, I'll be in and out even before the first bump and grind." He laughed not knowing what was in store for him. Gloria shared in the laughter, but her's was a forced smile. Her guilt would not allow for anything else.

There was a rousing round of applause when Freddie finally got to the bar. However, it had taken a while for him to arrive and, at least a few of his fellow officers were already feeling no pain. That was to be expected. There were always those few who used alcohol to buffer the clandestine hardships that permeated their existence. It created a fake dynamic of worry-free living and an "I don't give a damn" attitude. That was great until the effects of the alcohol wore off and one realized that the original problems were still there. Additionally, the drinker was now actually supporting a new problem called "alcohol addiction." Of course, this didn't apply to all, but it definitely found a home with some.

===

People were having a good time. Everyone seemed to be enjoying themselves with Freddie being the focus of attention. Although alcohol played a significant role in bringing out the "best" in people, Rocco didn't need the influence of spirits to have a good time. He was enjoying the company, the laughs and the overall relaxed atmosphere. Gloria too was having a good time. At least outwardly she was, but it was getting close to the time when she would have to initiate the beginnings of a diabolic plan to ruin a person's life. So, although she laughed and joined in the activities, Gloria was in turmoil.

It was getting near that time, and the three-piece-band was playing their last set. Guys were gradually moving to the entrance of the back room. Suddenly, the band stopped playing and a drum roll began. The rolling drums led to the introduction of Freddie's best man who was going to close the "open" party with a toast to the soon-to -be groom.

Gloria and Rocco were standing next to each other and leaning on a table that held their drinks. Gloria knew that this was the time for her to act. Before the best man asked everyone to pick up their glasses and raise a toast to Freddie, Gloria reached into her pocket and grabbed the white pill. As she gave Rocco his drink, she had already and reluctantly dropped the pill into what was now a devil's potion. Bobby had been right about the pill. It dissolved almost instantly, and there was no sign of it ever existing. Gloria toasted with everyone else, but she was the only one with tears in her eyes.

Shortly after the toast, the best man thanked everyone for coming, and a cadre of guys headed for the back room. This was where the real party was about to begin and where Rocco's former life was about to end. Rocco turned to Gloria and let her know that it was time for them to separate. She knew it was coming and she said to him: "Rocco, don't have a good time!"

Rocco was little surprised by Gloria's statement: "Well, that wasn't very nice, Gloria. I probably won't have the best time, and all of a sudden, I am beginning to feel a bit tired anyway. Take that worried look off your face. The rest of the guys will be so absorbed in what's going on that they won't even realize that I am gone. Everything will be fine. Be careful driving home, you've had a few more than usual. I don't want to get any calls from Highway Patrol."

===

Gloria's guilt became overwhelming. She couldn't take it anymore, and she decided to tell Rocco what she had done. She could still save him. Just as she was about to grab his arm and confess, one of Bobby's friends, the ones who were going to "look after" her, bumped into her and came between Rocco and her. Rocco waved "goodbye," and Bobby's friend gently nudged Gloria toward the exit door. When they reached the street, her "protector" told her that he thought she might be getting cold feet. To avoid any sudden change in plans and to make certain that nothing happened to Kate Dancer, he thought it best if he intervened and removed any temptation that might be plaguing her.

Gloria was incensed and she let him know it: “Get your hands off me. I know what I’m doing, and I don’t need your help. Don’t you have anything better to do than to be at Bobby’s beck-and-call? What is he paying you for babysitting? You should be really proud of yourself for helping to ruin a man’s life.”

The alcohol was beginning to take effect and Gloria was becoming much too loud. Her comments could bring unnecessary attention to them and the whole operation. Bobby’s henchman gently squeezed her arm and continued to apply pressure forcing Gloria to keep her mouth shut. The applied pressure was a sobering measure, and Gloria realized that there was no way out for her. The man brought her to her car and told her to “use her head.” He turned and left, but she knew that he and his partner would not be far behind her.

===

Rocco entered the back room with the majority of guys who were at the “open” party. One could see the enthusiasm in the eyes of the soon-to-be participants in a sexual escapade. There were a lot of comments and some “oohs and ahs” when they saw the young women who were going to entertain the hungered flock of excited men. Rocco found a corner to sit in and be as inconspicuous as possible. He had no idea that no matter where he was in the room, the well-paid distributors of sexual temptations and favors would find him. Of course, most of their attention would be directed toward the soon-to-be married man, but they would find the time to do what they were privately paid for.

There were three woman who started gyrating to the recorded music that they had brought along. It was Rocco's plan to start his exit when the dancing began; however, he felt lethargic and incapable of thinking clearly. He couldn't understand why he was feeling so out-of-sorts. He hadn't had any amount of alcohol that would influence his usual frame of mind, but he definitely wasn't himself. He almost felt that he didn't have the strength to raise his hands or move his legs. He heard the howls and yelps of his fellow officers, but he couldn't really focus on the activities.

Before he knew it, Rocco felt the closeness of one of the females who had her untethered breasts resting on his face with the nipple lying on his lips. He tried to push the individual away, but his actions were far too weak to prevent further sexual behavior and the advancement of even another female. This woman unbuttoned his shirt and exposed Rocco's chest that was now being kissed by still a third individual. The females took turns situating themselves in various positions that would definitely arouse certain feelings in the male genitalia of most men. An objective observer would surely say that the pictured male participant was having a grand old time for himself. The way that he was positioned and the female performance that took place was undeniably an activity where others would assume that the interactions and displayed promiscuity was more than welcomed by the male attendee.

===

At the end of the night, Rocco was still out of sorts. In fact, one of the other guys had to drive his car to his home and help him into the house. Rocco was out as soon as he hit the pillow. His night had been something that he wouldn't remember, and one that he wouldn't want to remember. If someone were told about the evening's events or actually saw the goings-on, it would be difficult for the apparent participant to deny his involvement.

When Rocco arose the following morning, his head was throbbing and his mouth was totally dry. He was experiencing the same effects that someone would have with a bad hangover. He knew that he did not drink enough to have had a hangover. He wondered if someone had spiked his drink. He couldn't think of any other reason why he would be feeling the way he was, but he couldn't believe that any one of his friends would do that. He was at a loss to explain why he was out of it.

Bobby Santiago got the verbal report from Gloria. He also spoke with the women who had participated in the sexual activities and who had contracted to take the photos. His scheme had worked perfectly. He couldn't be happier, and he couldn't wait to execute the next part of his perverted revenge scheme! Bobby was waging a war that he was sure would end in his favor. He wished that he could be there when Janet first sees the photos and when she questions her fiancée about his activities. There could be nothing better than seeing Rocco Deloberti crash and burn.

Chapter Thirty-Three

Going to the Source

Rocco was off the following day, and he needed the time to recover from a very rough night. Slowly, things were beginning to come to mind. He couldn't recall all of the specifics, but he remembered enough to realize that it wasn't a good night for him. In his mind's eye, he saw flashes of women gyrating with hardly any clothes on their bodies, and these same women unabashedly exhibiting their wears right in front of his face. Ordinarily, he wouldn't have participated in any kind of behavior like the kind he was remembering; however, from what he was recalling, he didn't do anything to stop the sexual flirtations. He couldn't.

The more Rocco thought about the night, the more he believed that he had been the victim of a spiked drink. However, he had very little to drink, and the only one he drank with was his partner, Gloria. He didn't want to believe that Gloria would have any part in a scheme to drug him. Also, what would be her reason to do such a thing? It was totally out of character for her to be involved in something like that. Rocco wouldn't accept the fact that she would put him in such a precarious situation where his reputation would suffer, and he would become the brunt of obvious ridicule. No, it wasn't Gloria, but who else had the opportunity to spike his drink? He was at a loss to figure it out.

===

As night time approached, he contacted Janet and arranged to see her later that evening. She inquired about the previous night's events, and Rocco told her that everything went well, and that he left before things could get out of control. She was happy to hear that he used good judgement, but that was what she expected from him. Janet asked if there was the usual sexual entertainment, and Rocco said that there were some belly dancers that arrived, but he left before anything like that started. Janet told him that she was sure he would have.

Rocco never felt more guilty, and when the time was right, he would tell her the whole truth. With her father passing, and her mother in the throes of saddening depression, Rocco did not think that this was the time to divulge how inappropriately he had apparently acted. The excuse that someone spiked his drink would not sit well right now with his fiancée. So, he skirted around some of the questions and gave lame, inaccurate answers to others. As time went on, it would be easier to explain. Anyway, there was no way that she was going to find out what had really occurred. Time would heal all.

Rocco was still a little shaky from the previous night's events, but he made certain that he was not going to give any indication that he wasn't one hundred percent raring to go. Janet always gave Rocco a warm welcome, and always reacted like she hadn't seen him in a very long time. It was heartwarming to Rocco, and he enjoyed every moment of the welcome. It was going to be a quiet evening with Janet and her mom. They decided on a particular movie and settled down to enjoy the entertainment. Janet had prepared some snacks which added to the pleasure of the night. Even Janet's mother seemed to be reacting favorably to the company, and recently, that was not always the case.

Just as the three of them settled in to see the movie, the front door bell rang. It was odd that someone would be coming to the door this time of the night, but Janet got up from her comfortable position and went to the front door. To her surprise, there was a delivery man with an envelope in his hands: "Hello, are you Ms. Janet Commings?"

"Yes, that's me."

"I have an envelope for you. Please sign."

Janet had no idea who would be sending an envelope to her that was so important that she had to sign for it. However, she signed for the delivery and took the envelope which had "Please Do Not Bend" stamped on the outside. She was more than curious about what she had received, but she felt that delaying the movie wasn't fair to Rocco and her mom, so she put the envelope on the kitchen table and went to join the others. Her mom inquired as to who was at the front door, and Janet said that it was just a mail delivery. Mrs. Commings voiced her surprise that the mail was delivered during the evening hours. Janet informed her that it was a special delivery, and that she wasn't expecting anything important. She shrugged it off and said that she would look at it later. With that, the group settled in to watch the movie.

They had chosen an entertaining movie that lasted approximately two hours. They drank and snacked throughout the presentation, and Mrs. Commings seemed to be having a good time. Janet was happy see that her mother was enjoying herself, and she attributed her mom's good attitude to Rocco's constant joking and interjections about the movie. However, it was a long movie, and the three of them were tired. Janet and Rocco decided to call it a night. Janet's mom retired to her bedroom, and Janet led Rocco to the front door. As they passed the kitchen entrance, Rocco reminded his fiancée to open her mail, but she said that she was in no hurry to open what she thought was just another "important" advertisement. Rocco acknowledged her comment and continued to the front door. Janet thanked him for bringing some joy to her mother's evening. They kissed "good-night," and Rocco went on his way.

After waving "goodbye" to Rocco, Janet proceeded to the kitchen to tidy up a bit. Her clean-up task only took about ten minutes, and she was ready to retire for the evening when the special delivery envelope caught her eye. Although she was tired, her curiosity peaked, and she decided to see what she had signed for. Janet sat down in the dimly lit kitchen and proceeded to open her mail. The first item that she came upon was a note that was typewritten. It said: "Is this the type of man that you would want to spend the rest of your life with? I don't think so. You are better than that!" Janet was confused until she unwrapped the rest of the envelope's contents. There were twelve, 8"x10" color photographs of what looked like an orgy. As she looked more closely, her curiosity turned into shock when she recognized her fiancée as a participant in what was pictured as sexual promiscuity with three half-naked females. Although she was disgusted with what she saw, she couldn't put the photos down, and she continued to look at pictures of Rocco apparently participating in sexually deviant acts.

===

Curiosity had turned into shock, and now shock had evolved into anger. In a disgusted and desperate gesture, she took the photos and threw them to the ground. It was her way of expressing the disappointment and disbelief in what she had seen. Tears filled her eyes, and Janet began to sob over what she believed to be the beginning of the end of her relationship with Rocco Deloberti. As she continued to cry out as a result of growing anguish, she subconsciously fingered and twirled the engagement ring that was supposed to acknowledge a wedding day that would lead to the start their life together. She took the ring off of her finger, something that she had not done since Rocco had put it there, and was about to throw it against the wall when she heard footsteps behind her: "Janet, what's the matter? I got up to get a glass of water, and I thought I heard you crying. Is everything all right?" Mrs. Comming's question didn't have to be answered as she observed the photographs lying on the kitchen floor.

"Is that Rocco? It can't be. He wouldn't do something like that." In total disbelief, Mrs. Commings bent down and picked up a few of the photos to look more closely. She remained totally silent.

"Mom, I'm sure as you continue to look, you will definitely recognize the person who was once my fiancée." That statement said it all. There was no way that Rocco was going to be able to justify what Janet had seen. In fact, there was no way that Janet was even going to give him a chance to offer an explanation. She didn't want to hear it, and as far as she was concerned, she wanted Rocco Deloberti out of her life for good. She decided that she would mail him some of the photos that she had received. There was definitely enough of them. Along with the disgusting photographs that she was going to send, Janet decided to include the engagement ring that he had given to her. She would mail the envelope the same way she had received it – special delivery.

===

Bobby Santiago couldn't wait to hear from Gloria about the potential demise of the relationship between Rocco and Janet. The wait was well worth it because when Gloria relayed to Bobby what Rocco had told her, Bobby Santiago was in his glory. His plan had worked even better than anticipated. Also, it was Gloria's understanding that Janet wasn't even going to give Rocco a chance to explain. As far as Janet was concerned, the relationship was dead.

Although the relationship between Janet Commings and Rocco Deloberti was completely dissolved, Janet couldn't stop thinking about the shocking and unbelievable experience that continued to plague her stream of consciousness and which had turned her life upside down. Apparently, she continued to wonder who had sent her the photographs and why Rocco had decided to participate in the disgusting activities that took place on that evening.

Janet only had one real dependable contact within the police department. She decided to call her friend, Bobby Santiago, to see if he could find out who sent her the photos. He was there for her once before, and she hoped he would be there for her again. Maybe he could even find out why Rocco decided to partake in activities that seemed totally out of character for him. No matter the excuse or reason for his actions, and as far as Janet was concerned, Rocco Deloberti had crossed over the line of decency and trust.

Chapter Thirty-Four

Kate Shocks Everyone

Shortly after the movie night that Rocco had spent with Janet and her mom, he received a very distressing phone message at his home. It was definitely Janet, and she told him, in no uncertain terms, that their relationship was over. She also made reference to some photos that she had received which pictured Rocco in some very awkward positions during the recent bachelor party. Apparently, someone had photographed his sexual frolics with the invited female entertainers. The photos were developed and either delivered or mailed to his fiancée. One way or the other, Janet had proof that he was unfaithful and had lied. The phone message was so devastating that Rocco decided not to even try to mend fences.

To further enforce his decision not to contact Janet, he had also received an envelope in the mail. It not only contained some photos, but even more incapacitating, it included the engagement ring that Janet had worn all this time. He knew that, at least for now, there was no coming back from what Janet had seen. He was hopeful that, at some time in the future, he could successfully argue his case, but he knew, that for now, the odds were against him. He needed to find out who had spiked his drink and who was behind the whole idea to destroy his reputation and his relationship with Janet.

===

Detective Bobby Santiago was doing well in his new assignment at the Organized Crime Prevention Unit. Even though he had only been there for a short time, in his devious and corrupt manner, he had already made unofficial contact with a few of the mobsters. These organized crime thugs were willing to enter into arrangements that benefitted both the crime family and any police officer who was willing to stray from the norm. Detective Bobby Santiago was definitely one of those officers who could be placed in that category. In fact, it had been through his new contacts that Santiago was able to buy the additional services of the female strippers who entertained at the bachelor party. Because he knew that other officials were also involved in corruption that permeated the organized crime unit, Bobby worked with what he believed was total immunity. Although he was correct about his assumption, unbeknownst to him, there was a separate and independent active and on-going investigation regarding the mob contacts and their connection to police personnel.

===

Rocco Deloberti's former plainclothes partner, John Hallerin, was now the Acting Lieutenant in the Special Operations Unit of the police department. He was the ranking supervisor who was leading the investigation on the possible corrupt activities involving the police and organized crime. Lieutenant Hallerin needed investigators who he could trust, and who would not be swayed or tempted by the opportunity to accept tainted money.

Hallerin remembered Rocco and was aware of the reputation that he had gained as a police officer. He also remembered that Rocco had been involved in a number of successful investigations. The lieutenant recalled Deloberti's staunch stand against what he believed, at the time, was police corruption. John Hallerin decided to take a chance on Rocco to see if he would be interested in a transfer to the Special Operations Unit. John Hallerin was well respected in the department and with his influence, he could have Rocco Deloberti transferred and promoted to the rank of "Detective." John was pretty sure that he could depend on Rocco.

===

Rocco was still suffering from the devastating effects of his separation from Janet, and his partner, Gloria, was forced to endure his pitiful rantings everyday as they patrolled. Her feelings for Rocco were impacted by the fact that she was the one who had allowed the bachelor party fiasco to take place. She was the one who set her partner up for a fall from which he might never recover. It was getting harder and harder to live with what she had done. She got no relief from her guilt because Rocco had really only her to confide in, and he couldn't help himself from talking about it every time they were together.

Gloria came close a couple of times to revealing to Rocco the whole plot that was forged against him, but something always interrupted her determination. She had to tell someone, and she decided to confide in her soul mate, Kate, who seemed to be at a standstill with her emotional feelings. Gloria had hesitated in telling Kate because of Kate's slow recovery, but now, she had to confide in someone or she would burst at the seams from the ever-present guilt that plagued her conscious thought every day.

Apparently, her guilt also fortified her planned response to her cousin, Bobby. Gloria was going to tell Kate everything, and she was going to let Bobby know that she decided to do so. She rationalized that it would be better to let him know up front than to do something behind his back. He would be incensed either way, but the resulting actions toward her would be less severe if she let him know before she did anything.

When the tour was over, and she and Rocco were about to split for the day, she looked at him and said: "Have faith partner. Things will get better. I guarantee it. You can only go up from here."

"Yeah, thanks, Gloria. I know I've been bending your ear, but I really don't have anyone else with whom I can talk, and who understands who I really am. I don't know what I would do without you."

That's all that Gloria needed. Talking about "piling on." If she wasn't at the edge of a cliff before, she now had one foot in the air: "No sweat, partner. You can always talk to me. That's why I'm here, and besides, I am sure that there were many times that you had to endure my constant jabbering." They both laughed and went to their cars.

Gloria had been staying with Kate, and as soon as she got home, she checked on Kate and found her asleep. That was a fortunate break for Gloria because she wanted to tell Bobby first before she let Kate know anything. As she continued to deal with her guilty conscience, she became more determined and decided to let Bobby know that if she became even more overwrought with guilt, she was also going to let Janet know exactly what had happened. It just didn't sit right with her that she had ruined not one person's life but two. Sure, she was tempting fate and risking her safety by telling her cousin, but what was he going to do, kill her? The way she felt now, she could take whatever Bobby was going to dole out as long as her conscience would be relieved. She punched in his number: "Hi, Bobby, it's me, Gloria. I need to talk to you about the whole situation involving Janet and Rocco. I have to get some things off of my chest."

===

By the tone of his cousin's voice, Bobby became concerned: "Gloria, you don't have to get anything off your chest. Just keep your mouth shut and things will be fine."

"No, that's just it, Bobby. Things are not fine. I am having a very difficult time living with what I did. The guilt is killing me, and I have to see Rocco every day and hear about how miserable he is. It's just not right. I have to tell someone what I did or I will go insane. I decided to confide in Kate. At least I can unburden some of my guilt by getting it out in the open."

Bobby reminded Gloria about his warning: "Gloria, did you forget about out little talk. I can't afford to let anyone know what we did. Do you really think that Kate would just listen to what you have to say and keep it all to herself. The first thing that she would do and probably insist that you do is to tell Janet and then Rocco. Do you think I can let that happen? The answer is 'no!' And If you can't keep your mouth shut, I will shut it for you. Do you understand what I am telling you, Gloria."

Gloria decided to throw caution to the wind: "Yeah, I heard what your said, Bobby, but that doesn't help me or my problem. I am going to speak with Kate, and after I get it all out, I am seriously going to consider talking to Janet. You'll just have to deal with the consequences."

"Let me get this straight, Gloria. You're telling me that no matter what I say, you're going to do what you want. Dear cousin, you're playing with fire and you're going to get burned, and I will be the one to light the match."

Gloria responded: "You don't scare me, Bobby. There's nothing that you can do that will stop me. I have to unburden myself."

“Oh, there’s definitely something that I can do to stop you, and it will also unburden you from the nasty guilt that is occupying your every thought.”

Gloria didn’t want to hear anymore: “Goodbye, Bobby. We just don’t see eye-to-eye. I am going to do what I have to do, and I guess you will have to do what you have to do. So be it.”

With that, Gloria disconnected the call and went into Kate’s room to see if she had awakened from her nap. Kate hadn’t moved, and there were no signs of her waking up. Gloria couldn’t wait any longer. She had to tell someone what was going on and what she had done. She decided to nudge Kate and get her up. Gloria pushed on Kate just a bit and called out her name, but again there was no response. Gloria looked more closely and became concerned that Kate wasn’t breathing. She grabbed Kate and tried to wake her, but again, there was no response. Gloria immediately called 911 and started administering CPR. As she was attempting to revive Kate and waiting for the ambulance, she glanced at the night table and noticed an opened and empty bottle of pills. She now realized that Kate may have intentionally overdosed. Gloria knew that Kate was having a difficult time progressing, but she had no idea that Kate was at the point of taking her own life.

The ambulance crew tried to save Kate Dancer, but their efforts were unsuccessful. Kate was pronounced dead at the scene. The fact that she had mistakenly taken another officer’s life just weighed too heavy on her mind, and she couldn’t deal with that reality. However, not even the psychologist thought that she was at the point of ending it all. Gloria was uncontrollably distraught and had to be attended to by the EMTs who had responded. Kate was her soulmate, her confidant, and her reason for living. How could she not have noticed that Kate was at this point. Gloria started blaming herself for what had happened. She also started to feel that it was God's punishment for what she had done to Rocco.

In the midst of her grief, Gloria became angered at her cousin, Bobby, and decided at that moment that he was not going to win. Her mental angst influenced her to entertain the theory that in some way, Bobby had influenced a divine power to stop her from confiding in her mate about the bachelor party. However, that was not going to stop her now from relieving her guilt. She decided that she was going to go even farther and tell all to Janet Commings. One way or the other, she was going to attempt to ease the pain of a guilty conscience which had been influencing her everyday existence. Putting things in proper perspective, however, Gloria's tell-all confession would have to wait until after she took care of the funeral arrangements for the love that she lost.

Although Gloria was devastated, she knew that Kate would want her to get on with her life and put the grief behind her. As hard as it was going to be, Gloria was going to do just that and wipe the slate clean! She had to unburden herself and tell all to both Janet and Rocco. She was also aware, however, that in so doing, she would have to face whatever consequences her actions would bring. She was well aware that her cousin, Bobby, did not make empty threats. Because of that, she would be looking over her shoulder at every turn.

Bobby Santiago was her cousin, but he was also an individual who hated losing. He never forgets and he is unforgiving. Sure, they were blood relatives, but Gloria knew that Bobby would not think twice about spilling some of her blood just to teach her a lesson. To Gloria, that was a small price to pay for the relief that a clear conscience would bring. She hoped, however, that she was not underestimating the price, a price that could be compounded by her cousin's rage and which could ultimately result in her demise.

Chapter Thirty-Five

Blood, Thicker Than Water

When Rocco Deloberti received the call from his former partner, John Hallerin, he couldn't believe his good fortune. After the devastating news about Kate, he needed something to boost his spirits. Fortunately, he and Gloria were able to console each other for the most part. Now, however, he had to add more grief to Gloria's day when he had to inform her that he would be leaving, and that she has to look for another partner. He was hesitating and trying to find the right time to drop the bomb. He realized, however, that there was no good time.

As he was passing the front desk searching for equipment with Gloria, one of the officers on the outgoing tour stopped him and said: “Hey Rocco, congratulations on your transfer. That will be a great move for you. Good Luck.”

There are no secrets in the police department, and Rocco learned that the hard way. Gloria stopped in her tracks and just stared at her partner waiting for an explanation. Rocco shook his head and said: “I’m so sorry, Gloria. I was just waiting for the right time to let you know. I accepted a transfer to the Special Operations Unit where my former plainclothes partner is the acting lieutenant. He wants me to work on some specific investigations, and he wants me to start as soon as possible. I didn’t want you to hear it from anyone else, and I don’t even know how anyone found out about it. I didn’t tell anyone. I wanted you to be the first person I told. However, that idea is out the window. I’m sorry you had to find out this way.”

Gloria was hurt to have to find out about her partner’s transfer from someone other than her partner, and she let Rocco know: “Yeah, it’s definitely a little rough to hear that your partner and friend is leaving. It’s especially difficult when you hear the news from someone other than your partner. I understand that you were taking my feelings into consideration, but it really hurts to find out this way. The best laid plans of mice and men.”

Rocco knew exactly what Gloria was talking about: “I know. I know. I didn’t want it to be this way. I am so sorry. I will miss you and the connection we have together. It is also difficult for me to leave during a time when you and I are both grieving the loss of Kate. Even though we might be a distance apart, you know that I will always be there for you. I am a phone call away. Anything you need or want, just ask."

Gloria didn't want to accept the fact that Rocco was leaving: "What I want, Rocco, is for you stay as my partner, but I also want what's best for you. If you think that the transfer is advantageous, then I wish you the best of luck in your new assignment."

===

The news of Rocco's transfer took its toll on Gloria, and she just couldn't go out on patrol and be one hundred percent. She decided to take the day off and try to cope with the grief and disappointments that were coming at her from all directions. Rocco understood and told her to go home, try to relax, and get as much rest as possible.

Unbeknownst to Gloria, this tour may have been the last one where the person sitting next to her in the patrol car would be Police Officer Rocco Deloberti. John Hallerin was anxious to get Rocco working on the investigations, and when the department wanted something done, it got done quickly. Rocco figured that by the end of his tour, he would receive his transfer orders, and that shortly after his transfer, Hallerin would make good on his promise to promote him.

Rocco was right on the money. When he turned in his equipment at the end of the tour, there was a note for him to check the telephone message book. There in big, black, bold letters were the transfer orders that took effect at midnight. Rocco looked at the orders with mixed emotions. He was happy to be going into a unit that specialized in investigations; he was happy about his potential promotion; and he was enthused to be working for a good boss, John Hallerin. However, he was saddened with the thought of leaving Gloria and her having to face a very dismal future alone. He made a promise to himself that he was going to keep in close contact with her, and meet with her whenever he could. She was a good person and always had his best interests at heart. Little did he know that he was leaving the very person who initiated his personal downfall. However, the way Gloria was dealing with her guilt, it might not be that long a period of time before Rocco knew the truth about the bachelor party night.

As soon as Rocco got the orders for the transfer, he contacted Gloria to let her know. Since he hadn't had a chance to really say goodbye, he asked if he could stop by for just a few moments later on in the evening. Of course, Gloria told him that she wanted to see him. So, they made arrangements, and Rocco was going to see his partner before he left. He felt so much better that he had the chance to personally say "goodbye." He didn't want to leave and say goodbye on the strength of a phone call alone.

Shortly after seven o'clock, Rocco rang Gloria's front doorbell. He was surprised to be greeted with a strong hug and flowing tears. He maneuvered his way into the house with Gloria holding on for dear life. He mentally compared the welcome and the passion as if it was a soldier leaving for his tour of duty overseas. Finally, when Rocco was able to pry his way free, he assured Gloria that he would stay in constant contact with her.

He emphasized the fact that in addition to being partners, they were also friends. And friends do not forget each other. Gloria's outward flow emotions were slowly working their influence on Rocco's feelings, and he began to "tear-up" just a bit; however, he had to remain strong for Gloria's sake, and so he held back the flood.

Gloria collected her thoughts and controlled her emotions so that she could speak to her partner: "Rocco, you have no idea how much I will miss you. You are my pillar of strength, and you made working on patrol, not only a comfortable experience for me, but something I looked forward to every day. Not to burden you with any guilt, but what am I supposed to do now? No one is going to match up to the relationship that we had, and I don't think anyone else will be able to tolerate my constant jabbering." She smiled a soft smile.

Rocco tried to play down her anxiety: "What do you mean 'what am I supposed to do now'? You will do the same thing that you did with me. Show whoever becomes your partner how lucky that individual is to have you sitting alongside him or her. You've earned a good reputation in the precinct, and I really don't think that you will have a hard time finding someone to replace me. In fact, I know a number of cops who would not hesitate to jump into my seat."

"Rocco, get this straight. No one will ever replace you, and I'm not looking for anyone to do that. As long as I can get along with whomever it is, I will be happy. Of course, it will never be the same, but I will tolerate the situation. I've learned a lot from you, and I appreciate all that you have done for me."

The remarks from both of them were bittersweet: "Gloria, the door swings both ways. We've learned from each other. I only hope that your new partner is as loyal to you as you were to me."

===

It was this last statement that stabbed Gloria right in the heart. Loyalty was the last thing that Gloria showed to Rocco. She had all to do from holding back and telling him everything, but she wanted to get to Janet first. There would be time to straighten things out with Rocco. Gloria was more determined than ever to let Janet know what happened that evening. She didn't care what Janet thought of her after the explanation, but she wanted to make sure that when Janet knew the truth that she would reach out to Rocco.

Following a few more comments and recalling some good times, the partners knew that the time had come to face the reality of leaving. Once again, they both rose and hugged each other. Gloria whispered: "Rocco, don't say anything. Just hug me for a little while, and I don't want to hear 'goodbye'."

Rocco listened and happily complied with Gloria's request. They hugged and took deep breaths, but neither one said anything at all. When the time came to leave and when Rocco reached the front door, he turned to her and said: "I'll see you soon, partner."

Gloria could say nothing in return. She just smiled with tears rolling down her face and nodded her confirmation. Rocco turned and left. Gloria had the strongest urge to run out of the front door and stop Rocco to tell him what she had done. In fact, she took a few steps toward the door when her cell phone started ringing. Just the person she didn't want to talk to, Bobby Santiago, was on the line. She answered the phone with hate in her heart: "What do you want?"

Santago was taken aback: "Hold on, cousin. You sound like you are ready for war or that you lost your best friend. What's bugging you?"

Gloria couldn't believe how cold and inconsiderate her cousin was: "You have to be kidding. Not only did I lose my best friend, but because of you, I really screwed him over. But don't you worry, cousin, I am going to fix that. There's nothing you can say or do that will deter me from making things right with Rocco and Janet. Okay, I said my piece, and I hope you listened carefully. You called me for a reason. Now, what do you want?"

Bobby answered: "I had a question for you, but you have already answered it. You sound like you are at a point where there is no turning back regarding a confession. That is a shame. Unfortunately, you are not leaving me much of a choice, so let me say 'goodbye' for the final time."

"If 'for the final time' means that I will never have to deal with you again, that's fine by me. Goodbye, Bobby."

Gloria was so incensed by the brief but pointed conversation that she had with her cousin that she decided to act on impulse and contact Janet. When Janet got on the phone, Gloria had second thoughts about telling her anything over the phone, and she asked if she could meet with Janet that very evening. Janet knew about Kate's death, and she assumed that Gloria wanted to talk about it with her, so she gladly invited Gloria over to her house.

Gloria got dressed in a hurry and tried to mentally prepare herself for what might very well be an accusatory and unfriendly conversation with Janet Commings. She went to her car and quickly took off for Janet's home. In her haste, she didn't notice that the lights on the car across from hers turned on right after hers. Not wanting the feeling of true confession to leave her, she drove at breakneck speed to arrive at Janet's house as soon as she could. The trip took about forty minutes, and when she arrived at Janet's home, she turned the car off and just sat in the driver's seat trying to bolster the necessary courage to carry out her goal.

===

After about five minutes of careful thought and contemplation, Gloria Santiago exited her car and stood in front of Janet's house. Her thoughts, however, were shockingly interrupted by the sound of an engine from a quickly approaching vehicle. Reacting like a deer in headlights and before Gloria realized what was happening, the vehicle was up on the sidewalk and sending her air-bound for about twenty feet.

The collision was loud enough to catch Janet's attention, and she went out of her front door to see what had happened. Janet heard the moans of a female who was lying just outside of the fence line of her home. When Janet got closer, she realized that she was looking at the broken body of Gloria Santiago who was moaning in pain. The shock of seeing Gloria froze Janet for a moment, but then she quickly bent down to help Gloria. As far as Janet was concerned, the hit-and-run victim was in very bad shape. Janet heard Gloria trying to say something, so she put her ear close to Gloria's mouth. In almost an inaudible whisper, Gloria spoke: "Janet, I am so sorry. Rocco is innocent. He is a good man. He didn't..." Gloria Santiago's eyes closed, and she went limp in the arms of Janet Commings. Police Officer Gloria Santiago, the victim of a tragic hit-and-run accident, expired. She was foolproof evidence that in the eyes of some, blood is not thicker than water.

Although Gloria, in Janet's opinion, had referred to that fateful bachelor party night, death had robbed Janet from finding out the actual story that ultimately led to the severing of her relationship with Rocco. Janet now had statements of a dying woman, but was in a quandary as to what they really meant. Janet's mind was working overtime, and she had to find out if the assumption that she was making was correct.

Once again, Janet thought of her police contact, Bobby Santiago. She decided to contact him but hesitated because she was sure that he would be wallowing in the grief of having lost his cousin. She also knew that Bobby would be totally involved in the funeral arrangements for Gloria, so contacting him would have to be put on hold for at least a little while.

Janet understood that Bobby knew his cousin better than anyone else, and that maybe he could make some sense out of her dying comments. He was a detective; he knew his cousin, Gloria, very well; and he had a relationship with the few people who were involved in the shocking party scene. Maybe, just maybe, he might be able to get to the bottom of this plaguing event. Gloria, apparently, knew something, and if Bobby's cousin had some information, then there was a good possibility that Bobby might have it too. If he didn't, Janet was sure that he would, at least, look into things for her. Detective Bobby Santiago was being called to the rescue, once again. In Janet Comming's mind: "Thank God for Bobby Santiago!"

Chapter Thirty-Six

The Internal Investigation

When Rocco first got the news that Gloria had been killed by a hit-and-run driver, he wanted to know who was investigating the case and what evidence the detective had uncovered. To his dismay, the investigating detectives had very little to go on. There were no witnesses to the accident and very little material evidence left behind. Rocco knew that Bobby Santiago would surely get involved in the case, and even though there was no love lost between Rocco and Bobby, Rocco felt that he should contact Santiago and offer his condolences. However, just prior to Rocco making the phone call, he was asked to come into his boss's office. Rocco had just recently arrived in the unit, and John Hallerin hadn't had a chance to properly welcome him.

The boss wanted to thoroughly review what he expected Rocco to do.

John Hallerin gave a warm welcome to Rocco and made him feel totally at ease. John started the meeting with a general overview of what the office is charged with and how confidential the investigations are. As the boss continued speaking, Rocco got the general idea that much of the investigative work centered around department personnel possibly getting involved in questionable activities. The description had all the earmarks of what an internal affairs investigating unit would do. However, Hallerin assured Rocco that the Special Investigations Unit was not an Internal Affairs Office. Although the investigations by the two entities could, at times overlap, they were two very distinct divisions of the department. Rocco was more than glad to hear that. He did not want to be part of any internal affairs unit. He wasn't going to be a sycophant who tried to catch other cops. That kind of police work was not for him.

After listening carefully to all that John Hallerin had to say, Rocco still wasn't sure where he fit in, and what the boss wanted him to do: "Lieutenant, (Rocco was very much aware of protocol and rank, and even though they had been partners at one time, now, he was speaking to the boss) I really appreciate your asking me to come on board, and I can't thank you enough for having the confidence in me to advance my career, but I am still not certain what my immediate responsibilities would be."

The lieutenant nodded in the affirmative: "That's Rocco Deloberti, all business and getting right to the point. Okay, let me fill you in. There is a strong possibility that a few of our investigators assigned to the Organized Crime Prevention Unit have taken their involvement in their investigations to a compromising level of interest. To be frank, the department is concerned that some of the detectives are actually helping members of organized crime avoid arrest. In fact, we are very much concerned with a relatively new detective assigned to the unit who apparently had some dubious connections prior to his transfer into that unit. In the short time that he has been assigned there, it seems that he might be the main contact who is possibly involved in suspected corruption. I want fresh eyes and ears to pick up on this internal investigation, and I need someone who has proven that he would not falter when it came to corruption. Rocco, you are that person. You have proven it to me before, and I have no doubt that you will prove it to me again."

Rocco listened and became concerned that he was getting involved in the specific area that he wanted to avoid, internal affairs: "Boss, it sounds to me like you want me to get involved in an internal affairs operation. With all due respect, that is not where I want to be. I would be investigating possible corruption on the part of members of this department, and that, boss, is an internal affairs investigation."

The lieutenant understood where Rocco was coming from: "I appreciate what you are saying, Rocco, but our main focus is to destroy a particular element of organized criminal activity, and our efforts are possibly being hampered because of the corrupt activities of some of our officers. So, yes you will be involved in determining if our investigators are involved, but you will be working toward the final goal of disassembling an apparent operation of organized crime. Rocco, can I count on you?"

"When you put it that way, Lieutenant, I will do whatever I can to assist in taking down an element of organized crime. You can definitely count on me."

Lieutenant Hallerin was relieved: "I knew I could. Although you will be working with other team members, right now, you are the one who I am depending on to confirm whether or not police investigators are working in tandem with organized crime members."

"I got it, boss. You mentioned that a newly arrived member to the Organized Crime Prevention Unit is of particular interest in this investigation. Who might that be, Lieutenant?"

Then lieutenant knew that sooner or later it was going to come to this: "Rocco, I believe you know the individual. He is Detective Bobby Santiago, who is presently out on bereavement. It seems that his cousin was the tragic victim of a hit-and-run accident. He has been handling the funeral arrangements and taking care of her personal effects. He should be back to work any day now. He could possibly be our main target and the connection that is assisting organized crime members ."

Rocco was, of course, taken aback by the news that one of his targets, actually the main one, was none other than the same person who vowed to "win the war." He had to let the lieutenant know that there was some bad blood between him and the person who he apparently would be investigating. He had to let him know that there might be a conflict of interest. So, he went ahead and informed Lieutenant Hallerin about the history between him and Bobby Santiago.

"Lieutenant, just so you know, I and Bobby Santiago have had some problems in the past. I wouldn't want the investigation to be jeopardized because of our previous involvement. I guess it might be best if I were assigned to another case."

John Hallerin was not at all surprised by Rocco's revelation: "Rocco, as you should know, I am well aware of your relationship or lack thereof with Detective Bobby Santiago. That having been said, I am also keenly aware of your dedication to doing the right thing. If I thought that your involvement with Santiago would, in any way, compromise our investigation, you would not be working this case. However, I know that you are more than capable of putting your emotions to the side and running a straight and narrow investigation. So, let me worry about any monkey wrenches. You just put the pedal to the metal and get going on giving me an unbiased conclusion to the possibility of police corruption."

The lieutenant made it perfectly clear that no matter the connection, Rocco was the right man for the job: "Yes sir, I'll get on it right away, and thank you for your vote of confidence."

"No thanks necessary. You've earned the reputation that you have, and make sure you don't tarnish it."

Rocco nodded to the Lieutenant and proceeded to the door. Before leaving, he turned to John Hallerin and said: "I never got a chance to thank you for being in my corner when things got a little rough for me. Without your influence, I could have very easily forfeited my job. I owe you big time, and I will not let you down."

"No thanks necessary, Rocco. You're not doing it for me. You're doing it for every other cop who toes the line and wants to garner the respect that the shield should command. Having said that, however, you're welcome."

Rocco smiled and left the lieutenant's office. When he walked into the squad room, the general area where most of the detectives had their desks, he was met by the senior detective in the unit. He was prepared for a lengthy speech geared to letting him know that this was the detective who was the unofficial boss in the squad. However, Rocco was pleasantly surprised by the friendly attitude that the detective displayed: "Hey kid, it's not often that the boss will go out of his way to get someone assigned to this unit. He must be really sure that you can be trusted, and if he is sure, then we all are. I know you were officially assigned a couple of days ago, but with everything going on, I didn't get a chance to welcome you and introduce myself. I'm Detective Jamie Forest; however, most people call me 'trees.' It's not because of the last name, but rather the size of my legs. Most of the guys commented that my legs looked like tree trunks, and I guess the term 'trunks' didn't fit the bill. So, it's 'trees'." With that, the detective pulled up his pants and displayed muscular legs which were aptly referred to as tree trunks.

===

The squad members seemed to get along really well, and that was a definite reflection of John Hallerin's supervisory and leadership skills. Rocco already felt comfortable even though he knew that this new assignment was going to bring him into a very precarious situation. Cops did not like other cops investigating their activities. No matter how well documented the case, if it meant that a cop or cops were going to go down, the investigator is tainted forever throughout the department. As far as the rank and file were concerned, Rocco Deloberti's reputation was about to take a major hit.

Rocco still had to make a phone call to Bobby Santiago. No matter how he felt about Bobby, offering his condolences was the right thing to do. Not only did Bobby Santiago suffer the loss of his cousin, Gloria, but the burden of finalizing funeral arrangements rested on Bobby's soldiers. As far as Rocco was concerned, Bobby was a snake in the grass, but offering his regrets made Rocco feel like he was respecting Gloria's passing. Rocco looked for some private space and punched in Bobby's cell phone number.

"Well, hello, Rocco. I imagine you're calling about Gloria since you have no other reason to contact me."

"Yeah, that's right, Bobby. I am really sorry about Gloria. I thought the world of her, and we had a special relationship. I will truly miss her every day."

"That's real nice of you, Rocco, but you really didn't know her that well. However, I appreciate your contacting me. Also, I understand that it's not only me who might need some consoling. I have heard that a former girlfriend of yours is also is in the market for some tender loving care. But don't you worry, I will let her know that my services are available."

At this point, Rocco felt that he should have never made the call: "Hey asshole, don't make me regret calling you. I was going to offer my help with regards to Gloria's funeral arrangements, but I don't think I could stand your company. It's so hard to believe that someone like Gloria could have been connected to you. Disregarding her unfortunate relationship to you, I will miss her. Goodbye." Rocco disconnected the call.

Just as the conversation with Rocco ended, Bobby's cell phone rang again. Ironically and like manna from heaven, he looked at his screen and smiled: "Hello, Janet. I was just thinking about you."

Chapter Thirty-Seven

The Trap Revealed

Janet had wanted to wait for a period of time before she contacted Bobby Santiago, but her desire to find out what Gloria was trying to say as she was dying was overwhelming, and she couldn't wait any longer. She gave in to her curiosity and dialed Bobby's number. He was more than happy to hear from her and accepted her condolences.

Following just a short dialogue on small talk, Janet brought up what had been on her mind, and one of the main reasons she called him: "Bobby, the night Gloria was unmercifully mowed down by an unscrupulous individual, I heard the commotion and quickly went out to the scene. When

I got to Gloria, she was in very bad shape and probably knew that she was dying. When she realized who I was, she started speaking to me, but she was so weak that I could hardly hear her. So, I put my ear to her mouth and I heard her whisper: 'I am so sorry. Rocco is innocent. He is a good man.' She couldn't finish the next sentence that started with, 'He didn't.' Bobby, I am kind of confused. What was she sorry about, and what did she mean when she said that Rocco is innocent? I need someone who I can trust to help me solve this problem. Do you know anything about this?"

"No, Janet. I can truthfully say that I really don't know what Gloria was trying to tell you. However, I will do some soul searching and give it some thought. Maybe, something will come to me. I understand that Gloria was killed right outside of your house. I guess she was on her way to see you. Do you know why she wanted to come over to talk to you?"

"Unfortunately, Bobby, she didn't live long enough to tell me, but she didn't want to talk about it over the phone. She was killed just before she was about to enter my house. I can't believe something like this happened."

"Yeah, it's a damn shame that a good person like Gloria was tragically killed like that. Let me think about the last few days I spent with Gloria, and then I'll come over, and we can discuss it."

"Great, Bobby. That sounds like a plan. Thanks again for being there. You're a true friend."

===

When Bobby got off the phone, he smiled like the cat who caught the canary. Things were working out better than he had thought they would. He had some regrets about Gloria, but he justified what he had done by recalling the fact that he gave her every opportunity to change her mind and not confess to anyone. His good judgement on keeping a tail on Gloria paid off well. His henchmen were in the right place at the right time. He was able to deter a situation that could have been disastrous for him. It was at the expense of his cousin's life, but it was a matter of self-preservation for him.

Bobby had heard about Rocco Deloberti's transfer and was not happy that they were both in a specialized investigative branch of the department. Rocco was much closer now, and that didn't sit well with him. Santiago was sure that they would cross paths as investigative cases unfolded. For Bobby, Rocco was too straightlaced to have around. Bobby would have to be more careful with his outside dealings. He knew that if Rocco could grab him on something, he would jump at the chance, and if it were reversed, Bobby would do the same.

The bad blood was more intense now, and that intensity could influence either one of them to go the extra mile for revenge. This tension existed without Rocco ever knowing that Bobby had planned the whole disastrous bachelor party ambush. However, Bobby was feeling a lot more confident now that the one who could have betrayed him was gone. There wasn't anyone left who could gain anything, at this point, by revealing what truly occurred that night. Although he had to be careful, he was a lot less worried.

Bobby was going to take care of all that he had to regarding Gloria's effects and funeral, and then he would contact Janet for a meeting. He hoped that it would be the beginning of a long and fruitful relationship. Of course, he didn't have to do any investigating to find out what Gloria had been trying to say. She had mentioned that Rocco was innocent and a good man, and that she was sorry. Bobby was sure that her next statement would have been something regarding the fact that Rocco was drugged and set up. Thank goodness, that will never be revealed. Bobby was going to wait a bit, and then call Janet for a meeting that would hopefully lead to many more of them.

===

Rocco was well on his way to being indoctrinated not only into the squad but into the foundation of the case that he would be working on. Bobby Santiago and his partner, who was probably as deeply involved as Bobby was, made many unscheduled trips to various addresses that were known to be mob hangouts. Rocco and his team set up a surveillance schedule that kept close tabs on the movements of Santiago and his partner. However, there were a number of times that Bobby Santiago went to one of these addresses unaccompanied; so, it was assumed that he was keeping certain things from his partner.

The team was able to document instances where Santiago met with a certain individual for dinner and drinks. Apparently, Bobby Santiago was very tight with this individual, who by the chart outline on organized crime in the detective squad room, was quite high in the hierarchical structure.

When Bobby met with this individual, who was known as Mickey DeCampo, it was usually at the same restaurant location. Previous surveillance had indicated that this restaurant was a favorite meeting place for various criminal figures and heavily supported by the "family." Mickey was especially fond of the location. Armed with this information, and although it had taken a while, the Special Operations Unit was able to place an undercover officer in the restaurant working as a waiter. As was the routine, before each meeting at the restaurant, the mob soldiers would always check the location for "bugs." However, the undercover waiter was well aware of the routine and was able to place a new bug right after the place had been "cleared."

As a result of the placement of these listening devices, the Special, Operations Unit had recorded many conversations. And now they were getting even more incriminating evidence that could be used against the mobsters, Santiago, his partner, and a few other officers who had been named. Bobby had gotten so close to his mob contact that the conversation, many times, drifted to topics other than illegal activities and protection. To an objective observer, the relationship could possibly be described as two friends catching up. They were getting so dangerously comfortable with the situation that they were getting sloppy. Mickey DeCampo, knowing that he had the cops in his pocket, and Bobby Santiago, enjoying the additional money and believing that he had his hand on the pulse of any organized crime investigation, were lulled into a state of false safety and security.

DeCampo mentioned that he had heard that a new investigator had been added to the roster of the Special Operations Unit. Since Bobby's unit and Special Operations sometimes worked closely together, Mickey was interested in finding out about the new guy. Santiago allayed any fears that his associate had and told him that he knew Rocco Deloberti very well. To demonstrate that Rocco was of no concern, Bobby told Mickey the entire story about the bachelor party night. At the conclusion of the story, they both laughed and put any worries about Rocco Deloberti on the back burner.

Although the latest conversation had been clandestinely recorded and submitted to the boss, Rocco had not yet heard the tape. However, Lieutenant Hallerin, who had heard it, worried that Rocco would explode when he did hear it. The lieutenant thought about keeping the tape from Rocco, but realized that if the shoe were on the other foot, he would want to know. So, at the weekly intelligence meeting where cases were discussed, John Hallerin played the newest tape that the team had recovered.

At the conclusion of the tape, Rocco fisted the table and marched out of the meeting. The lieutenant told the rest of the team to just give Rocco a little time to let his professional demeanor win out over his emotions. Once again, John Hallerin was giving Rocco the benefit of the doubt, and once again, he was rewarded for his thinking.

Rocco was sitting at his desk with both fists clenched and proverbial smoke coming out of his ears. However, he was in total control of any potential outburst that might have been building inside. The guys gathered around him for support and assured Rocco that sooner or later Bobby Santiago was going to get his due. They were able to calm the rage that colored Rocco's face, but Rocco couldn't wait until the day that Bobby's mobster connection bit him in the ass. Unbeknownst to Rocco, that day was just around the corner.

===

The weeks of recorded tapes produced enough information to build a solid criminal case against Mickey DeCampo and a career-ending corruption and a conspiracy-to-commit murder case against Detective Bobby Santiago. However, the department decided that it wanted more than just the two main targets they had been surveilling.

The police bosses made a decision to use the mob's police contact against the mob itself. Police officials decided to feed false information to the mob utilizing the mob's own bought and sold police connection. Through the assumed-to-be-correct revelations of the corrupt police detective, bogus information was going to be fed to the "family." If things went right, the department was hoping to take down anywhere from between five to ten high ranking mob bosses. With one fell swoop, the police department would get organized crime captains off the street and at the same time, clean its own house. Lieutenant John Hallerin was going to make sure that Rocco Deloberti would play a major part in the operation that brought Detective Bobby Santiago to his knees.

Rocco worked tirelessly to put Bobby Santiago and his friends out of business. He arranged all the tapes and surveillance assignments in chronological order. He identified the persons in all of the photos. He highlighted those areas of discussion that were involved in criminal planning, and he kept all of the detailed notes up-to-date. He was building an air tight case against Mickey DeCampo and his associates, and there was no way that he was going to let Bobby Santiago escape prosecution.

===

The department, through the unwitting efforts of the corrupt Detective Bobby Santiago, leaked certain "crucial" information that, if true, would negatively affect the crime family to which Santiago now had allegiance. As anticipated, Bobby informed his immediate crime contact about the upcoming department plans. This information led the hierarchy of the crime family to call for an immediate emergency meeting to counter the specific plans that the police department was developing.

Because of what they learned, the top family bosses mandated attendance at a planning meeting of their own to discuss the options that were available to them so that they could thwart any attempt by the police to interrupt their operation. This concern was totally based upon the information that Bobby Santiago had brought to them, the information that the department had planted.

Bobby Santiago was also invited to attend this highly confidential mob meeting to be available to answer any specific questions that the crime bosses might have about the upcoming police operation. As with most "family" meetings, there was always an array of food and drink offered to the attendees. The police undercover "trusted" waiter from the favorite "family" preferred restaurant was there as one of the servers. This was working out even better than the police department had planned.

After the initial screening for "bugs," the meeting began in earnest, but not before the police undercover had planted his device. With many voices participating in what could only be described as a developmental, defensive strategy geared to defeating any police action, the criminal cohorts labored over the exact maneuvers that they were going to employ. The meeting continued for more than two hours.

Bobby Santiago, having been tailed by members of Lieutenant Hallerin's unit, had led the police to the "secret" designated meeting warehouse where law enforcement quickly and surreptitiously surrounded the location. The police investigators patiently waited because they wanted to collect enough evidence to solidify an iron-clad case against the majority of the attendees. As Lieutenant Hallerin and his unit continued to compile incriminating evidence on the majority of the mob participants, they anxiously waited for the pre-arranged signal from the undercover. However, since there was so much information being exchanged among all of the participants, the undercover kept biding his time to collect as many incriminating facts as possible.

There was so much concern and worry regarding the information that Detective Bobby Santiago had revealed to the mob bosses that the undercover officer actually witnessed verbal fights that almost evolved into physical altercations. The mob bosses were really worried about what the police department had planned. They praised Bobby Santiago for getting the information to them. As far as Bobby was concerned, the praise only served to reinforced his connection to the "family," and he was happy about that.

Since the assault on the warehouse was taking so much longer than he had anticipated, Lieutenant Hallerin started to worry that maybe something had gone wrong. However, his worries soon dissipated as the signal finally came. The well planned police raid on organized crime had begun!

Chapter Thirty-Eight

He Didn't Need the Tapes

The organized crime group was totally surprised by the police onslaught, and they reacted accordingly. Their surprise resulted in guns being drawn and ill attempts at escape. However, the overwhelming number of police officers dampened any effort to flee the scene. Although weapons were in full view on both sides, the mobsters thought it best not to challenge the firepower of the advancing law enforcement officers. So, without much resistance, the "family" attendees and Detective Bobby Santiago were taken into custody.

Although Santiago was taken into custody just like all of the criminal thugs, the "family" hierarchy looked at him with a jaundiced eye. One could tell by their attitude that the leaders of the group were not totally convinced that Bobby Santiago didn't set them up for a downfall. Their thinking supported the idea that his being taken into custody was just a charade covering up his real mission. Mickey said nothing to Bobby, but looked at him with a sneer of doubt and the "how could you not know that this was all a trap" attitude. However, Bobby Santiago was as much in the dark as everyone else was. He realized, now, that he was used as a pawn to effect the arrests of the organizational bosses running the "family" business. He also realized that he was going to be hard-pressed to convince the mobsters otherwise. They were not a forgiving group, and they had no allegiance to a turncoat cop. He began to worry about his own safety, and the payback that the "family" was probably contemplating.

===

All crime families have excellent and well-paid attorneys on retainer. Because of this, those individuals who were not charged with serious crimes were able to be released on bail. Others had to wait and face a judge who would decide whether or not an individual was a flight risk. Bail was set according to the risk that attorneys were able to diminish for their clients, and a final decision was usually given at the arraignment.

Detective Bobby Santiago was not immediately charged with conspiracy or any other criminal violation including corruption. He was being interrogated by members of the District Attorney's Confidential Investigating Unit. This elite unit was called into action when a case of significant value to the community was about to go to court. Bobby Santiago was no slouch when it came to situations like the one he was presently in. He knew that the District Attorney would want as much condemning evidence as he could get to secure his case against the mob bosses. Bobby's cooperation would be a valuable asset to the District Attorney's case. The detective had a significant chip with which to bargain, and he would play his hand to win.

Bobby knew that he had important information and potential evidence that the District Attorney could use. Not trusting anyone, Bobby had his own set of recordings involving himself and other mob figures that were even more chock full of valuable tidbits that could help in slamming the door on many of the defendants. Knowing the value of what he had, Bobby wanted guarantees that no criminal charges would be brought against him, and he wanted access to the witness protection program.

These demands were outrageous and, at first, were not agreed to by the District Attorney's office. However, as the attorneys examined what they had against the criminal conspirators, they realized that Bobby's evidence and testimony was more valuable than they originally thought. Santiago stayed rigid in his demands and ultimately a deal was brokered. Bobby Santiago would lose his job, but no criminal charges would be brought against him regarding the organized crime activities. Additionally, he would be eligible for the witness protection program because of his testimony and involvement in the organized crime activities.

For these guarantees, Bobby would turn over all recordings and any other evidence including photos and/or correspondence that involved the activities of the crime family. He also had to cooperate in court and face the people with whom he had associated and who had somewhat trusted him. These were the same people who, undoubtedly, would ultimately order his death. Bobby was aware that his life would be in jeopardy. He realized that the cops despised him for what he did, and the mob hated him. The fact that he was still breathing was a failure as far as the "family" was concerned. He would have to be kept in protective custody until it was time for him to testify in court. That would be a most distasteful assignment for any cop. The department would be protecting someone who could care less about cops and who worked to defeat efforts to combat crime and criminal behavior. No one was going to volunteer for that protection assignment.

===

Since Lieutenant John Hallerin's unit was intricately involved in the police operation that saw the mobster arrests, he was charged with guaranteeing Bobby Santiago's safety and his appearance in court. Hallerin had no problem following the orders, but he mandated one strict rule: Officer Rocco Deloberti was never to be assigned to guard Santiago. That situation would be too volatile to control. The court could not hear the testimony of a dead man, and Rocco might very well be capable, at this point, of ending Santiago's life.

Without the lieutenant knowing and with the help of some of the guys in the squad who empathized with Rocco, he was able to visit Santiago at the location where the turncoat detective was being lodged. Rocco gave his word that nothing would happen to Bobby, and that he only wanted a few words with the corrupt detective. The other guys in the Special Operations Unit knew the circumstances surrounding Rocco and Bobby's relationship, so they kept a close eye as Rocco approached the former detective who was in protective custody. To demonstrate to the detectives who were guarding Santiago that Rocco had no bad intentions, he left his gun with one of the detectives.

Rocco approached the one who had made his life so miserable: "Hello, old friend. I see you got yourself into a little bit of a mess. You should be more careful with whom you associate. Not only did they lead you down a shaky road, but they probably want to kill you. I don't blame them, and If I had my way, I'd leave the door wide open for them."

Santiago sarcastically responded: "Well, if it isn't old straight-laced himself. I figured you would come to see me sooner or later. By the way, I had a call from a mutual friend. Yeah, Janet called me to help with deciphering what Gloria said as she lay dying in the street. She said that it was something about Rocco being innocent. Isn't that a riot? I told her I would do some soul searching and get back to her. In fact, I planned to meet her at her house, but I got involved in this shit."

"You know, Bobby, you think you're a lot smarter than you actually are. I will have no problem convincing Janet of my innocence, and it will be words that came from your mouth that will clear the way for me. I just came by to thank you."

Rocco turned and walked away. He heard Santiago yelling after him, but Rocco just ignored the rantings: "What the hell are you talking about? What do you mean words from my mouth? I'm not going to tell her anything. I may not wind up with her, but neither will you. You'll never win the war!"

Rocco kept walking with a smile on his face. Bobby Santiago was unaware of the many tapes that the undercover officer was able to retrieve. There were tapes that had Bobby telling all to his criminal associate. Not only did he reveal the criminal activity that he had been involved in, but he told the story of how he set Rocco up for a fall. More than that, he admitted to having given the order to murder his cousin, Gloria.

===

The agreement between the District Attorney and Bobby Santiago pertained to his involvement in organized crime activities. The agreement did not include anything about his having Gloria terminated. It was just a slight oversight by Bobby, an oversight that would cost him dearly. In fact, it was Bobby Santiago at his best and in his own words, confessing to murder. So, the smile on Rocco's face had a lot more to do with the results that a murder conspiracy conviction would bring than what an agreement with the District Attorney cemented.

Although Rocco had all the evidence that he needed to convince Janet that he didn't voluntarily enter into any of the activities that she assumed he did, he wasn't allowed to let her hear any of the tapes until the trial was concluded and the case was closed. However, he did contact her and assured her that before long, he would be able to show her that she was mistaken in her belief that he was unfaithful. He did explain to her what the tapes would demonstrate, and that was enough for Janet to be able to open her mind to other than an accusatory frame of reference.

Rocco called her every day, and they spoke about many things including a rethinking on marriage arrangements. It seemed that even without the hard evidence that the tapes would reveal, Janet was back on track. Rocco was glad to see the one hundred and eighty degree turn that she had made. He was glad because he really wasn't sure if he could ever allow Janet to hear the tapes that were used as evidence in a criminal trial. In fact, he was never going to bring up the tapes again, and he hoped that his word would be good enough to eliminate whatever doubts Janet had lodged in the pathways of her mind.

Chapter Thirty-Nine

There's Always a Leak

Time passed quickly, and the trial was in full swing. Now, promoted Detective Rocco Deloberti made certain that he attended the sessions whenever possible. The District Attorney had prepared a well-researched case, and the defense was at a loss to demonstrate that the defendants did not play an integral part in organized criminal activity. The evidence against the mob figures was strong and indisputable, but the testimony from the undercover officer added an additional level of involvement that definitely influenced the jury. The undercover officer testified to the many conversations that he overheard, but the defense kept hitting on the point that it was testimony from a third party who possibly erred in his interpretation of what was heard.

Examination and cross examination went on for what seemed like forever.

The Special Operations Team had kept Bobby Santiago safe and sound. Shortly, it was going to be the District Attorney's chance to bring out the big gun, disgraced Detective Bobby Santiago. Everyone in court knew that Santiago was going to testify, and it was assumed that his testimony would be the final nail in the coffin for a "guilty" verdict from the jury. Knowing how organized crime operates, many of the jurors were surprised that Santiago was alive and still willing to testify. The police department knew that there might be an attempt on Bobby Santiago's life because that's the way organized crime operates; hence, the protective measures and the around-the-clock police protection. There would be a heavy contingent of police officers guarding Santiago until the point when it was his time to testify. It was a known fact that if Bobby Santiago testified, the jury would most likely be persuaded to render a "guilty" verdict. The "family," therefore, had to figure out a way to prevent the District Attorney's ace-in-the-hole from testifying.

===

During the past year, the Civil Service Police Sergeant's Examination was given. Like a multitude of other officers wanting to better themselves, Rocco Deloberti registered and took the exam. The results of the examination had recently been certified, and Rocco was in the upper echelon of those who passed the test. There was an excellent chance that before long,

Detective Rocco Deloberti would become Sergeant Rocco Deloberti.

Things were looking up for Rocco: there was a very strong possibility that before the year ended Rocco Deloberti and Janet Commings would, once again, be closer to their marriage ceremony, Rocco might soon be promoted to the rank of "Sergeant," and more than likely, the detective who brought nothing but havoc into Rocco's life would not be seeing the light of day for a very long time. All in all, life was shaping up for the once beleaguered public servant, and that scared him. He was plagued by the old adage that said: "all things in life cannot remain good before something negative breaks the chain." So, although he was happy with the way things were going, Rocco Deloberti was waiting for the other shoe to drop.

===

It was shocking, thus far, that there was no intelligence on a possible mobster hit on Bobby Santiago. The police department used all of its confidential informants and squeals, but nothing surfaced. They knew, however, that it wasn't "if" but "when" it would happen. No one was letting their guard down, and all the officers assigned to the special protection detail guarding Santiago were being extra cautious and on high alert. In fact, Bobby Santiago was moved to an undisclosed remote location that only those officers who were involved in the protection detail knew about. It was a secluded safe house that had both external perimeter security officers as well as internal security personnel. The Special Operations Unit of the police department was now sharing the protection efforts with the

United States Marshals' Office whose deputy marshals were well experienced in guarding State's witnesses. They had specific procedures that had proved successful in the past; so, the detail now followed the marshals' policies and procedures.

One of the marshals assigned to the Santiago detail was a young man who coincidentally came from the same small Mexican town that Bobby Santiago and his family had come from. So, when Marshal Angel Hernandez was on duty and in close proximity to Bobby, there was a constant and somewhat friendly flow of conversation. This conversation was mainly voiced in Spanish. A loose translation of what transpired indicated that Bobby Santiago was pleading with Angel to understand how it was necessary for him to interact with certain members of organized crime. He supposedly executed these efforts in order to gain significant intelligence to combat the actions of the criminal "family." Angel was sympathetic to the comments of his hometown neighbor, but asked Bobby if he realized that he might have gone over the line.

Santiago continued with his pleas: "Angel, you don't understand how difficult it is to deal with organized crime and remain within the guidelines of the legal limits that are cast upon you. No one, not even you, could operate successfully while adhering to such legal restraints."

Angel listened carefully and responded: "No, Bobby, I do understand. What I don't understand is why you ran interference for the mob and put other law enforcement officers in danger. From what I've been told, it seems that, at every turn, you prevented the good guys from winning. Again, from what I understand, there were a number of opportunities for the good guys to make arrests, but because of something that you said or did, the opportunity disappeared. Maybe, you may have forgotten. We are the good guys!"

These last statements bothered Bobby, and he lashed out: "Hey, Angel, come down from your lofty perch. You are a Deputy United States Marshal. What do you know about undercover work and infiltrating the mob? Don't lecture me if you have no understanding of what it takes to be successful."

Deputy Marshal Angel Hernandez pushed on: "So, let me get this straight, Bobby. You were working undercover so that you could acquire intelligence information that would ultimately lead to the downfall of the crime family. Also, you did what you had to do, even if it meant that you had to break the law to continue to operate in your successful undercover role. Is that what you want me to believe? You are a disgusting representative for our own hometown and the police department? Really, is that what you want me to believe?"

Bobby Santiago did not like the tone of Angel's comments, and he interpreted them as threatening. Bobby rose from his chair and confronted Angel: "Are you calling me a liar, Angel?"

Angel didn't back down and answered Bobby's challenging question: "It's more than that. You are a corrupt, lying, disgrace to us as Spanish police officers, and you are a disgrace to the people of Mexico who have taken great pride in what we do. Your existence is an insult, and I can only hope that your buddies in the "family" find a way to get around our security and render the appropriate justice that you deserve. I wish I had the nerve to do what they want to do. If I did, I wouldn't hesitate!"

With that remark, Bobby Santiago leaped up and attacked the unexpecting marshal, and they both fell to the floor. As they scuffled on the floor, other marshals quickly responded in an attempt to separate the two. However, Bobby had enough time to rip Angel's weapon out of his holster and was now pointing it directly at Angel. He yelled to the other marshal's to stand back as he threatened to kill one of their own. The marshals drew their weapons but did not proceed any closer. Santiago kept a threatening gun-hold on Angel and ordered the other marshals to clear the way. With the potential threat on Angel's life, they reluctantly complied.

With Marshal Angel Hernandez in tow and a warning to the other marshals not to follow him outside, Bobby Santiago grabbed the car keys to the government auto and fled. When he got to the car, he pistol whipped Angel into unconsciousness and got into the car. He started the car and headed toward the highway where he hoped that he could get far enough away so that a search for him would not yield positive results.

The location where Bobby Santiago was being held was a clandestine location known only to those who were assigned to the protection detail. However, as any law enforcement officer can tell you, there is always the possibility of leaks. So, at times, the secure, secretive location may not be as secure as one might believe. As Bobby left the location, he felt quite confident that his escape was a success, and that he would be able to avoid re-capture.

===

As he proceeded to the highway, he passed two vehicles that were parked on the side of the road and out of obvious sight. However, as soon as Santiago passed these vehicles, he failed to notice that both vehicles came to life, got onto the roadway and closely followed directly behind him. They stayed behind him for a while as they proceeded along the highway. After looking in his rear view mirror a number of times and seeing the same vehicles closely behind him, Bobby became suspicious and started to accelerate in an effort to lose the vehicles that he assumed were following him. His efforts were unsuccessful, and the vehicles closed the gap.

One of the cars stayed right behind Bobby while the other driver maneuvered his vehicle directly alongside Bobby. The last thing that Bobby saw when he looked over at the driver who pulled alongside him was the barrel of a gun that discharged two rounds which penetrated Bobby's skull. Bobby Santiago was no longer in control, and he could not stop his vehicle from crashing over the guard rail and on to an embankment. The car continued to roll down the hill and into a stagnant body of water below. The government vehicle, which now acted as the final resting place for Bobby Santiago, slowly sank beneath the dark murky waters.

Bobby succeeded in helping organized crime, once again. His attempted escape allowed for his never being able to testify against them. The District Attorney had lost a valuable witness in the case against the "family," and Detective Rocco Deloberti had lost the opportunity to seek personal revenge. That might have been a good thing!

Epilogue

One Year Later

The day finally came for Janet Commings and Rocco Deloberti to exchange wedding vows. It was a long time in coming but the two of them couldn't be happier. However, the day did produce some mixed emotions for both Janet and her mom. A very important person in the family was missing, David Commings. Mrs. Commings was feeling the effects of her husband not being present, and Janet was teary-eyed over not having her father to walk her down the aisle. The one high spot, however, was the fact that David Commings was a twin, and his twin brother was there to walk with Janet. Sure, it wasn't the same, but it was a close enough substitute for Janet to feel that, in some way, her father was there.

On the groom's side there was the best man who had always looked out for Rocco. John Hallerin stood alongside Rocco as they waited for Janet and her uncle to approach the alter. According to Rocco, Janet never looked so beautiful, and John agreed. After giving the bride away, Janet's uncle sat with Mrs. Commings who couldn't control her tears of joy that were now, thankfully, overpowering the emotional sadness that she previously felt.

The church was filled with many different people. Some were friends and acquaintances of Janet, while others, mostly police officers, were friends or officers who had worked with Rocco. Since both Rocco and Janet had very small families, there weren't that many relatives present, but the few who were there made their presence known by the rousing round of applause at the end of the ceremony. The final touch of pomp and circumstance occurred when the newly married couple exited the church to walk under an umbrella of raised police batons. It was a bit of official protocol interlaced with ceremonial elegance, and it was much appreciated by both the newlyweds and the surprised guests.

===

Following his honeymoon, Rocco Deloberti came back to the news that he was being promoted to the rank of "Sergeant." Since he had experience in investigations and, most likely, again through the influence of now permanently promoted Lieutenant John Hallerin, Sergeant Rocco Deloberti was going to remain in the detective division. There was a squad commander's position that became vacant as a result of a promotion in a certain detective squad, and Lieutenant Hallerin pushed for Sergeant Deloberti to get that position. Although the position was one that was high on the list of preferred assignments, Lieutenant Hallerin's influence, again, secured the transfer for Rocco.

When Sergeant Deloberti arrived at the Brooklyn South Detective Squad, he was greeted by Lieutenant Robert Lauder. The lieutenant was the son of Captain Bret Lauder, the task force commander who was killed during the siege of the Three Kings Shopping Mall that took place on Christmas Eve a number of years in the past. Rocco was familiar with the Captain's name because the attack had been well publicized and had been one of the top stories for a long time. In fact, the siege and ultimately successful conclusion of the attempted take-over had become one of the tactical topics for discussion in the police academy training curriculum.

===

"Hello, Sergeant Deloberti, I am Lieutenant Robert Lauder, and I had the privilege of supervising this squad for quite a while. You'll not meet a finer group of investigators."

Rocco was appreciative of the enthusiastic welcome by the lieutenant: "Glad to meet you, Lieutenant. The reputation of the squad is well-known, and its history is even more celebrated. I am honored to be placed in such a prestigious position. I'm sure that supervising the Brooklyn South Squad will be an experience that will remain with me forever. I know it was a long time ago, lieutenant, but I am sorry about your father."

The lieutenant was somewhat surprised that Rocco knew the specifics: "Thank you, Sarge. He was a good man, and I miss him every day. Come with me and let me introduce you to some of the detectives who will be working for you."

With that, the lieutenant walked Rocco to the desks of the detectives who were present. The lieutenant gave a brief introduction and a description of what each detective had been working on and the particular strength of the individual investigator. Having visited with each detective, the lieutenant headed toward the rear of the squad room where there were two other detectives who had their desks facing one another. As Lieutenant Lauder and Sergeant Deloberti approached the two detectives, Rocco noticed that one of the detectives had a vase on his desk with a single Daffodil rising out of it. It was an odd thing to see, and Rocco made a note to ask the detective about it.

The Lieutenant pointed to the desk on his left and said: "Sergeant Deloberti, this is Detective Martin Iniddor Jr." Rocco nodded to the detective, and the lieutenant then pointed to his right and said: "And this is his partner, Detective Anthony (Tony) Uhrich Ossur. These two are your 'go-to' guys. If something really needs to get done, give it to them. Have confidence that they will not let you down. They will do it. They have a lot of experience, and both come from a family with a law enforcement background."

Both detectives rose from their chairs and shook Rocco's hand. There was a good feeling all around, and Rocco could tell that he was going to depend a lot on these two investigators who, apparently, were also favored by the lieutenant. Rocco was still curious about the Daffodil, and he thought that the time was right to ask about it: "Tony, I'm curious about the Daffodil. It's something you don't often see on a detective's desk."

"You're right about that, sarge. It's sort of a tradition that I inherited from my father. My dad looked at the Narcissus, which is the formal name for the Daffodil, as a symbol that represented both beauty and strength. It is gold like the detective shield, and it blooms in late winter. When other flowers died, the strong daffodils flourished. My dad felt that the flower was a reflection of who he was. I only hope that I can follow in his footsteps."

Rocco wasn't ready for such a detailed explanation, but it jarred his memory: "Iniddor and Ossur, I remember those names as the detectives who foiled the infamous attack on the Three Kings Shopping Mall. Tony, I'm sorry about your dad, but from what I heard, he died courageously as a hero. Well, between the two of you, I couldn't be in better company. Good meeting you both, and I'm looking forward to working with you."

===

Lieutenant Lauder and Sergeant Deloberti walked back to the Lieutenant's office talking about the detectives and the squad as a whole when they heard someone yelling after them. Marty and Tony were standing as they voiced something aloud to the new squad commander: "Hey Sarge, your reputation precedes you. We understand that you fear nothing, won't take 'no' for an answer, and you're not for sale. Well, that's what your new wife said anyway."

There was a deafening silence, and then the entire squad room burst into laughter, including Robert Lauder and Rocco Deloberti. The lieutenant turned to Rocco and said: "Well, that's a good sign. They just welcomed you into the Brooklyn South Detective Squad!"

Sergeant Rocco Deloberti had come a long way since the days of "Trouble." At least, that's what he thought. However, an unrelated combination of events had positioned him as the supervisor of the Brooklyn South Detective Squad. The squad, although highly touted as an effective and efficient asset for law enforcement, had a past history of trouble. It was rumored that, in the past, one detective had been involved in the commission of a felony - trouble; also that the detective's partner never reported it and worse, covered it up – trouble; and that the sons of these two detectives wanted to follow closely in their fathers' footsteps - trouble. No, trouble was still an obvious part of Rocco's life, but it seemed to make demands on him that ultimately resulted in his success. So, with opened arms he welcomed the anticipated challenges – a.k.a. "Trouble."

===

While Sergeant Deloberti was meeting with his team and learning the operations germane to activities in the Brooklyn South area, another young man, many miles away, was also conducting a meeting with his associates. This meeting was taking place in one of the rooms of a structure that recently survived the bombing efforts directed at the Gaza Strip. The young man was focused and emotional as he addressed the small group of loyalists: "We have been too cautious for too long. It is time to strike back both at home and abroad. We need to hurt our enemy here and attack the security that the Americans still feel that they have. It is time to increase our activities and bring Israel and America to their knees as those who went before us tried to do. I am calling for all of our groups to come together under one leader and prepare for our battle against tyranny and for freedom."

The small cadre of soon-to-be loyal followers agreed with this relatively unknown self-appointed leader, and since he was a stranger to most present, one of the listeners asked: "If you are to lead us on this righteous path, what shall we call you?"

The young leader rose and with focused determination and a chilling stare addressed the question: "Out of respect for one who came before me and who valiantly tried to slay the dragon, you may refer to me as my father was known. I am "Dunait."

Many years ago his father attempted to bring both the United States and Israel to a weakened compromised state by attempting to take over the Three Kings Shopping Mall on Christmas Eve, and holding numerous shoppers as hostages for the release of prisoners that were being held in Israeli jails. Although the attempt had failed, lives were lost, and it set both countries back on their heels. One of those lives lost was the senior Dunait. Also, it was during this siege that Detective Tony Ossur also lost his life.

Apparently, fate had now dictated that one rebel leader and one New York City Detective, both of whom lost their fathers, might very well be involved in another attack and definitely involved in a personal war to avenge the violent extermination of their fathers. The rebel leader would depend on those who would blindly follow him, and the New York City Detective would lean on his partner as his father did. Unfortunately, it seems that neither one of these determined, head-strong individuals had learned from history, and therefore, it had become inevitable that history was going to repeat itself.

He did not have to look for it; in most cases, it found him!

"Trouble"

Acknowledgements

Thank you to my wife, **Lisa**, for being there to help with my constant questions and remarks. You're never bothered and always offer a positive outlook when problems arise. You turn a sometimes daunting task into an enjoyable journey into the unknown. You keep me on track, as always. A big thank you to my son, **Martin**, who volunteered to complete the tedious job of proof reading and suggesting recommendations to clarify and magnify the theme of the book. His law enforcement experience added to the accuracy and attitude of my writing. Thank you again to **David Manzolillo** for lending his unique expertise to the cover of this book. His work is always eye-catching and revealing. Your talent never goes unnoticed. Thank you to both **Officer Rick Purnhagen** and **Officer Dan Gavigan** who inspire me to be at my best because of their curiosity, pointed questions, and interesting discussion. It is their enthusiasm that often influences my attempt at putting thoughts to paper. Also want to thank **Chief Nick Stillman** for his keen outlook on all matters involving law enforcement, and his unselfish sharing of police policies and procedures. A big thank you to my **fellow officers** who unknowingly gave me much to write about. It is their stories and experiences that have influenced my writing. As usual, I want to thank **Avi Gvili** and **Aliyah Manuel** for ushering my work through the publishing process of Boulevard Books and forwarding a honed product of which I can be proud.

www.ingramcontent.com/pod-product-compliance
Lightning Source LLC
LaVergne TN
LVHW052335100826
845147LV00020B/1070

* 9 7 8 1 9 7 2 9 1 9 0 1 9 *